Don't Delve Too Deep

L. J. Hutton

Published by Wylfheort Books 2019

Copyright

The moral right of L. J. Hutton to be identified as the author of this work has been asserted by her in accordance with the Copyright, Designs and Patents Act 1988.

All characters in this book are fictitious, and any resemblance to actual persons living or dead is purely coincidental.

All rights reserved. No part of this publication may be reproduced, stored in a retrieval system or transmitted in any form, or by any means, without the prior permission in writing of the author, nor to be otherwise circulated in any form or binding or cover other than in which it is published without a similar condition, including this condition, being imposed upon the subsequent purchaser.

Three weeks earlier

The men stumbled through the tangle of trees, all of them desperate to get away from that dreadful place on the other side of the ridge.

"Keep together, lads!" Toby called, worried at the way they were starting to wander. But then he was having increasing trouble keeping his own thoughts straight and getting his feet to follow.

Over to his left, Karl had Flynn with an arm draped over his shoulders and was more carrying him than supporting him. God, Flynn didn't look well. His breath was harsh and uneven, and he was a terrible colour. Toby wiped the sweat from his eyes and looked to his right. Young Tom and Josh had Craig between them – and Craig was another one who looked bloody awful – while Simon and Ash were stumbling across the rough ground just about holding one another up, and he himself had a supporting arm around Tufty, although it looked as though they would be carrying him soon.

"Si! Come and help with Tufty!" Toby ordered, and Simon thrust the First Aid box into Ash's hands and came to link hands with Toby as they hoisted Tufty off his feet.

What a bloody state to get into, Toby thought exhaustedly. This had been supposed to be an easy army exercise, one they'd all been silently grateful for, even though aloud many had said that they felt they ought to be going to Afghanistan with the rest of the battalion. How had it gone so wrong?

"Take five," he called, and the men sank gratefully onto the ground, panting, sweating and dark-eyed from strain.

When he could lift his head up, Toby scanned back along the steep trail they'd come down. No sign of that weird creature. Nothing white and faintly luminous up there, or was that actually what he was looking for? God he was struggling to remember! Already his thoughts were a jumbled mess. What was it that they'd seen? Had it been real?

He looked at them all, seeing that every one of them was a mass of bleeding cuts. No, some figment of his imagination couldn't have done that. Worse, a tremor of stark terror ran through him at the thought of something that was back up that trail. Something he was having increasing difficulty remembering, but one which was haunting his subconscious something shocking and would not fully let go. Had it been white? Part of his addled thoughts said yes, but another part was screaming at him that no, it had been black, black as oil at midnight and then some. Something not just dark in colour, but dangerous and yet …and yet …His mind wouldn't quite form the thoughts anymore, but in his soul he felt that that blackness was also something akin to the deepest mourning, a despair so deep and so profound you could fall into it and never surface. And that wasn't him, his own feelings, that was something left behind inside him. Something that had lanced into his soul along with the cuts that were on his arms, both of which now ached beyond anything he'd though he could ever endure, yet he was one of the better ones, and worse, he was now in command.

Another uncontrollable shivering spasm ran through him, and he recognised that he had to get the lads up and moving again because they were all getting worse.

"Up! Up! Come on, lads! Get moving! The road isn't far away! Get moving!"

Chapter 1

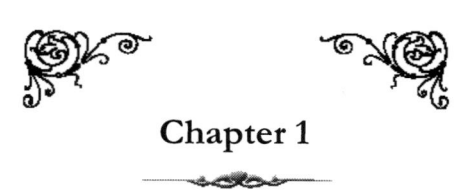

Tuesday

It all started with Trish. If she'd never made the phone call none of what happened afterwards would have occurred – or at least that was what Stella would think later. She was opening the tin of dog food for Ivan when she answered the phone on that fatal day, hurriedly chopping the meat into the soaked kibble as he drooled hopefully by her side as if he'd never seen food before, rather than only that morning. It was the rescued dog's inevitable response to food if they'd been starved before, and so she was distracted by reassuring him when she got Trish's usual cheery greeting,

"Hi mate! How's it going?"

Nothing in that to suggest what was to come. In fact Trish managed to talk for nearly twenty minutes about the stuff they always chatted about, like their jobs and what they had planned for the weekend. It was only after Stella had been lulled into a false sense of security that Trish sprung the trap.

"Look Stella, I have to ask you something and you're not going to like it."

Stella's heart sank. It had to be about Toby, her ex-husband, and Trish was right – she didn't even like the thought of it before it had begun.

"What's the little shit done now?" she asked with more acerbic bite than she realised.

She heard Trish sigh sadly, and wished for the thousandth time or more that Trish wasn't Toby's cousin, or that if she had to be, then at least that she hadn't taken it upon herself to play big sister to him even when he was the elder. But then that seemed to run in Trish's family. Trish's dad had felt obliged to try and help his feckless sister Molly bring up Toby, even though she got through a considerable alimony from her ex-husbands in record time each month, while he worked hard to support himself and Tess.

Maybe it had been because they were both living with their dads when the other kids of divorced parents inevitably lived with their mums, but Trish and Stella had been best friends long before Toby and his mother had appeared in their lives. As the only two girls of nearly the same age on a small housing estate it was natural that they'd gravitated to one another as children, but as teenagers (and in different classes at secondary school) they had found that their friendship had grown and stayed while others came and went.

Looking back now, Stella realised that Toby had been a charmer even then. It hadn't taken him long to win them over, despite disrupting almost every aspect of their lives. Molly had already spoilt Toby rotten, but he hadn't been obnoxious with it then, though he'd already developed a good line in lost puppy expressions to use on any female he came into contact with. His family had been ecstatic when he and Stella had started going out and then married, albeit ridiculously young considering neither of them had been out of their teens. The family at large had been far less enthusiastic and supportive when the marriage had died its death ten years later. However at that point Stella and Trish had agreed that they'd been friends first and in-laws second, and that whatever else had gone on they would remain that way.

Which was why Stella felt rotten for snapping at Trish before she'd even had chance to say her piece.

Trish knew how she felt about Toby these days so it must be something serious in Trish's eyes, even if it turned out to be another of Toby's manipulations.

"Oh go on then," she sighed resignedly, "what's made you bring him up."

"He's back from Afghanistan," Trish told her guardedly.

"Yes, I saw on the news that the Mercians were back home, what of it?"

"Well Toby came back a bit before that..."

"...Oh? How'd he manage that? Teflon Boy manage to wangle some special dispensation again?"

"...He's been injured. He's in Selly Oak Hospital on a military ward."

Stella gasped. "Selly Oak? Crap! ...Sorry, Tess, I had no idea. Is he going to be okay?"

"I think so, although the doctors will never give you a categorical answer. It's a shrapnel wound amongst other things, I'm told, so they're hauling all sort of bits of metal out him."

"Bloody Hell! Well give him my best for getting better and ...well, ...whatever. I know I said I could have killed him for what he did to me, but ...oh, you know what I mean ...I wouldn't have wished it on him ...not out in Afghanistan and all that."

Trish could be heard taking a deep breath. "Mmm. Not that simple, hon', ...sorry! You see it's not just the physical stuff. He's really messed up psychologically this time, and not just because of some of the things they saw out there. One of the lads with him lost both legs, and another is in a worse way than Toby even though he's not an amputee." She took another audible breath. "But the worst is ...they lost Dav."

Stella felt herself going cold. "Dav? Lost? ...What do you mean? Dead? ...I haven't heard of anyone being missing in action the way they used to report about the Gulf War, or back when Vietnam was in the news – like back in school when we did in that project on it and read all those newspaper reports on MIAs. So was he killed? I don't recall his name coming up on the news, and they usually name dead soldiers once their family's been told, although that's hardly relevant in Dav's case."

"Oh God, Stella, I don't know. I can't make any sense of what Toby says when he gets going on that, and I'm not exactly Dav's family, so I can hardly push the Army to tell me."

Stella groaned. Dafydd had been Toby's best friend and someone she'd liked a lot. Actually, after the first few years a lot more than Toby, because in her eyes he was a far nicer person. In total contrast to Toby, Dav had been a quieter and kinder man. He'd also been a godsend when she was getting the divorce sorted, having gone through the process already himself, and for a while Stella had half hoped they would get together as a couple. In the end that hadn't happened, but they'd kept sporadically in touch when army postings allowed, and now Stella found herself feeling far more distraught about Dav's unknown fate than Toby's. More than that, she felt a dreadful sense of obligation falling on her. Dav had no family of his own, having being orphaned when, as a small child, the rest of his immediate family had been wiped out in a multi-car pile-up. So there was no-one to kick up a fuss and demand answers about what had happened to him.

"I've still got some contact with the chap who was our Families' Officer," Stella heard herself saying with a strange sense of detachment. "He's retired now, but I bet he's still in contact with the right people, and he knew how close we were to Dav. He'll understand if I ask him to make inquiries. I presume that's what's got you bringing this up? I mean, I'm more than willing to do the chasing for Dav's sake, and I guess Toby knows that too – manipulative little git that he is! But under the circumstances I'm not going to say 'no' just to spite him, and I guess he's already figured that one out too, damn him!"

"It's even a bit more than that, hon'," Trish said apologetically. "Toby wants to speak to you. In person! In fact, he's been getting right worked up about it. The doctors asked me to ask you to come up to Birmingham to see if that would calm him down."

Stella winced, pulled her office specs off and dumped them on the phone table, then rubbed her eyes with her spare hand. This was the last thing she wanted. The divorce might be seven years in the past, but the wounds weren't so well healed that she was prepared to risk opening them up again. Yet the circumstances put a whole different spin on the request. Taking a deep breath she asked,

"The *doctors* have asked you? Them specifically? ...This isn't just *Toby* telling you that that's what they've said?"

"Christ, Stella! He's a wreck! You surely can't think he'd be pulling a fast one? He couldn't fake anything at the moment."

Stella found herself growling, "Where Toby's concerned I'd believe him trying it on with the bloody undertaker while they were screwing the coffin lid down!"

"I thought you were all over that now!" Stella heard Trish starting to well up with tears. "Anyone else acting like this I'd be calling them selfish and bitter. But I know you. Anyone less selfish I've never known. ...God, I had no idea the wounds went this deep. I'm sorry... I suppose I should have realised. ...I shouldn't have said anything..."

Stella's heart took the final plunge into the floor somewhere under her feet. She hated it when Trish got upset over being caught between them.

"Look, Tess, hold on! It's not you I'm mad at... You know that! But for God's sake...! It's one thing for me to have picked myself up and made a new life. In that sense, yes, I am over it. Over it because I'm not letting it ruin the rest of my life. ...But can't you see that contact with Toby in person is a whole different thing? And Dav is a *very* different thing! Of course I want to know about *him* after all he did for me. It's just that if I'm going to make a trip for no reason other than to see Toby, and risk having all the old wounds reopened, then I want to make sure the situation is really as bad as it seems. ...So, ...*was* it the doctors who asked?"

Trish blew her nose before answering. "Yes. It was the junior doctor who's attached to the consultant who took me on one side when I went to visit yesterday. He said he'd already asked 'Co'po'al Donal'son's wife'," she mimicked a pronounced oriental accent.

"Oh, the delightful C.D.!" Stella said with acidic sweetness. "The nympho's still about then?"

That at least earned her a weak chuckle from Tess. "Oh yes!" Then her humour evaporated. "But something's wrong there too, and please don't say 'I told you so' or anything, Stella. The psychiatrists are worried at the way he's reacting to her, and yes, they do know about the kind of marriage they have, but there's something beyond that causing concern. It's you he keeps wanting to talk to, so in the end they asked C.D. to get in touch with you."

"*Pfff!* Like I'd take a phone call off her!"

"That's what C.D. told them, at the same time saying that she'd do many things for Toby but that that wasn't one of them."

"Well our hatred always was mutual! ...OK, so that's why you've been roped into this."

Her close friend sighed heavily. "What else could I do, Stella?"

"I know, mate, I know, but it still rankles with me that after all this time I can't seem to sever all the ties. ...Look, get the details and find out when the consulting team can meet me up there. I'm guessing that the evening is pretty rushed for visitors, like all hospitals, so I'm not going to come tearing down now. It can wait until the weekend and I'll catch a train up on Friday if they can see me with him then. But I want one thing clear, Tess. I'm not coming down to see him alone! If he thinks I'm going to sit at his bedside just mopping his fevered brow he's got another thing coming! It's with at least a junior doctor present or not at all – you tell him *and* them that! Now cheer up and tell me the rest of the gossip...!"

Yet Trish had no heart for much more chat and soon rang off with a promise to ring Stella to confirm the arrangements. It was Tuesday today, and if Trish visited tomorrow and rang Stella back to say all was well, there was still time to buy a train ticket before Friday morning.

Stella wandered out to the west-facing front garden to where Ivan, her large white lurcher, was basking in the sun on the patio. Luckily her neighbour adored Ivan and would be only too pleased to keep an eye on him for the day. She could hardly take him to Birmingham with her as she would normally, if this time she was going to be spending time in the hospital instead of the normal trips she made, which usually included walkies on the Lickey Hills. This time she had no intention of lingering longer than possible, but also felt that if she got truly upset in the process, driving back on the M5 alone was not a good idea.

"Oh Ivan," she sighed, leaning over and ruffling his ears, "how come he always manages to come out of these encounters with one over on me?"

Ivan rolled over onto his back and exposed his tummy for rubbing with a baleful expression, making Stella smile despite herself. As the only man in her life these days, Ivan was blissfully uncomplicated – feed him, walk him and give him some love and attention, and he was uncritically bonded to her for life. She went inside and poured herself a glass of wine and put a Bonnie Raitt CD on, opening the front door from her lounge so that she could sit outside and still hear it. Sad songs appealed just now and *Valley of Pain* and *Wounded Heart* really caught her mood perfectly.

Part of her felt guilty over the way she'd reacted to Trish's news. After all it did sound as though there was something severely wrong. On the other hand, though, Toby had been in the army since leaving school, and this was far from being the first time he'd been in some dangerous place. And that was partly the trouble for Stella. She knew from personal experience of being around when he got back in the past that, while others often returned battered and distraught, Toby had never yet shown any signs of long-term damage. This was in no small measure due to the fact that he was just too selfish and self-centred, she was sure. If something didn't impact directly on Toby, then he was capable of turning a totally blind eye to it – that and the fact that he had no imagination where his own mortality was concerned – and he had, after all, survived to tell the tale yet again.

"I doubt it's anything much different to before," she muttered darkly, taking a restorative drink of the crisp, cool white wine and allowing it to linger in her mouth with relish. That and the flower-scented air soothed her. Trish and her husband Graham had lived in Norfolk for many years, and so had not seen Toby firsthand on his previous returns, which no doubt accounted for the way Trish had been manipulated. That almost certainly would end up accounting for Trish's distress, and with any luck Stella could say 'I told you so' and return the same day.

However, Stella was also reflective enough to recognise that she was capable of over-reacting, seeing trouble where there was none. It was similar to the way a previous colleague had talked about physical pain. He'd had years of intense back pain before the problem had been sorted out, and Stella had been astonished to observe that by the time she met him he would pop pain killers at the slightest twinge. When she'd asked how he'd survived in the past being like that, he'd told her that, since he had a very real idea of what pain could be like, he was terrified of going through it again. And that was just how she thought of her own experiences now. She knew only too well how badly Toby could hurt her with just a careless comment, so that even the thought of going back into that mental torture chamber caused her to react violently.

It was also why she'd never got involved with someone else, and often seemed to keep people at arms' length. She had tried making new friends when she'd come to live here but inevitably, once they thought they knew her, the invite would come to some supposedly casual barbecue or the like, only to find some eager male being very pointedly introduced to her. At which point Stella had found herself struggling to disentangle herself without causing outright offence. So these days she liked to keep her options open and her friendships distant.

That was why working as a supply teacher suited Stella. She liked the flexibility and today she was glad of it. She had nothing booked yet for next week because it was the summer half-term anyway, so she could take the week off without the additional grief of having to explain why to inquisitive colleagues. There was some marking upstairs which she'd have to finish tonight and take in with her by Thursday, but the chap she was covering for would be back on Friday when his course finished. Other than that her weekend time was all her own. However, it was only a little after seven in the evening and there was plenty of time to get it done before she went to bed, and so she settled into the swing seat and allowed herself time to calm down further and enjoy the early-summer sunset. The ground fell away steeply from here, with barely enough room for Stella to squeeze her old car up against the garden wall in the tiny cut-out parking space that took up half of her garden, but there wasn't another house properly in sight from this high up on the Malverns – just fields and knots of woods, and the distant hills viewed over the roofs of the houses below hers, and plenty of room to breathe.

She loved her life here. This open view from the front was the reason why she'd bought the cottage, and yet she could get to Worcester, Pershore or Evesham without much trouble, and at a push Gloucester or Hereford, so that she was never without options for work. Beyond the garden fence she had an uninterrupted view out across the western countryside to the Brecon Beacons and the Black Mountains of Wales, currently in shades of amber as they were bathed in lowering sunshine.

In a month or two they would turn purple with the heather. It was a glorious view, and had the cottage not been the middle one of a terrace of three she would never have been able to afford it, despite earning a reasonable amount. As it was, the two end ones had been extended several times with their price increasing accordingly, but with hers there was nowhere to go and with only two bedrooms it had come on the market at her kind of price. It was her sanctuary, her place of calm.

Yet now, just the thought of coming face to face with Toby again had her jittery and all on edge, and try as she might she couldn't fully relax. It wasn't that she was frightened of him, far from it. Rather, it was the case that she felt a desperate need to be constantly on alert whenever he made the least of contacts for any new manipulations he might try on her.

"The bloody man never gives up!" she muttered darkly to Ivan, who had come and plonked himself companionably at her feet and now gave a sympathetic thump of his tail on the slabs. "For all Trish says he hasn't engineered this situation, what's the betting I get up there and find he's been winding them all around his little finger like always?" Ivan's tail beat another short tattoo on the slabs. "I tell you, Ivan, I'm doing this more so that I can find out what's happened to Dav than for his lordship. God, it would be so unfair if Dav has been killed and Toby's *still* running around screwing the world over!"

Chapter 2

Friday

However, early on Friday morning she found herself on the fast train to Birmingham, leaving her home and security behind. She felt passable until the train got into the outskirts of Birmingham, but after that her anxiety increased bit by bit until they pulled into the University Station. It did little for her composure that this was horribly familiar territory. As girls she and Trish had sometimes walked up to this station, and taken the train into the city centre as an adventurous change from taking the bus to do their lengthy Saturday window-shopping. Days when Toby had seemed such a catch! Just the thought now made a shiver run down Stella's spine.

Once out on the road which ran from the station to both the university campus and the enormous and still expanding Queen Elizabeth Hospital complex, Stella rang Trish on her mobile and then called another taxi to take her to the older hospital. Under other circumstances she would have walked – Selly Oak wasn't that far away when you knew the back roads, and the day was pleasant – but she didn't dare give herself a chance to turn around and get on the next train back. It was therefore just coming up to lunch time when she met Trish outside the hospital and they embraced in a friendly hug.

"You should be staying with us!" Trish remonstrated. "You know you're always welcome. Graham's horrified that you're travelling up and down."

But Stella shook her head vehemently. "No! There's no way I'm staying with you. Not for this! If he thinks he can use you as a way-station for me, he'll expect me to be coming up and down like a yo-yo." No need to say who 'he' was.

"Oh Stella, that's harsh!" Trish protested.

"Maybe, but I bet it's the bloody truth! Now, ...what's all this about C.D. and himself being at each other's throats?"

After they'd split up Toby had married his last and longest standing affair – a nurse whom Stella had detested upon sight. Chloe James, as she'd been then, was a tall willowy blonde with no sexual restraints or morals that Stella had been able to discern. Her own problems with Toby had always begun with his inability to keep his flies done up, and she'd found a savage kind of glee in the knowledge that in Chloe he'd found someone as promiscuous as himself. If he was never going to be faithful to any woman, neither was she ever likely to be a one-man woman. 'An open marriage' was the euphemistic way he'd described it to Stella over the phone as an opener to another one of their vitriolic arguments. A situation which, as she'd told Trish, meant that at least they weren't making two other poor souls' lives a misery as well.

C.J., as Chloe had always wanted to be known, had become Chloe Donaldson upon marrying Toby and had promptly become C.D. – a nickname which Stella had problems with, for she could never resist pronouncing it as 'seedy' since that was the way she viewed the marriage. Never had a nickname rung so inadvertently true! And now Stella had a sneaking suspicion that C.D.

had had a word with her medical colleagues, and had realised that at least in the trouser department, Toby might not be performing to his old standard for some time. Something which wouldn't go down well at all with either of them, because unless Toby had become a total fool over C.D., he would surely know that she'd be off getting satisfaction elsewhere if he couldn't provide it. Stella restrained a mirthless grin at the thought – serve the bastard right if he found out how it had felt for her for all those hellish years!

However, it wouldn't do to gloat in front of Trish, who was regaling her with the tale.

"He's been home – back in England, that is – for over a month now, and C.D. *was* calling in to see him whenever she went on or off shift. She maintains that she's done all she can to help him but he's being totally irrational with her. Wants to know what she's been doing if she's a few minutes late."

"I bet he does," Stella murmured softly, imagining Toby lying in bed watching C.D. breeze in with the scent of some other man still on her. He'd had a nose like a bloodhound for any woman likely to be sexually active, so he'd be unlikely to miss it on his wife unless he was completely sedated.

"C.D. says he's told her that he doesn't trust her any more. She's really cut up about it."

"You don't say," Stella snorted, this time unable to keep her amusement hidden. "She must be scared to death that he's going to divorce her before she does him. Wouldn't do for her to be painted to a judge as the nympho' who leaves her hero husband in the hospital bed to go off shagging her arse off round the town, would it?"

Trish looked horrified. "There's no need to be crude, Stella!"

"Oh, don't look like that, when did you turn into a prude, woman? You know that's the truth. What drew Toby to her was that white nurse's uniform pulled tight over the huge tits. They don't have a damned thing in common apart from humping one another's brains out. The only thing which surprises me is that it's lasted this long, and that's probably only because Toby was away so much. They'd have tired of one another long ago if he'd had a nine-to-five job and been home every evening. So what's he expecting? To make nice with me so that I'll come back and wipe his arse for him, and be the good wife who cares for him now that life's come up and bitten him at last?"

By now they were coming up to the ward and Trish just looked at Stella, sighed, and shook her head as she led the way in. At the nurse's station Trish was greeted by name. Clearly she'd been coming here pretty regularly.

"This is the ex-Mrs Donaldson," she said introducing Stella to a tall motherly woman with a staff nurse's badge on.

"Stella *Fox*," Stella introduced herself emphatically with a tight smile. "Mrs Donaldson is someone else entirely these days!"

The staff nurse took in her expression and broke into a warmer smile in return. Maybe Toby has already irritated the living daylights out of this one, Stella thought hopefully? A huge West Indian woman who must have stood six feet tall in her socks, the staff nurse certainly wasn't the kind of woman Toby would have looked twice at, so maybe he hadn't tried to turn the charm on either.

The junior doctor scuttled out of a side ward forestalling any further comment, a diminutive man whose accent was nowhere nearly as broad as Trish's mimicking had made out.

"Mrs. Donaldson, thank you for coming," he said at great speed.

"I've not been Mrs. Donaldson for seven years, and I've no intention of returning to it either," Stella growled uncooperatively, making him stop in his tracks and look at her perplexed.

"Look doctor, I don't have time to give you the whole catalogue of miseries that little shit inflicted on me, so let me just put you straight on this: I'm here reluctantly, alright? Tess, here, is the only reason I've got on the train and dragged myself all this way. You've got me for the rest of today. After that I'm going home no matter what! But if you've any daft ideas of me picking up the pieces of Toby Donaldson's life you can think again. Whatever rehabilitation he needs to do is going to be done without me, okay?"

"Oh dear," the little junior doctor seemed quite taken aback. "I didn't expect you to be so hostile."

"Really?" Stella said with sickly sweetness. "Told you I was a little mouse, did he? Spun some cock and bull story about how sorry he was to have lost his respectable, quiet, doormat of a woman?"

The junior doctor's pink cheeks told Stella she wasn't far from the mark, but behind her she heard the staff nurse's throaty chuckle – at least I have an ally there, she thought.

Going into the ward, however, sobered her swiftly. Mercifully Toby was in the first bed, but beyond him were some heartbreaking sights. If Stella felt no sympathy for him, she was far from being unmoved at the state of some of the younger men on the ward, and she knew she would have been hard-pressed to retain her indifference if Toby had been surrounded by them. As it was Toby was still something of a shock. It wasn't that he was swathed in bandages or anything. His visible wounds were comparatively small and covered by neat dressings. It was how gaunt he was for a start, and then when he turned his gaze to them it was most unsettling. All the old Toby bounce and ego seemed to have been seared away in the haunted eyes which looked back at her. Maybe, just maybe, Trish had been right and he wasn't the man he used to be anymore.

"Toby," she said flatly, quirking an enquiring eyebrow his way.

The junior doctor looked at her and the way she was standing with her hands firmly thrust into the pockets of her jacket. Clearly he'd been expecting something more emotional from her. Well that was his tough luck.

Toby blinked at her and forced a smile. It was forced too, Stella noticed. None of the old Toby smoothness, none of the automatic default to charmer whenever life bit him.

"Don't I get a hug and a kiss?" he asked, flicking a glance which might almost have amounted to worry in the junior doctor's direction.

"No," she answered shortly.

Now she could see he was bothered. He really hadn't thought this through at all, and she felt her anger bubbling up inside yet again. The selfish bastard had clearly wiped all memory of the reality of their marriage from his mind. It suited him to think her irrational, and that his current situation would change things for her. That was instantly confirmed as he said,

"What? Even after I've come back to a hospital bed? You used to be more…"

"...of a doormat?" Stella grimaced and in turn glanced to the intern. "You've got some kind of nerve, Toby!"

"Stella!" Trish remonstrated.

"No! I've had it with him! What did you expect, Toby? What have you told these strangers? I bet you haven't told them about the one thing I kept back during the divorce proceedings."

Trish whipped around to stare at Stella as her husband Graham came into the ward and rested a hand on her shoulder. "Kept back? Oh Lord, Stella, there wasn't more was there?"

"You …you promised!" Toby spluttered, for the first time showing some real animation.

"Yes I promised. I promised that I would never say a word because you said it would go against you if the army found out. You said that if I wanted a settlement worth anything you needed to keep your job. I agreed to that. But do you remember what the price of that was, Toby? In that twisted version of life that you keep filed away in your head, can you remember what the deal was? It certainly wasn't that I was so money grasping! Come on, tell the good folks here what it was!"

Toby blushed scarlet. "That I was never to call on you for anything ever again. That I'd leave you alone to…, to…"

"Pick up the pieces, I think were the words I used," Stella said frostily. "And have you done that? No! First you were constantly at me to try and weasel out of the small amount you were paying out to me. So once I got my teaching going I let you get your way. Clearly not my brightest idea! I thought that with the money not connecting us any more you'd piss off, but you just like yanking people's chains, don't you!" She paused and took a deep breath. "So what did you *think* you could ask me to do?"

Toby said nothing, so Stella turned to the young junior doctor.

"What about you, then, doctor? What did *you* think I was coming down to do?"

The poor man was utterly undone, and it was the older nurse who answered for the medical staff in a voice which held the undertones of amusement in it.

"Oh he said that you could be *relied* upon. I think it was after the current Mrs. Donaldson argued with him whenever she was here, that he said that you were …quieter! That you two might be divorced but that you would always do the right thing. That there was still a spark between you, even though he'd been a bit foolish having an affair."

Stella's jaw had dropped further and further with each sentence. "The right thing! Jesus, Toby, you've got a fucking nerve! And as for a spark…! The only spark you'll get from me is when I light the match before sticking a bomb up your arse!" She turned to Trish and Graham. "I told you! I bloody told you, but you wouldn't believe me! Well now you're going to hear his nasty little secret. What I kept quiet about was the fact that he shoved me down the stairs when I challenged him over his affairs!"

Trish clapped her hands over her mouth and began shaking her head.

"Oh yes, Trish! You see I found out that I had Chlamydia. It came as a nasty shock when the doctor told me, because I knew there was only one place I could have picked that up from. So when this dirty little shit here got back home, I challenged him about it. He got so angry when I told him that he had to get in touch with the girl who'd given it to him. Angrier and angrier until he thumped me and put me down the stairs. If you don't believe me it's a matter of hospital records, because I crawled to the phone and got a taxi to the hospital, while he went to the pub and got smashed on vodka again."

The tears were rolling down Trish's cheeks now, while Graham was pale and embarrassed, although Stella guessed it was in part due to the realisation of just how badly they'd been sucked in by Toby's tales.

"When I got back I moved into the spare room. Did you never wonder, Tess, how I got a place in the university halls of residence despite still being married? I showed them the medical reports and told them that getting my teaching qualifications was the way out. That's what pissed him off even more. That someone took me seriously! And of course he couldn't tell the person who had given him Chlamydia – but not out of pride or machismo, though. No, he couldn't tell them because he didn't know which one of the *many* women he'd had one night stands with had been the one! Anyway, he sure wasn't about to get in touch with all of them – especially as some of them were the wives of men he was in the army with! That's the other thing he asked me to hush up for our divorce hearing! I could divorce him on the grounds of infidelity, and he wouldn't fight that hard as long as I didn't say that he was the mystery man in *Dav's* divorce and others!"

"Oh Toby, how *could* you?" Trish sobbed.

"Pretty bloody easily, I would say!" Graham said with an iciness Stella had never heard from him before. "You know, I always used to think that you and Stella were equally to blame for the marriage going wrong."

"Gee thanks, Graham!" snorted Stella, but Graham maybe hadn't heard her, or chose to ignore the comment because he carried on,

"But you really are a complete arsehole! Well you can forget coming to our house to convalesce! I'm not having you under our roof!" He tried to pull Trish away but she resisted, and so he turned on his heels and walked out with the parting words of, "I'll be in the car when you're ready, girls."

"You'd better make nice with C.D., too," Stella said calmly, "because I'm not having you with me, either." She turned to the doctor, and the nurse who'd been joined by a couple of colleagues, clearly hanging on her every word. "I'm sorry to have to be brutal about this, but it was the only way I could get you to see what he's like. I could have answered phone-call after phone-call and you still wouldn't have understood me, because he would have put a spin on every message I gave back. I meant what I said when I arrived. You have me here for the rest of today and then I'm gone. ...Now then, ...I'm going for a coffee downstairs to give you all time to think. When I come back, you can tell me if there's anything you can reasonably ask me to do for this miserable specimen."

She turned and fixed a steely gaze on the squirming Toby, who was evidently not so shocked or damaged as to not to be acutely aware of how badly he'd miscalculated the whole situation. "I understand that Dav is missing or hurt. If you can summon a thought for anyone other than yourself, think about him and what you might want me to do on *his* behalf. In that respect at least you're right, I will always do the right thing by him. And it's not because there was something going on behind your back between us, despite the mud you kept on trying to throw at me over our friendship. I'll do anything I can to help Dav, because the bottom line is that Dav is a decent, kind and honest bloke. Something you'll never be if you live to be a hundred!"

And with that she turned and marched out of the ward. This section of the old Victorian hospital was in the final stages of moving across to the newly built military wing at the Queen Elizabeth up the road, and its melancholic atmosphere suited her moods. As she got further away from Toby's ward she felt her anger evaporating to sadness. She had a nasty suspicion that she'd made things difficult for Trish with Graham with her revelations. That was rotten for Tess, although Stella was still insulted that Graham had evidently thought her some kind of frigid hysteric who had forced Toby to other women's company. To hell with him! She wouldn't be holidaying with them anymore, (although that was less of a wrench now that they were back living in Birmingham, rather than on the Norfolk coast).

In the cafe she got a cup of what purported to be coffee, although the taste was as nondescript as the colour. Sitting in a corner she nursed the cup, and found herself feeling surprisingly calm. It was letting out those last deep buried truths which had brought a new sense of peace inside, she decided. The last efforts of pretence that things hadn't been as bad as they had been were finally gone. The last cord had been cut.

Looking up she saw C.D. standing just inside in the door, watching her with a smirk on her face. Stella looked down again and as she anticipated, C.D. came over to her, unable to resist the opportunity to gloat. Biting her lip, Stella let C.D. make the opening.

"Well you didn't think I was going to start nursing at home as well as at work, did you?" The peroxide pony tail got a flick with her head. "But you're the good girl, aren't you! He said you'd be desperate to be in the right over me! Well don't expect me or anyone to hear you whining the next time!"

Stella looked up into C.D.'s gloating face and rose to her feet herself. "Oh I knew you wouldn't be wanting him once he couldn't keep it up all night, every night," she replied with a grin she had no trouble in forcing. "But you've got me wrong. In fact you *always* got me wrong, C.D.! Your trouble was that you believed exactly what Toby said about me without filtering out all of the crap even you must know he puts in to everything to make him look snow-white all the time.

"So don't you worry about me! I'm not having him back either! In fact I'm booked on the train home this very night, so as the current Mrs Donaldson you'd be better deciding what you're going to do about him!" Stella pushed the chair back under the table and picked up her shoulder bag, giving her time to enjoy watching C.D.'s expression melt from synthetic smile to worried frown. "Oh …and I wouldn't frown like that too long! You'll get wrinkles, and they wouldn't do much for your chances of catching a replacement for Toby, would they!"

Walking back along the corridor and up the stairs, she got to the ward and heard something which sounded rather heated going on in the nurses' office. Clearly the decision over what to do about Toby's treatment was not going smoothly! She smiled softly to herself and looked about for Tess, but her friend was nowhere to be seen, and Stella guessed she must be in the meeting with the doctor and nurses. That meant that she would have to go and sit with Toby on her own and she didn't want that.

It wasn't out of spite. It was simply that she wanted to avoid any image which might make people think that she could still be won round. So she wandered along the small corridor, aimlessly reading notices pinned up on the walls. As visiting time came round families filtered in and the ward became more animated with conversation. She was filled with sympathy for the worried parents and girlfriends who came in to see the young soldiers. Clearly the men were getting the best possible care, but it wouldn't make it any easier if it was someone you really loved lying in one of the beds.

She was so lost in her thoughts that at first she didn't register the voice that was calling softly, but then she realized that someone was calling for some water. A natural nurse she might not be, but giving someone a drink was something even she could do, and none of the other people in here had done her any harm. Whoever this was, at least he wasn't Toby.

Chapter 3

Friday

Looking about her, she realised that the voice came from a side ward – a tiny space cut out of the big old ward by modern partition walls. Sticking her head around the partly open door, she saw screens around the bed still shielding the bed from view.

God I hope he isn't on the commode, or worse, she thought!

"Can I come in?" she called softly, feeling that she ought to ask first.

"Aye, come in," the voice responded with a definite hint of the north-east in it.

Slipping into the room Stella found herself confronted with an impossibly young-looking lad. Was he really old enough to have been out fighting? She was hardly ancient herself, but even to her eyes he looked way too young! Then her eyes caught the tented sheets, and the way they dropped flat to the bed where his legs ought to have been, and felt a lump come in her throat. Yet when she caught his eyes she knew instinctively that she needed to get a grip. He must have had more than his share of family weeping over him.

"Water," she said, for want of anything else, and walked round the foot of the bed to the cupboard where a jug and a standard non-spill hospital mug sat. "You are allowed it?" she suddenly asked, having a momentary panic that she might inadvertently kill him with kindness.

"Aye, I'm allowed water. Wouldn't mind sommat stronger, mind!" he added with feeble humour.

"I bet you wouldn't!" Stella quipped back, not having to force the smile now.

She poured some water into the mug and then carefully handed it to him, watching for any signs of shaking hands or other clues that he might need help. He was a little shaky, but managed to have a long drink without other help.

"Have you no visitors today?" Stella asked, suddenly aware that other families were starting to say their goodbyes and stream out of the ward.

The lad's face fell. "Me mam and dad come every day, but me mam only manages a couple of minutes before she starts cryin'. And then she has to go out. Me dad sticks it out a bit longer, but then feels he has to go and find her."

"Oh, that's rough …on all of you!" Stella could imagine only too well his mother's anguish, but also how this lad must be wishing they could hold themselves together a bit more for his sake. "Would you like me to sit with you for a bit?"

"Aren't you visitin' someone yourself?"

"Not exactly. It's a bit complicated. My ex-husband is in here and I was asked to come and speak to the medical staff because his current wife isn't being helpful." She rolled her eyes theatrically. "Quite a lot of the drama queens going on there! I think they thought I'd be easier to deal with."

"Was he out there?" the lad asked.

"Yes, Sergeant Donaldson. Did you know him?"

The lad frowned. "Donaldson? Naw, doesn't ring any bells. Probably not with our lot."

Seeing the Mercian cap-badge sitting forlornly on the cupboard top, the cap itself no doubt long disposed of as bloodied and wrecked, Stella was sure that wasn't so, but put it down to the lad's considerable trauma. He already seemed exhausted by the short conversation and his eyelids were drooping. By now Stella had gone round to sit at the seat on the other side of the bed, and she gently reached out and touched his hand. With surprising strength he gripped it back, and so she had little choice but to sit there until he relaxed into sleep. Clearly he'd been desperate for just that bit of human contact, and Stella found herself happier to sit with him and provide such a small thing than to go and find the doctors and Toby.

Eventually, though, she realised she had to make a move, if for no other reason than the nursing staff coming and finding her in a stranger's room and wondering why. And she really did want to get home tonight, so better to get things over and done with. However she didn't want to go blundering out of the room straight into some nurse, and so she sidled up to the door and paused to listen.

What she heard, though, was not the soft soles of a nurse's shoes, but the heavy tread of military boots striding down the corridor towards her. She barely had time to shrink back so that the door masked her fully before an older man's voice called out,

"Captain?"

Immediately she heard another set of boots coming from the corridor, turning into this first section of the old ward, and coming to a halt abruptly outside the partition she was behind. She didn't need to see anything to know that there had been a crisp salute going on out there too.

"Colonel? What can I do for you, sir?"

The older man's voice now dropped to a confidential hiss.

"What in God's name is going on here? Visitors? Can't you keep control of the situation, Captain?"

Stella could almost hear the frustration in the captain's reply, although he did a fair job of keeping it hidden as best he could.

"Sir, this is out of my jurisdiction! This ward has men from all over the place – we can't just shut it off! And it was not my decision to have the men on an open military ward, but I couldn't ask for them to be segregated without giving the staff here a good reason why. My orders when I left the facility were to integrate them into the rest of their regiment coming home, so this was all I could do. Have the orders changed?"

The colonel gave a disgusted harrumph. "No. The orders stand. But you'll have to keep control of the men. Under no circumstance can we have them blabbing about where they've been and what they've done."

This time the captain really did groan out loud. "I'm sorry, sir, but what do you want me to do? Half of them are off their heads so far I doubt they'll ever come down! I was just with Biggins, trying to talk to him, when he started giggling hysterically. When I asked him what was wrong, he said, 'Fuck me, serge! That rabbit costume's awesome. Never had you down as a Playboy bunny!' And when the nurse heard him and asked him what that was all about he said, as if she was the crazy one for not seeing it, 'The great big fluffy rabbit there! Look! The white one waving his willy at you!' ...How in God's name do you want me to control that ...*sir*?"

Far from being sympathetic, the colonel instead growled, "You know how vital it is that no word should get out about the tests! That cannot happen!"

"To be fair, sir, given the outrageous crap most of the lads I brought in are spouting, they could be telling people they've been to Area 51, or to Kansas with just a click of their heels, and no-one would bat an eyelid! In amongst all the rest of it, who on earth is going to take notice of one more loony claim?"

The colonel was silent for a moment. "Are they all like that?"

"To be honest, sir, yes. Even the more lucid ones fade in and out. Sometimes they're perfectly reasonable, and then out of the blue they're talking total crap! Completely without warning!"

"Like what?"

"Well Donaldson's been telling the ward staff that his ex is going to be looking after him."

Even as Stella struggled to muffle her gasp of shock, the colonel was snorting in disbelief.

"Man's a bloody fool! I saw the report on their divorce – the Families' Officer said quite clearly that he was lucky to get away without a criminal prosecution. The regiment's got more to be worried about from the current wife, by all accounts. She's a nurse, isn't she?"

"Yes, sir, but her speciality is paediatrics and gynaecology. She's not involved in this kind of ward at all."

"Thank Christ for that! ...Very well, captain. Carry on, but keep me informed! Anyone who looks as though they might be trouble, let me know. Immediately!"

"Yes, sir!"

And there was another clatter of boots and then the sound of the colonel retreating. Stella heard the captain give a sigh of relief, and then turn and walk back into the main ward. So while she knew his back would still be turned to her, Stella slipped out of the room, and then walked over to the nurses' station hoping she would look as though she had just walked in from the main corridor.

"Has anyone been asking for me?" she asked the nurse there, and having given a quick explanation, was left to contemplate what she'd heard while the nurse went and found out.

What on earth had all that been about? It sounded very much as though some of the patients in here hadn't been out to Afghanistan at all. Was that why Toby had come back so soon? He'd never been there in the first place? But if not, then where had he been?

Her frantic thoughts were interrupted by the young oriental doctor's appearance.

"Mrs …errm, Miss…?" He was suddenly awkward, not knowing what to call her.

"It's Miss Fox, or Stella if you want. I've no quarrel with you, doctor. I'm only too aware of how convincing Toby can be when he's after something. I've just had more practice than you at spotting it when he's spinning one of his webs of lies. …So is there anything I can actually do to help you, doctor?"

He 'umm'd and 'aaa'd for a moment but then admitted that really all he could ask of her was to come and visit.

"We have to acknowledge that we've been totally misled over you taking care of Sergeant Donaldson," he confessed, "and to be honest, finding someone to send him home to was our first priority. As that's clearly not going to happen…"

"No, it's most definitely not!"

"…then he'll be here for the foreseeable future, until we're convinced he will be able to look after himself, or we can find convalescent care elsewhere."

Stella had to stop herself from saying there never had been any chance of that. It would sound petty to anyone who hadn't known of the full extent of the misery Toby had put her through. Grating though it was, she realised she would have to offer some kind of concession.

"Well I suppose I could come up a couple of times this coming week, seeing as it's half-term. But after that, I'm sorry, but I have to work full-time and I don't live locally, at best I can offer to call in once in a weekend. That's not being difficult, doctor. I simply can't afford the petrol or the rail fare to come traipsing up here twice in a week. When he divorced me he left me without anything. No alimony, nothing! So I can't spend what I haven't got just because after all this time he's decided he needs me."

The poor doctor blushed furiously, horribly aware of the situation he'd been dumped in.

"No, Miss Fox, I quite understand."

Stella was feeling really sorry for him by now.

"Would you like me to go in and sit with him for a bit now?" she offered through gritted teeth. Her day was utterly spoiled anyway, so as long as she made her train, what difference did it make?

The way he jumped at the offer made her think that Toby was definitely one of his more difficult patients, and so, squaring her shoulders, she strode back into the ward. Caught unawares by her, she found a much more sombre Toby than she had expected. He was staring down the ward towards where one of the other soldiers seemed to be having some kind of fit. The nursing staff piled in, and the screens were already being drawn as Stella got to Toby's bed, but he continued to gaze worriedly down there oblivious to her presence.

"One of your lads?" she ventured to ask.

Toby visibly jumped at the sound of her voice.

"You came back!"

"Yes. Don't get your hopes up. The doctor asked

me to, and I've an hour or so before I need to go and get the train."

"Oh."

Stella could feel her irritation rising again. "God help us, Toby! What did you expect?"

"Was I really that bad?"

She looked at him as disgust and disbelief vied for top place in her emotions. "That bad? You have the almighty nerve to even ask? Have you so totally rearranged our past in that thing which passes for your brain that you don't know what the truth is anymore? Or are you so damned selfish that you can't see how you're pissing me off?"

Whatever she was expecting, his answer stunned her.

"I can't remember, Stell'. God's honest truth! Some things from the recent past are so muddled I can't seem to get a grip on them at all. The further back I go the better it is. But..." his voice cracked and although he screwed his face up, he couldn't stop tears from starting to run down his face, "...but none of it's good. Nothing's ...right! Nothing's *all* there! Not you. Not Mum, and I can't even see Dad's face anymore."

For the briefest of instants Stella was going to laugh and tell him to pull the other one, yet there was such distress in his face that it stopped her before she could even snort in derision. In all the misery of their separation, and the grim reality of their life together, she had never seen him like this. And then it dawned on her. He was scared. Not just a bit frightened. She'd seen him like that when he'd been worried that she would tell the truth at their divorce hearing. When frightened Toby got aggressive, but he certainly wasn't now, and if she was honest with herself, Stella had to admit that she would have said he was damned near terrified, and that all of itself changed how she felt.

Plonking herself down on the visitor's chair, and throwing her jacket and bag onto a chair behind her, she looked at him hard.

"What happened to you, Toby? What really happened?"

His "I don't know," came out as a plaintive whisper, and suddenly she remembered the overheard conversation.

"Toby, look at me! Did you ever go out to Afghanistan this time? Ever? Were you with the rest of the lads out there?"

He raised frightened eyes to hers. "I don't know. Truly, Stell', I don't."

"Can you remember anything which might give you a clue? Like sand? Can you remember lots of sand? Or being in mountains? I'm told that there are mountains out there. Big snowy mountains. Do you have any sort of hint that you saw anything like that?"

He shook his head dejectedly. Which made Stella think that maybe he'd never left this country. Surely he would have some vague impression left on his mind if he'd been out in another place, and somewhere where the conditions were as extreme as Afghanistan? Had it been to somewhere like Germany she would have understood his bafflement a bit more, because at the end of the day there was a certain amount of commonality within modern European countries, but not a Third World one.

"Who was with you, Toby? Are all the lads in this ward from where you were?"

Suddenly he was able to be more decisive. "No!"

"How many, then?"

Toby looked around the ward. "Him definitely," he said with a nod to where the screens were still pulled around the far bed, and where the sounds of someone in extreme distress were coming from. "The lad over in the far corner. And the chap halfway down on the far side with the black hair."

Stella followed his gaze and was chilled to see that the two still visible to her were sitting staring into space in an almost catatonic stupor. Other patients fidgeted in their beds, one was reading, another furtively playing a game on a high-tech mobile phone while the nurses were distracted and couldn't tell him to switch it off. But however battered and broken the others looked, none had the mental vacant look of those two.

"Are there more in other wards?" she asked.

"I don't know," Toby answered mournfully. "I can't remember their names, so I don't know who to ask for. The only one I can still remember is Dav."

Stella felt her blood run cold. "Oh no! Oh please don't tell me Dav was there with you?"

He nodded and once more his face creased unbidden into grief. "I can't find anyone who knows where he is."

"When was the last time you saw him?"

Toby gave a weak shrug. "Hard to tell. Not long ago, but not recently either."

That made a warped kind of sense. Dav and Toby were no longer the close mates they had once been, and much of that was down to how Toby had treated her during and after the divorce. So if they had been stationed together, the chances were that hadn't spent much off-duty time together. Then another though occurred to Stella.

"Toby, what's the official reason you're in here?"

She got another of his blank stares. "I mean what are they treating you for?"

He pulled the lightweight blanket down and hoisted up the pyjama top so that Stella could see the multiple wounds. She might not have had much in the way of medical knowledge, but even she could have made a fair guess at him having been in some kind of explosion. There were some nasty looking puncture wounds, and of the ragged kind which hinted at flying shards of something or shrapnel. But also there were many unpleasant-looking grazes, and patches which were definitely burns. Not the life-threatening sort, but still bad enough to blister and look angrily red.

And yet ...the more Stella looked the more she couldn't help but think that it looked like he'd been in something closer to domestic disaster than a war zone. It seemed more like he'd been hit by glass and splinters of wood as well as metal, than anything more military, and not one of the visible marks looked even vaguely like a bullet wound. Again, she was no expert on what the fresh wounds looked like, but from her time in married quarters and those rare summer days when the lads had been outside without their shirts on, she had seen the scars which bullets left, and these didn't look like those at all.

Curiosity piqued, she went to the chart at the bottom of the bed and began reading. As she worked back through the notes it became clear that when he had been brought in, Toby had been a very sick man indeed. There were mentions of blood transfusions, and in amongst the technical jargon which meant nothing to her, Stella nonetheless got the distinct impression that Toby had been left for some time before being rescued and brought to a hospital. That was understandable out in the wilds and with an implacable enemy firing at you.

But if Toby had never even left these shores, then it was inexcusable!

Slipping the chart back where she had found it, before anyone noticed she'd been taking a more than expected interest in her ex-husband's health, Stella sat down again, but shuffled her chair right close to the bed.

"Toby! Try to focus on what I'm saying! Can you remember being in an explosion? Never mind where for now. Can you just remember being blown up?"

He screwed his eyes up, the picture of a small child going through such an exercise. "Yes. ...Well not exactly. But I have this vague sensation of flying through the air in my head, and landing hard ...but more as though I'd just been hit ...shoved ...punched. ...And maybe me getting up to go and fight something again. Nothing more than that. Not anything like an IED."

Stella patted his hand. "That's enough! Don't worry about the rest. Now in that moment, were there lots of you? More than the four of you here, I mean?"

Toby now looked haunted. "I think so. I can't tell you why, but I think a lot more. I can't say names or numbers."

"Was Dav one of them?"

"I think so."

Chapter 4

Friday – Sunday

Getting back to her peaceful home, Stella immediately changed into her old jeans and boots and took Ivan out onto the hills. She had a desperate need to get out into the clean fresh air after such a day. Trish and Graham had been nowhere to be seen when she had come out of the ward, and she was rather glad of that. Trish would have put all the wrong interpretations on Stella's interest in what had happened to Toby, and what Graham would think she didn't even want to start on.

Yet there was no doubt in her mind now that there was something very dodgy going on. She was ninety percent certain that the hospital staff were in complete ignorance of whatever it was. So trying to wheedle anything out of the young doctor would be a waste of time. The nursing sister might be someone she could confide in, though, but not for finding out what the army were trying to cover up. And that there was a cover-up was something she was increasingly convinced of.

That made her angry. Whatever had happened to her personally, she was genuinely supportive of the lads who went out to fight on their country's behalf. And, if someone was siphoning men off to use them in some underhand experiment, or for some covert use without telling them first, then that made her angry.

But what really made her blood boil was the thought that if they then came to harm, that those responsible were dragging their heels over getting them the medical help they needed straight away. That colonel had been far more worried about what would be said if things got out, than of the health of the men he'd come to see; and however much of a shit Toby was, he deserved better than that. He'd given the army more than a decade of his life, and for that alone he had earned better treatment.

And what was going on with regard to Dav? She really felt sick about that. If they – whoever 'they' turned out to be – were dragging their heels over the men actually in the hospital ward, she could easily imagine that nothing much at all would be done about men who had gone missing, or killed, unless a family member got shirty and started kicking up a fuss. And by a fuss Stella was thinking of someone going as far as turning to the major newspapers and other media, not just complaining in writing or in person at the regiment's main base at Lichfield. Moreover, if Birmingham was hardly on the doorstep for her here in Malvern, Lichfield on the other side of the city was quite a way away if someone's parents lived over Hereford way; or even for the lads from Nottinghamshire, because the regiment had a very broad recruiting area these days, and that might make it harder to keep pounding on some senior officer's door too. The days when Toby's regiment had been recruited locally, and been known as the Worcesters, had long gone in the army reorganisations of recent decades.

Plonking herself down on the soft, sweet grass, with Ivan coming to loll companionably by her side, she said to him, "And what on earth am I going to do about Dav, eh? I can't let this one rest, Ivan, not if he's missing. Who else is going to demand answers about him if not me? Bugger it! I'm really going to have to go back up to that hospital now, aren't I? Thank heavens it's only six more weeks once I go back to work and then the long holidays." She ruffled Ivan's ears. "Might be short commons for your summer walkies this year, though, my love."

Her great solace was the summer break, when she could pack a tent into her car, and she and Ivan could go off into the wilds together. It had started as something she did to prove to herself that she wasn't the weak thing Toby had taken her for. And so it had become something of a challenge to walk at least some of the same territories he used to come home and talk to her about. That included the not so distant Brecon Beacons, but also the wilder parts of Yorkshire and parts of Scotland. Of course in his case it was always embellished. He could never have just marched up a hill. He had to yomp up it at the head of the pack, always reaching the top, or whatever goal had been set, in the best time, or ahead of whichever bloke in his company who had done it best before.

There had been a savage satisfaction in those early days as she'd realised that he couldn't possibly have done what he said he'd done on so many of those routes. It had felt like vindication for her scepticism over other things he'd told her. And she'd increasingly understood why – back in the days when their house seemed to always be full of Toby's mates at the weekends when they were based in the UK – Dav had often rolled his eyes and grinned at her while Toby was spinning some yarn, or had just shook his head and walked away chuckling to himself. Of course that had been while Dav and Toby had been best mates; what his reactions had been later on to Toby's endless one-upmanship she hadn't witnessed, but she suspected it must have started to grate on his nerves as much as hers.

"I might go up on Sunday," she said thoughtfully to Ivan. "I bet there are lots of visitors on that day. Might be the best time to sneak a peek at other lads' records, or ask one of their relatives if they've been suspicious of anything. That captain will be run ragged trying to watch everyone when the ward's rammed with outsiders, and he can't stop the regular lads having visits, can he? Not without giving the game away."

She got a sticky lick on her hand as an answer, but took that as Ivan being in agreement with her. "You'll have to go to Dai Thomas' again," she warned him, and his whiskery face broke into a grin. Ivan wasn't daft. He knew Dai's name and that it meant far more biscuits and treats than Stella allowed him. As if reading her expression, Ivan's tail began beating a tattoo on the ground and then rolled onto his back for belly rubs, for all the world as if to say, 'I know it's naughty, but I can't help myself. I like biscuits!' His lolling grin made Stella laugh, and the last of the day's tension drained away.

"Come on, you terrible hound," she laughed. "Time for your dinner!"

However, two mornings later she dropped Ivan next door and set out, this time feeling happy enough to drive herself. She felt as though she had more control over the situation now, given that she had an objective of her own to work towards – whatever Toby might say would now be secondary to her to finding out what had happened to Dav.

At the hospital she struggled to find any parking, confirming her assumption that Sunday was a popular visiting time, and she ended up having to park a couple of roads away. Actually she didn't mind that. If C.D. was around then she wouldn't spot Stella's car, which was pretty obvious given that it was a bright banana yellow.

That hadn't been Stella's choice, it was just that it was the right car in other respects and came at the right price – cheap! But it also meant it was hardly anonymous, especially as she had tried to cover some of the worst paint chips with bright flowery decals after her attempts to touch them up with paint had failed miserably. No, if C.D. was on shift, Stella definitely didn't want to be spotted, with her making assumptions and coming to all the wrong conclusions.

Feeling faintly ridiculous as she shiftily made her way into the wing where Toby was, Stella relaxed when she saw how many families were coming and going. Also, it was a different nursing team on today. Nobody who'd been in on Friday was there to recognise her, and that was all to the good.

Making her way to Toby's bed, she paused before pulling up a chair. He had his eyes closed and hadn't seen her, so she was able to watch him for a moment. Yes, something had definitely taken all the bounce out of Toby. His usual relaxed sprawl when in bed was gone, and he was curled up on his side in an almost foetal position – one she'd never seen him adopt before. And there was a tension about him even though he seemed to be asleep.

Then he stirred when a child further down the ward began squawking, and Stella realised he'd just had his eyes closed against the world.

"Stell'? How long you been here?" he asked, blinking up at her blearily.

"Just got here. I was wondering whether to wake you."

He wriggled around in the bed so that he was facing her more as she sat down.

"I meant what I said …you know …the other day, when you came."

"Meant what?" Stella's heart was already sinking.

"About not remembering."

"Oh." What could she say to that? "Toby, about that... I'm not going to go on about when we were together. If you honestly don't remember, then when you get home I'd suggest you read the divorce papers and the reasons I gave. I'm not going to argue with you here. ...But I did come because I want to find out what happened to you. I said I'd try and find Dav and I meant it. ...Where the hell have you been?"

Toby's face crumpled into a distressed frown. "I don't know, Stell'. I wish I did."

"Hmmm... Do you think you came straight here? I mean, can you remember being anywhere else before waking up in the hospital? A field hospital, for instance? Being under canvas while they patched you up? Being hot? Hotter than in England I mean."

Toby bit his lip, thinking hard. "No, I don't think I do. Ever since you asked me the other day I've been trying to remember, and I think I can just about recall being in an ambulance, and that it was going at speed. I think what brought me round was the siren being switched on."

They talked for a few more minutes before Stella observed, "You're very pale," noticing for the first time that compared to some of the other soldiers on the ward that Toby looked positively pasty. "Look at him over there. Brown as a berry! You're not like that. And you said that lad in the far bed was with you? Well he's really pale too."

Toby blinked owlishly. "Christ! I never spotted that before! Bloody hell, Stell'! What happened to us?"

"I don't know, but I'm going to find out. ...Look, that lad over there ...he's another of the ones you said was with you, isn't he? The one with all the family around him?"

"Yeah, I think so. His face looks as familiar as anyone's."

"Okay, then I'm going to wander over there and ask his family if he's said anything. I'm going to tell the truth – that you have no memory, and that's why I'm asking. Who knows, maybe he's not so knocked about as you?"

She eased herself up off the chair and walked casually over the other bed, positioning herself to come up by a man who looked like the lad's father. The mum and sisters were all focused on the lad, but the man looked like he'd be glad of the distraction as he desperately tried to hold himself together, and be the strong one for the others.

"Excuse me," Stella said gently. The man jumped at her words. "I'm sorry to intrude. My name's Stella and that's my ex-husband over there. I'm really sorry to bother you, but can you tell me what happened to these guys? Being his ex I've been told nothing, and his current wife won't even answer my calls." That was stretching it a bit, but Stella wanted the man to think that she still cared and had perhaps been abandoned rather than kicking Toby's miserable behind out of her life.

He coughed and cleared his throat, then held out his hand. "I'm Bob, used to be in the regiment myself when it was still the Worcesters."

"Yes, Toby joined right at the end of when they were still a separate regiment alongside the Sherwoods," Stella said, summoning up what she hoped was a comradely smile.

It seemed to work, because Bob breathed a sigh of relief, and Stella guessed he was glad to talk to someone who wasn't about to dissolve into tears at the drop of a hat.

"Hasn't the Families' Officer been in touch?" he asked.

"Oh the chap who I knew has retired," Stella said truthfully, "and I'm hardly on the current person's radar. But Toby's not only my ex, he's my best friend's cousin, and I've got increasingly concerned that as his closest relatives, they seem to have been told nothing either."

"Bloody hell, you're a breath of fresh air," Bob said with visible relief. "I've been saying to my Jane over and over that I can't make out what the hell happened to our Josh and his mates, but all she keeps on about is how ill he is, and whether we'll be able to get him home soon."

Bob shook his head. "I've never come across the like. Honestly I haven't. I know that sometimes they can't tell you exactly where the lads have been because of ongoing operations, but this? This is like the army's just clamped down!"

He gestured for Stella to step a little aside with him and lowered his voice a bit. "See that lad over there and the one next to him? Well they were flown in from Kandahar. Don't know where exactly they got wounded, but they were in Afghanistan for sure. At least their families know that much. I had a look at the one lad's records, see? And it said what he'd been given medically to stabilise him on the long flight. It said it specifically, 'in flight' and the repeats over the hours. Well there's nothing like that on our Josh's record."

"No, there's nothing like that on Toby's," Stella confirmed. She'd taken instantly to Bob. He was like the older staff sergeant who'd been around when she'd been married to Toby. Someone dependable and straight, someone who told it like it was with no messing around. A bit blunt for some of the wives, but Stella had always liked his honesty, and that was what was drawing her to Bob now. If anyone was going to help her it might very well be him.

"Don't you think they look a bit pale, too?" she asked Bob softly. "I mean it's June, and even allowing for the time spent getting back here, surely it's started hotting up a bit over there by now? Look at those other lads? They look like they've been out in the sun a while, but your son and Toby, and a couple of the others look like they've hardly seen daylight."

It was Bob's turn to blink and look at the three other beds which contained the ones Toby thought had been with him. In a modern hospital with smaller wards it wouldn't have been so obvious, but this was one of the huge old Victorian wards with multiple beds, and so Bob instantly saw what she was getting at.

"That's what's been niggling at me!" he said with relief. "I couldn't put my finger on it, but that's it!"

As the poor lad who'd had something like a seizure when Stella had last been there began to spasm again, and all of the nurses piled in to deal with it, Bob picked his son's charts off the base of the bed and gestured Stella back towards Toby. Stella grabbed Toby's charts and they began to compare them.

"What's this stuff, do you know?" Bob asked, pointing to an incomprehensible long name, but which looked like the name of a drug. "Because whatever it is, they're both on it."

Stella dug her smart phone out of her bag and, shielding it from the view of the nurses, typed the name into Google.

"Look at that," she breathed, turning the phone so that Bob could read it.

"Anti-psychotic? Why on earth would they need an anti-psychotic?"

Stella scrolled down. "It says here it's used for people who've been on drugs and been affected. ...Blimey! I mean, I know things like LSD can do permanent damage. I'm a teacher and we have to be aware of the kids taking some of these weird and wonderful pills which can permanently alter moods and stuff. But why would you give a bunch of soldiers these? Toby, you never took drugs, did you?"

Toby gave a puzzled shake of his head. "Got pissed a lot, but drugs, no."

"And our Josh wouldn't touch the damned things," Bob said firmly. "That's not being a blinkered dad. He lost his best mate at fifteen like that. Went to a party and Chris got persuaded to 'just try one'. The next thing they knew, Chris had collapsed and Josh was ringing for an ambulance. Poor lad died two days later in hospital. Ever after that Josh's been totally anti-drug, so I *know* he wouldn't have taken anything voluntarily."

The way he said the last word made Stella swallow hard. Had the army given them something? Was that what that colonel had been on about? Some kind of chemical warfare test that had gone wrong? Bloody hell!

"Did Josh write to you?" it occurred to her to ask. "I mean, Toby and I have long got past that, but you seem like a close family. Surely he wrote to his mum or you?"

Bob gave a growl of disgust. "The last we heard, he was telling us that he'd been selected for something special. He couldn't tell us what it was, but he was really excited about it. He said that all he could say was that he wouldn't be where we thought he was – not in the obvious place, which I took to mean Afghanistan."

"And have you been given any reason for him being here?"

Another growl. "Load of bloody eyewash! Wounded on a training exercise, they said. What bloody training exercise produces wounds like this, eh?" and he flung his arm out to encompass the other lads too.

"I thought that," Stella agreed as they furtively replaced the two charts. Drawing Bob back over to Toby, she said, "Lift up your top, Toby, let Bob see your injuries."

As Toby did so, Stella pointed to two long gashes. "Does that look to you like it was done with something wooden? Because to me those side marks look like splinters came off something. ...And that lower one looks like a metal cut, but nothing done with a knife or a bayonet. It's too ragged."

"Looks like a shrapnel wound," Bob agreed, "but not one I've ever seen the like of. The nearest thing I ever saw to that was one of my lads who got caught up in a car bombing in Northern Ireland. Luckily he wasn't in the car, but he got hit by chunks of metal being ripped out of it. That's what that looks like – like something exploded and he was in the way. But no training sergeant would have people that close to an explosion, it defies all the safety procedures. Wherever that happened, I'd bet good money on it not being within a camp, or out on a formal exercise."

Stella turned to Toby. "Look, I'm going to go and talk some more to Bob, but I don't want to do it here. If they stick something into you and you inadvertently start talking, I don't want someone to tell the army and them to start covering their tracks on this, okay? If I'm going to find Dav, I've got to get to the truth before it gets destroyed."

"Okay, Stell'. Thanks."

As Stella and Bob moved away to the ward entrance, where they could see who was coming and going, Bob asked,

"Who's Dav?"

"Well once upon a time he was Toby's best mate. But Toby has a habit of behaving like a dick and driving people away. When Toby and I divorced, Dav was an absolute gentleman to me. I don't know how I'd have got through it without him. But the thing is, Bob, Dav is now missing! The one thing Toby is sure of is that Dav was with him wherever that was."

"And this Dav's family aren't kicking up a fuss?"

"Dav doesn't have any family. Nobody! He was an orphan, but his parents had alienated both sides of the family by marrying. His mum came from a Welsh family – so his name's really Dafydd – but although her dad was West Indian, both parents were absolutely die-hard chapel goers. I mean real Bible thumpers! So they weren't happy at all that Dav's mum married a chap whose mum was Chinese Buddhist and whose dad was Anglo-Indian Buddhist, and the feeling was returned. By the time his parents died in a car crash they hadn't spoken to anyone on either side for more than a decade. Dav told me that Social Services tried to find someone, but either they couldn't or the old wounds hadn't healed and nobody wanted him."

"Poor little sod!" Bob breathed sympathetically. "Not a bloody soul to kick up a fuss, then?"

"No. Dav had been in care since he was ten. Mind you, as is the way sometimes, that mix made him a stunning bloke to look at. I mean, you wouldn't miss him – couldn't miss him! He was a good six feet two, built like a brick outhouse, the kind of skin that looked like he'd always got a tan, with jet black hair and eyes. When he'd been out in Iraq he was someone they sent out to do the covert stuff because, apart from his size, with his colouring he could pass for more of a local than most of the lads. They let him grow his hair because of that, and when he came back he looked like some American Indian male model.

"Honestly, Bob, Dav turned heads wherever he went, but he wasn't a nightmare with women like Toby was, and he was really liked by all the other squaddies too. Possibly helped that he was a cracking rugby player and helped his team win a lot of the internal trophies, but he's a genuinely good bloke too. I can't understand how he could just go missing and nobody notice."

Chapter 5

Sunday

"So your mate, Dav ..he's definitely missing?" Bob wondered. "Or might he be dead? I don't want to upset you, but I don't want you to get false hopes."

"Oh believe me," Stella sighed, "I've thought of that too. Cried a few tears over it in the last couple of days too, if I'm honest, because if Dav's dead then that's a bloody cruel twist of fate. But what's worrying me sick, Bob, is more if he's alive and nobody's doing anything to help him."

The ward was starting to empty of families.

"Look, is there somewhere I can meet you to talk? Away from the hospital altogether, I mean. I've got something to tell you, but I'm really wary of anyone overhearing me here."

Bob looked slightly startled but said, "Okay, we don't live too far away. How did you get here?"

"I drove."

"Right …do you know *The Green Man* in Harborne? It's a biggish pub and it's got a car park. My local's a great pub, but there's nowhere to park there, and anyway, I don't want some nosy tosser seeing me meeting a woman on the sly and making something of nothing. Jane's got enough to cope with without thinking I've got some bird on the side."

"God, no! I wouldn't want to cause her any more grief!" Stella agreed readily. "Could we just not make it too late? I've got a bit of a drive to get home — I live on the other side of the Malvern Hills, you see."

"Fair enough. How about six o'clock? I think we're going to get a meal somewhere now, but by then I'll have dropped everyone back at home."

"Six will be fine," Stella agreed, although mentally wincing at the thought that she, too, would have to afford a pub meal somewhere now, because by the time she got home it would be too late to cook for herself. "I grew up around here, so I know *The Green Man*."

"I'll see you there, then," Bob said, being almost instantly being reclaimed by his family, and as they went on down the corridor, Stella heard one of the daughters asking Bob, "Who was that?" in a rather suspicious tone, and Bob's placating answering of, "Just one of the other soldier's wife."

As she made her way back to ask Toby a last few questions, Stella felt her heart sinking again. The way Bob's family had reacted made her wonder if everything was fine between him and his wife. She really didn't want to get hauled into someone else's messy divorce, her own had been bad enough.

Back at her car she had to stand with the door open for a while to let it cool down. The sun had been on it and it was like an oven with the steering wheel painfully hot to the touch, but at least it gave her time to think. *The Bell* by St Peter's church, she thought, that's where I'll go. She knew the old pub which was almost in the churchyard from years ago, and although it would no doubt be rammed on a nice Sunday afternoon like this, she suddenly longed to back somewhere familiar and comforting and associated with happier days. The pub had a nice garden at the back, but even if she had to take her drink and sit on the wall of the next door church car park, that would be fine.

She had to park further along Old Church Road from the pub, knowing that on a Sunday the clergy would take a dim view of drinkers taking up the space on the church car park. That was fine, though, as it gave her a chance to wander through the old churchyard in the dappled shade of the venerable horse chestnuts which encircled it. St Peter's had been here since Norman times, and its solid sandstone walls gave off an aura of permanence and solidity, while some of the Victorian tombs were quite ornate and decorative.

In the spring there was always a good show of spring bulbs here, but by now the cover from the trees had taken over, and there were just different shades of green punctuated by grey and white marble, making it feel very calm and peaceful. Stella had never found graveyards morbid. Rather she found it fascinating to look at the names and wonder what their lives had been like, and today that was a most welcome distraction.

At the pub she found it as heaving as she'd anticipated, and having booked a basic fish and chips, which she could eat perched just about anywhere, and been told that there would be a half hour wait, she took her glass of Coke and went out to the back. A group of elderly men were playing bowls on the pocket-sized green which took up half of the garden, and she worked her way around to the far side of the green for a while, watching for any vacant seat. She was doing her best not to speculate for the time being, for much would depend on whether Bob even turned up. If he didn't then she was going to really be on her own, but if he would join her on this …well what was it? A quest? Research? It would help no end if she could just get a grip on even the basics of what she was going to have to do.

Start making a list, she told herself, and when a space came up at the tiniest of tables, she shot in and claimed her space, then got her notepad out of her shoulder bag.

How do I find Dav? she wrote. *Need to find out where he was last seen!*

Yes, that would be a good start. If someone had seen him boarding a plane for Afghanistan then that was going to scupper her plans pretty fast. Following him to foreign parts wasn't within Stella's financial reach. Even Cyprus would be nigh on impossible, because although there were military bases out there where he might have gone, travelling there at this time of the year was going to be hideously expensive now that the main holiday season had started, not to mention that all of the flights there were probably booked up months ago. On the other hand, knowing that he definitely *hadn't* gone with the other lads might be as good an indicator as she was going to get at this stage. Was there anyone she could remember from among them who might talk to her?

Mentally she began going through the men she had known all those years back and their wives. Many of them were probably divorced by now if they'd stayed in the army, because postings abroad were notoriously hard on marriages. And who amongst them would have had their opinions of her coloured by whatever Toby might have said about her since then? She could only hope that her desperation to find Dav, eternally well liked, would counter anything negative that had come from Toby.

'Soapy', she wondered, would he help her? Soapy had been nicknamed that after earning his wife's wrath by dumping foul-smelling kit in her kitchen after a foray through a rat-infested farmyard on a manoeuvre; had been told that he could clean his own rotten kit; and had then covered the entire kitchen in bubbles when he'd used the whole packet of detergent in the washing machine. Stella couldn't help but smile at the memory.

Don't Delve Too Deep

Poor Cath's kitchen had looked like a kids' bubble machine had had a fit in there, and she'd been one of the wives who'd piled in to try and clean the place out. Amazingly Soapy and Cath were still married – or had been when Stella had had a card from them this Christmas. Soapy had recently left the regiment, so he wouldn't be out in foreign parts – a plus – and he probably had current mates who he could get in touch with to ask about Dav.

That was one boon about the way mobile phones had become so universal. It posed a nightmare in one way when it came to security within the army, but on the other hand it was going to make Stella's life a whole heap easier if Soapy could text a mate, and he could confirm that he'd seen Dav only the day before. She wasn't going to be asking for the ins and outs of any operation, after all.

On the other hand, that wasn't a phone call she wanted to make from a bustling pub garden, where she'd struggle to hear what Soapy or Cath said to her. She had the dreadful premonition of her bawling into the phone, "*Who's* dead?" just as there was a lull in the general racket and everyone turning to stare at her. No, that would be a call to make from home.

The fish and chips came, and as she was dunking a chip into tomato sauce she suddenly thought of Little Andy. He'd been like Dav's shadow for years, but unlike Dav, Andy was so unremarkable you hardly knew he was there most of the time. It wasn't because he was that small, it was just that there was another Andy who was bigger than him; but a quiet personality coupled with mousy hair and a bland complexion meant that Andy was one of life's wallflowers. He was married to an equally unremarkable lass called Wendy, and if Stella wasn't mistaken, they were still in the house she'd known them at. It had been on the same estate as the married quarters she'd lived in, but Andy and Wendy had bought a house there so that their kids could stay on at the local school, rather than moving on to another posting. Yes, that was something she could do over this half-term, because the chances were that one or the other of them would be at home with the kids this week.

That cheered her up a little, and feeling considerably better she made her way back to the car and drove the short way to the other pub. As she wandered inside and began scanning the various sectioned off areas for Bob, she was amazed to see him with another man. Half wondering whether to go across, she had paused when Bob saw her, and the way he smiled and waved her towards them made it clear that she wasn't interrupting.

"This is Ade," Bob introduced her. "His son is another one in the same way as our Josh and your ex. I asked him to join us because we met in the car park this afternoon and he took me on one side and said he was bothered by all of this, because he's ex-regiment too."

Stella took the other man's outstretched hand and said, "Glad to meet you, Ade. The more heads working on this the better as far as I'm concerned."

Bob kindly went and got Stella an orange juice and soda, and then they sat down and began to tell one another what they knew. Ade couldn't add a lot to the pool of knowledge, but he did say,

"My lad's always been a bit quick off the mark, if you know what I mean. Got his head screwed on, and though he's a loyal soldier, he's not blind to some of the less savoury things that go on. He told me before they went off on this whatever it was, that he thought he'd been selected because he's good with armaments. Always did have a way with guns and stuff on the mechanical side, and that's why he thought he'd been picked."

Ade puffed his cheeks out and shook his head. "Well, a few weeks back we get a postcard. All battered and bent it was and I knew straight off what it was. He used to use a blank postcard as a book marker, you see. But he said that if he ever thought he was in real trouble it was something he could send to us."

"Oh God!" Stella gulped, and Ade grimaced, but fished into a side pocket of his cargo trousers and came out with a very dog-eared postcard wrapped in a small plastic sandwich bag.

Very carefully Stella took it off him when he held it out. *Hi Mum and Dad*, it read. *It's cold, dark and wet here. Haven't seen daylight in days! Just out for a run, not in the army now! Tom.*

Stella turned the postcard over and looked at the post mark on it, then gasped.

"Harlech? What the bloody hell were they doing in Wales?"

"That's what I want to know," Ade said bitterly. "I daren't tell anyone in authority that my lad sent this, because he could get into a world of trouble if I do. But I know Tom, and he wouldn't have sent this unless he was feeling pretty bloody desperate. He wouldn't break an order lightly."

"What I don't like are those words, 'not in the army now'," Bob said grimly. "He was brought into the hospital two and a half weeks ago as a squaddie, so what made him think he wasn't? This was written when he was in his right mind, not all befuddled like they all are now, because in the state they're in none of them could have written anything that coherent."

"I know," Ade agreed. "I reckon he sneaked out under the pretence of wanting to just go for a run, or maybe just got out on the sly. Maybe he got to a post-box. Maybe he met someone and asked them to post it for him. He'd have had that stamp on him, I'm sure of that – especially if he was getting the feeling that something wasn't kosher about what was coming."

Stella reverently handed to card back to Ade. "Keep that safe! It might be the only evidence we have, although whether we can ever use it is, as you said, another matter."

She paused to take a sip of her drink. "But what leapt out at me is the rest of what he said. Cold, dark and wet? Well we're in an English summer – it can often be chilly and wet, but dark? We're into the longest days now. Even on the soggiest of days you'd hardly call it dark. Not like it can get on a winter's day, for instance. So why would he say it was dark? But when you couple it with that 'haven't seen daylight in days' it sounds like they were indoors, doesn't it? Like they were cooped up somewhere?"

"That's what we were just saying when you arrived," Bob agreed. "It would account for why they're all so pale. And I think Tom was very clever with what he wrote, just in case his message was found. Anything too wild and he knew there was the danger he wouldn't be believed, that Ade might think his card had been found by some mate who was playing a daft joke or something. He's kept it very cool, very understated, but he's put in just the right things to make Ade, and now us, wonder where the hell he was."

"Wales, though," Stella said with a bemused shake of her head. "And Harlech? We don't even know if he was anywhere near there, do we? I mean, for all we know, he could have thrust it into the hands of some farmer who was out early on his way to market there. So that leaves a vast tract of Snowdonia and down to the south of it where they might have been. There are lots of hidden places round there where I bet the only person who goes there from one end of the year to the other are the sheep!"

"That's a lot of hillsides and valleys," Bob agreed.

"And you're not going to be any happier when I tell you what I overheard," Stella continued, and proceeded to tell them of the overheard conversation between the colonel and the captain.

"Fuckin' hell!" Ade snorted angrily when she'd finished. "What have those bastards done to our lads?"

"I can see why you didn't want to tell me on the ward," Bob added. "That's explosive stuff. ...You say this captain was hanging around the ward?"

"Well I don't know about hanging around," Stella admitted, "but he was there for far longer than just the visiting times. I think I might be able to ask one of the nurses about him. She seemed an approachable sort. And I tell you something else, he was in civvies, not uniform, because afterwards I was on the lookout for him, and it was only by chance that I heard him speak to someone and recognised his voice. I was really shocked because I thought he'd already left, not having seen anyone in uniform."

"Could you point him out to us?" Bob wondered.

"If he's there at the same time as us, sure."

Bob looked to Ade. "I think we should be keeping an eye out for this sneaky Rupert," ('Rupert' being the catch-all nickname for any officer amongst the non-commissioned ranks).

"I tell you another thing that's bugging me now," Bob said. "When I thought it was just an accident, I wasn't surprised that only the five of them were brought in. I'd have been a hell of a lot more suspicious if there had been more, 'cause that would have implied a much bigger disaster. But now I'm thinking that they had to have taken at least a squad and more likely a platoon for whatever this was. So where are the rest of them? At full strength you're talking about twenty-seven men and an officer, Stella. How bad has this 'accident' been? Because you can't 'vanish' that many men without someone asking questions."

"What about other wards?" Stella asked. "That captain sounded pretty harassed. Maybe there are other men on other wards? They couldn't ask for them all to be on the one ward, could they? Not without giving the hospital staff a good explanation – like they were all particularly infectious.

"And then that would open you to all sorts of other questions, like how did they get that way, and where had they been? It'd be a lot harder to lie convincingly to a bunch of doctors, especially the army ones, than to pull the wool over the eyes of family members who've never been in the military. You two are unusual in that you've both served, but not all of the dads there will have.

"...Oh and I've just thought of something! Trish and Graham were told by someone – I'm guessing the captain – that Toby had been in there a month, but you said your lads were in only two and a half weeks. So clearly they've lied to those who they think they can bamboozle even about the length of time the men have been in hospital. That's a lot of secrecy going on."

Ade nodded approvingly. "Yes, that makes a lot of sense. And if this is a real Secret Squirrel job, then they won't dare tell the docs that something fishy has been going on, and that'll mean making no requests that would seem unusual or odd. They must have to be keeping up the front that this was just an accident to them, too."

"But hang on," Bob said thoughtfully. "How are they accounting for the lads needing that drug that Stella Googled? I mean, that can't be normal, can it? They must be covering up the need for that somehow? Even some kind of mortar exploding on a range wouldn't create that sort of need."

"I wonder if they've said there was some kind of chemical spillage?" Stella suggested. "Maybe something that would go up with a bang – which would account for the shrapnel-like wounds – but would also release toxic gases? If they've been really cunning and picked something where they've very few known cases of it going up in smoke, well that would account for why there's no set procedure for dealing with the after effects."

"That sounds plausible," Ade agreed. "There must have been someone on site who knew what they were doing, so they'd have been able to tell the ordinary Ruperts what and what not to say."

"It's all very cloak and dagger, though, isn't it?" Bob sighed. "What on earth were they doing that demanded that sort of secrecy?"

"Weapons testing?" Ade threw out, but shrugging as he did so. "Something they can throw at the Taliban? Something they could use miles from anywhere and hope nobody noticed? You'd hope to God it wasn't something they were thinking of using in the event of a terrorist attack, given what the fallout has been this time. What it would do in amongst a crowd of civilians doesn't bear thinking about."

"Or it was in its early stages of development," Stella said thoughtfully. "But in that case, what were they doing having ordinary soldiers involved? Wouldn't you want to have it closer to being ready to go before you started worrying about how you were going to use it?

Because that's the only reason you would want a bunch of regular squaddies involved as far as I can see. They could hardly be of much use on the development side. Toby hasn't any specialist knowledge, and I don't think Dav did – not the sort you'd want for something like that, anyway."

"And I don't like the way your friend Dav has seemingly disappeared off the face of the earth," Ade added. "Your ex is sure about that?"

"I double checked with him today," Stella confirmed. "He says as best he can remember – and admittedly that's very patchy – but one of his snatches of memories is of Dav bending over him and asking him if he was okay. That's why Toby's convinced he's disappeared. He can't see how he would have got out if there was another explosion, or whatever, when Dav was on his feet after the first one and he wasn't. If anyone was going to die it should have been Toby under those circumstances, but he does remember that Dav's face was all bloody, as if he had a scalp wound. So wouldn't you think that Dav would have been evacuated to some medical facility too?

"That's why I asked Toby if he remembered being somewhere else first. Somewhere like a field hospital, somewhere a bit makeshift. I asked him that again today, and he's with it enough to remember that I asked him that on Friday – so it's not his actual short-term memory that's shot to hell, it's what relates to him specifically getting wounded that's gone. But if there'd been a field hospital, then that would have accounted for where Dav went to, because he might not have needed full hospitalisation."

"But Toby's adamant that he went straight to Selly Oak," Bob mused.

"Yes, and I think he's probably right about that," Stella said, "if only because he said that he came round in the ambulance and then faded out again. If he was doing that, surely he would have done it if there'd been earlier treatment going on too? I know I'm no nurse, but wouldn't there be a difference between someone out cold and only waking up once they were in the hospital and getting treated, and someone who's badly hurt but surfacing every so often?"

"You have a point," Ade agreed. "Okay, so we're convinced – at least for the time being – that something happened, and that at that point the wounded were loaded onto ambulances and brought to the hospital."

"From that far into Wales?" Bob objected. "No! They'd have been helicoptered at least part of the way, especially if there was any urgency. I'd have expected them to be taken to the army field hospital at Llandudno, Stella. That's a proper hospital building. If that doesn't fit with what Toby or any of the others remember, then my first question would be *why* weren't they taken there? It's the obvious place if they were near Harlech. The folk there would have at least been able to stabilise any wounds.

"Otherwise, where were they patched up enough to survive the long ambulance trip all the way to Birmingham? That's hours away! If they were trying to avoid too many deaths, they'd want those lads treated a.s.a.p., not risk them dying on the way. I think you have to allow that Toby was probably out of it for several hours, in which time a lot could have happened, but I think he's right on one point. If his mate Dav was still on his feet right after the accident, then it makes no sense to think of a second whatever-it-was taking him out and leaving Toby alive lying on the floor."

Chapter 6

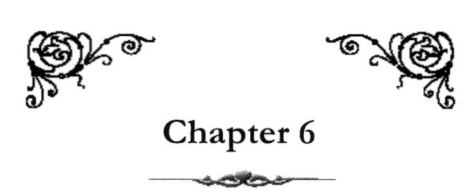

Monday

Stella left Bob and Ade not long after that, with promises made that they would all keep in touch and watch for the secretive captain on the wards. But the next day at home Stella felt the need to be doing something, and she felt she daren't go back to the hospital today. Tomorrow would be soon enough, and so she settled down with a mug of coffee, a notepad, and dialled Soapy's number.

It was Cath's cheerful voice which answered the phone, and to Stella's relief she was actually glad to hear from her.

"You've been a stranger for too long!" Cath remonstrated. "You must come over for dinner one day, we'd love to see you."

"Heavens, Cath, you're making me feel guilty now, because I've actually got in touch because you're the only people I can think of to ask. But I didn't want to put you two on the spot while Soapy was still serving with Toby."

Cath snorted. "You daft bat! After all these years we know just what Toby's like, and he's the one who wears out his welcome, not you."

"Thanks for that."

"Well it's certainly why he never made sergeant like Dav did. He's seen as too volatile and not stable enough. You know how the army likes its NCOs to be settled, married men. ...So what did you want to ask us?"

Taking a deep breath, Stella launched into how she had got dragged into the situation, and then her suspicions, ending with, "So it's not just me getting the wrong end of the stick, Cath. These two other ex-army dads are also worried sick about what their lads have got sucked into."

Suddenly Soapy's voice came on. "Cath got me over and put this on speaker, Stell', so I heard most of it. But did you say Dav is *missing*?"

"Yes, I did. God knows, I know all of Toby's faults, especially where women are concerned, but one thing's never shifted, and that's the way he feels about Dav. They're like the brothers each of them never had. Sometimes they argue like crazy, sometimes they don't speak, but when the chips are down they'll always look out for one another.

"So one of the first things Toby asked when he came round enough to start taking notice was, where was Dav? And he's got more and more worried as he can't find out. Nobody at the hospital has seen or heard of Dav, that's for certain. But some Rupert – and I'm guessing it was this lurking captain – spoke to him too, and he can't tell Toby if Dav's alive or where he is either. And given the way they seem to want to shut the men up, surely you would normally say, 'oh he's back at base' or something as an end to the conversation?"

"You'd think so, wouldn't you?" Cath agreed.

"I think that captain might not be the enemy you think he is," Soapy said perceptively. "I reckon he's as unhappy as anyone. Let's face it, you wouldn't want it on your career résumé that you lost a whole platoon, would you? If only out of self-preservation, I bet he's praying that something or someone starts sorting this mess out. That's why he's not lying about seeing Dav.

He doesn't want to be implicated in a cover-up, and he may well be genuinely worried stiff about his remaining men. Despite what Toby thinks, not all Ruperts are dickheads!"

"Well I may ask my two new allies, Bob and Ade, to look into that," Stella said. "Whoever he is, he'll take such questions better from blokes who were in the regiment than from some outsider. But what I really wanted from you, Soapy, was a few phone-calls to some of your old mates who are still in. Ask them if they've seen Dav lately. I think I have to know whether he really was with Toby in this strange place in the first place as my starting point.

"I mean, I know Toby's done his usual Teflon Boy act, and come out of this in one piece, if not totally untouched for once, but he's also had a nasty knock on the head. So before I start rocking the boat too hard I really need to know whether in reality Toby's remembering some other time when he got blown up, and Dav hauled his sorry arse out. I'm pretty sure he isn't, if only because Trish would have been wailing down the phone back then to tell me if he had. But I'm going to look a right twit if Dav's been working on his tan in Afghanistan all this time, aren't I?"

Cath gasped, "Wow, I totally see your point!" but Soapy was already thinking ahead.

"I know three lads who were in Dav's platoon I could reach out to. But I'll also reach out to my old lot. Somebody ought to at least be able to tell me if they were deployed at the same time, and if not, then why. They probably won't know where if it's all been hush-hush, but like you said, if they weren't on the plane with the rest of the lads, it'll have been noticed."

He thought, then added, "And I'll make enquiries about your two new mates. What were their names?

…Just to be on the safe side, Stell'. If you're going to be heading off on your own with these two, I'd rather know who they are."

She looked at the piece of paper where they'd written their contact details down. "Well Bob is Robert Ashford. I'd say he's late forties, so he may have been out for some time if he just did a twelve year stint. Looks pretty fit, though, as if he still keeps in training, so he might not have left that long ago, either – I'm guessing he was a dad quite young. Ade is Adrian Fernleigh, probably a bit older than Bob, so I'd put him in his early fifties. He, I'd definitely say, has been out a good while. Probably just did a basic stint if he didn't actually buy himself out early. Looks like he's been enjoying his wife's home cooking for a while now."

"You mean he's a fat git?" Soapy chuckled.

Stella laughed. "No, not fat, but Bob's still pretty lean, whereas you'd call Ade well-padded. If anyone's going to get his boots on and come trekking over the Welsh hills, I'd say it was Bob, while Ade holds the fort back in Birmingham."

"I might come with you," Soapy volunteered. "I wouldn't want to think Dav's been abandoned somewhere."

"You be bloody careful, then," Cath warned. "I had enough of gnawing my fingernails ragged while you were in the army, I don't want to start again now that you're out!"

"Hey, I'd have Stella with me," Soapy protested. "I'm hardly going to take her crawling through a minefield, am I?"

"No, suppose not," Cath conceded, somewhat mollified. "But you be careful too, Stella. If the army wants this hushed up you could be taking on some seriously dangerous people."

Leaving them with the promise of Soapy getting back in touch as soon as he'd heard anything, Stella went to refresh her coffee, feeling considerably buoyed up by the conversation. They hadn't dismissed her as just being paranoid, and getting back in touch in person had been so much easier than she'd expected. So with her mug refilled she sat down to call Little Andy.

However this turned out to be a very different call. The phone rang out for a while and then an unfamiliar voice came on the other end.

"Hello? Who's calling, please?" No name, no clue as to who was speaking.

"I'm sorry, is that Andy and Wendy's house?" Stella double-checked, wondering if she'd misdialled.

"Yes. Who are you?"

Good grief, that sounded a bit hostile. What was going on?

"My name's Stella. I used to live by Andy and Wendy when I was still in married quarters. I was married to Corporal Donaldson."

Stella was sure she heard a groan at the other end. Then the woman, whoever she was, said, "Look, it's very kind of you to ring up with your condolences, but Wendy's too distraught to come to the phone right now."

"Condolences? Oh my God! What's happened?"

"Oh! ...I thought you knew, and that's why you were ringing? Andy was killed three weeks ago in an accident."

Stella felt sick. "Oh no, not another one! Oh my God, I'm so sorry! ...Look Mrs...?"

"I'm Wendy's mum, Marjorie."

"Then please listen carefully to what I have to say, Marjorie. I'm not being over dramatic or anything, but Andy wasn't the only one in whatever happened. That's why I was ringing. My ex-husband is in one of the military wards at Selly Oak Hospital with about four other lads – he's in about the best shape of all of them, but whatever happened it was bad. I'm beyond sorry that Andy's been killed. Please give Wendy my genuine condolences, because I know how close they were. I won't come round and bother her now, but I will keep in closer touch, alright? But would you pass on this to her, too, please? Will you tell her that Dav is missing?"

"Someone is missing? Like how? Lost?"

"I wish I knew. He had no family to be informed, so there's nobody to ask if there's been a notification like Wendy's had. And after hearing about Andy, I'm worried sick that Dav might have been killed too. But the really worrying thing is that Toby, my ex, can't get any sense out of anyone. They won't even tell him what's happened to Dav, and he's not in such a precarious state that they daren't risk breaking bad news like that to him."

"Goodness me! I'm very glad Wendy hasn't been left in limbo like that. It's been a terrible few weeks, and all the worse for them telling her that we wouldn't be able to have a normal funeral service because there isn't..." Marjorie choked up. "There's not enough left..." There was the sound of her blowing her nose and Stella knew she was crying.

"Oh no! It's okay, Marjorie, I get what you're trying to tell me."

"All we can have is a memorial service, and that's not the same, is it? It's like he's not there to say goodbye to. That's what's tearing Wendy and the kids apart. I loved Andy like he was my own son, and I'm terribly upset, but they're at a whole other level of grief. Their Suzie was about to go to university this autumn, and he was so looking forward to being the proud dad at her graduation, and now he'll never…" Again Marjorie was too upset to continue.

"Look, I won't keep you," Stella said gently. "You don't need to go over the details to a stranger like me. Give Wendy my love and tell her I'll be in touch. If nothing else, I'll be able to help her get Suzie's place at uni' deferred for a year to give her time to come to terms with things." She wasn't going to say 'get over it', because a close family like that would probably never fully recover from the loss of Andy.

Feeling very shaken, Stella decided that for once a gin and tonic at midday was not decadent but very necessary. Once again it was one of the nicest blokes you could wish to meet who had suffered the worst, but where Andy went you'd be sure to find Dav, and that made her worried sick. And what was all that about there being no body to bury? Was that the truth? Because in that case, it implied a nasty explosion. Or was that a cover-up? A reason given to grieving families because no-one wanted a coroner sticking their nose in, or God forbid a civilian autopsy after exhuming a coffin from a normal cemetery?

What she wasn't expecting was for her phone to ring half an hour later, and answer it to find Wendy on the other end.

"Stella? It's Wendy." There was a sniff and a cough, but then sounding rather more resolute than expected, Wendy said. "I'm so glad you called. I had to ring back. …I don't know why, but it makes such a difference to know that my Andy," she choked on his name, "wasn't the only one. It's like part of the weight just got lifted off.

"You see the worst of it was wondering why him? Why was he the one caught in that explosion? Why was he put in that position? I know it shouldn't have been anyone, but why did it have to be *him* when he'd only got another six months left and then he was coming out? It felt so bloody unfair. Surviving all those years, all those tours abroad, and then to die here in some sodding accident. But when mum said Toby was in hospital and there were others…?"

"Oh there are others, alright," Stella said, doing her best to not sound too angry, even though she was moving from shock into fury at the thought of another old friend lost in this chaos. She explained what had happened and what she and Bob had started doing. "So I was going to ring and ask Andy if he'd heard anything, because I knew he was in Dav's platoon – or at least I was going to ask you to ask him."

Wendy gave another sniff. "Well you've answered something that's been upsetting me. I just couldn't understand why Dav hadn't been in touch with me. After all the years he and Andy were so close, what with Andy being one of his corporals for the last few years, I'd expected better of Dav than just silence. But it's a totally different thing if he's dead or missing."

Stella decided to risk a question. "I know this probably wasn't on your list of priorities, but have you asked about Dav? Did he come up in any of your conversations with anyone?"

There was silence for a moment, and Stella wondered whether she'd hit a raw nerve and Wendy thought she was implying she should have asked. But then Wendy came back, and had obviously just been thinking.

"Now you come to mention it, I'm sure that when they came to break the news I asked where Dav was. You see, I knew they were somewhere here in the UK. That was one of the reason why Andy said he was glad he'd got this posting – it got him out of another tour in

Afghanistan. Obviously he couldn't say exactly where, or what he was doing, but he told me that much to set my mind at rest. He said it wouldn't be dangerous!"

"Shit! That wasn't the case, though, was it?"

"No! But you see *that's* why I expected Dav to be one of the ones coming to break the news. And then when he wasn't, I'm sure I asked where he was. So when they didn't answer – didn't say he too had died, or was in hospital – I assumed he was okay and had somehow ducked out of coming to tell me. And that didn't sound like Dav. But then none of this has made any sense. The first time I've felt this horrible shroud of secrecy lifting was when you just called."

"Then I'm very glad I thought to call you." How much more should she tell Wendy? What would make the grief worse and what help? "Listen, I'm going to start telling you some stuff, but if you get to the point where it's all too much and you want me to shut up, just yell out, okay?"

"Okay, but what is there to tell, Stella?"

And so for the second time that day Stella went through the whole story, concluding, "I'm really sorry, Wendy, because I never thought to ask Soapy if you were one of those he was thinking of ringing. So you might get a call from him, but I can tell you now, he knows nothing of any of his old mates getting killed – I'm absolutely certain he would have told me if he had."

"No, that's okay," Wendy said, sounding better every time she spoke. "You know, I know more of the other wives than you do, and that was another thing I couldn't understand. If someone died when they were out in Iraq, or afterwards in Afghanistan, then we all used to pile round and help whoever the widow was. So I was feeling cut to the quick that nobody was bothering with me, and I've been too upset to start ringing round to talk to people. But suddenly I'm realising that they might not have a clue that anything's wrong. They think we're just ticking along as normal, and that's why they haven't been round."

Stella took a deep breath. "And you might not be the only one."

"Eh?"

"Well there might have been other casualties within the platoon, mightn't there? If yours is the common experience, there might be other wives sitting crying their eyes out and wondering why they've been forgotten?"

"Fuckin' hell!" That shook Stella. She could never remember hearing Wendy really swear, but when that was followed by, "The bastards!" Stella knew that Wendy had moved into being angry. Really furiously angry. "I'm going to start ringing round the wives right now!" Wendy said with real decisiveness. "Christ! To think there might be several of us all sitting at home feeling as bloody awful as I've done these last two weeks!"

Stella would have whooped with triumph under other circumstances. If she had lit the fuse which would ignite the wives of the platoon, then she'd done a good morning's work, because the successive moves from one set of married quarters to another united the wives just as serving together united their husbands. And a bunch of forces wives on the war path was something the army might find harder to hush up than they wanted to believe.

In the background she could now hear Marjorie saying, "Wendy? Are you alright, love? What's she saying?"

"I'll tell you in a minute, mum. …Stella, is this the best number to get you on?"

"This is my home, and I'm teaching, so I'm home for this week, but I'll give you my mobile number too."

"Good. I'll get back to you when I've had a ring around. Only four of the lads in Andy's squad were married, but I know a couple in each of the other squads in the platoon. ...God, all of a sudden I can face ringing them and telling them if they don't know! It's like you've blown a big dark cloud away, probably because now there's something I can actually *do*. Sitting on my bum crying my eyes out and feeling helpless was the worst part of losing him, you know. I doubt I'll ever get over it, but that feeling of being totally at sea with it all has vanished. Thank you, Stella!"

Chapter 7

Monday

After putting the phone down, Stella sat back and took another large sip of the G&T. Despite the dreadful news about Andy, she was actually feeling rather more optimistic. Wendy was right, she could ring up other wives where Stella couldn't – in no small measure due to some of them never having believed that she hadn't known whose bed Toby was in at various times, and had thought she should have said something. She hadn't. It was usually only when the rumours of Toby being the cause of someone's break up or terrible rows that Stella found out, by that stage already struggling hard to cope with the times when he was around, never mind when he wasn't.

But Wendy had been a popular member of the wives, always involved in the coffee sessions at someone or other's house, and if she rang up, the phone wouldn't be slammed down on her as it would be on Stella. And she was also glad that she'd been able to help Wendy. That put her in a much stronger position, not to mention portraying her in a better light when her name came up – they might just credit Wendy believing her, rather than thinking Wendy had been sucked in by a habitual liar (as many saw Stella) in her grief-stricken state.

However, with Soapy and Wendy well and truly on the case now, she felt that she was rather in limbo. There wasn't a lot she could do until either they, or Bob and Ade, got back to her if she wasn't going to the hospital today, yet sitting at home or going out all afternoon with Ivan felt somehow frivolous, and as though she was squandering precious time. Given that nobody was likely to call her within the next hour or so, she did pick up Ivan's lead to take him on a much needed good walk – Dai next door was in his sixties and wasn't one for treks over the Malvern hills, and normally when Stella dropped Ivan round to him she'd try to get out for a decent early morning walk first, but yesterday she'd been too preoccupied to go far. Yet now she felt as though a blast of fresh air might rattle something loose and give her an idea of what to do next.

So it was as they were coming down off Worcester Beacon, a howling wind whistling in from the southwest in her face, that it came to her. Farmland would be an unlikely place for any Ministry of Defence activities. They would never know when some farmer might come over the hills on his quad bike looking for a lost sheep. On the other hand, given the secrecy surrounding all of this, Stella had a gut feeling that whatever had gone on hadn't been on the usual MOD ranges either. That was largely due to that strange conversation she'd overheard, because why would the colonel have been so desperately concerned that the lads wouldn't talk when everyone else on the ward was in the forces, and subject to the same Official Secrets Act constraints anyway? That had to mean it was something they wanted to keep secret from the other army folk, so chances were that they'd been avoiding the usual bases in Wales.

Yet what else were there in the way of spaces which you could successfully seal off from the public? It might be some relic of an old mansion house with extensive gardens, but Stella had camped around enough of that part of Wales to know that those were few and far between. The wealthy men who had owned property in northern Wales hadn't wanted to live in a land of frequently rain-soaked hillsides and nothing much to do aside from riding to their neighbours' houses. And so their grand houses had usually been located elsewhere, in shires more amenable to sweeping parkland and the gentry's social lives.

What large houses there were in sufficient numbers for maybe one or two to be in suitably remote locations were the mine managers' homes – and that was what prompted Stella's revelation.

"Slate mines!" she gasped to Ivan. "Of course! How many mines are there up in that neck of the woods? And most of them disused too!"

But how on earth would she find which one? Most people thought of southern Wales when you mentioned mining, well aware of the huge coalfields which had once left vast scars on the landscape of the Welsh Valleys. Place like Merthyr Tydfil were instantly recognised and linked with a mining industry which had died the death in the 1970s and '80s; forever connected in the general consciousness with the increasingly violent and desperate strikes which had taken place, as the miners had fought tooth and nail to save the only work available in many of those places, battling the greed of distant owners who saw a means to make a bigger profit by moving operations to countries with fewer safety laws and lower wages. Along with many of the Yorkshire pit towns, parts of the Valleys had never recovered, but another mining industry had faltered and died out too, albeit somewhat earlier – the slate mines of northern Wales.

Once vital to the booming economy of Victorian and Edwardian times and even later, one of the mainstays of the slate mines had been the production of roofing tiles. You only had to walk down the street of any industrial town in Britain, and look at the rows and rows of terraced houses built to accommodate the factory workers, with every roof being covered with Welsh slate, to see how that industry must once have thrived. And Stella had driven past the huge spoil heaps of crumbling slate enough times to have a shrewd idea of just how many mines there must have once been, especially up around Blaenau Ffestiniog as you climbed into mountainous Snowdonia.

One of the largest set of caverns by Blaenau, Llechwedd, was now a major tourist attraction in the area, and there was another large tourist slate mine experience at Llanfair just south of Harlech; so Stella knew that the army wouldn't have gone close to them. But that was the exception, not the rule. Most of the slate mines had slid into obscurity and quietly faded away, the only evidence left of their existence being the records in old archives, and the spoil heaps, most of which had already been colonised by wild plants and were returning to nature, especially the smaller ones.

And of course, slate wasn't the only mine up there, Stella reminded herself as they got back to her cottage and she eagerly fired up her computer again. Another tourist attraction she had once gone around on a soaking wet day, when even Ivan had been glad to curl up on his big squashy bed in the back of her car, was the Sygun Copper Mine only a couple of mountains away from Llechwedd. Maybe not as plentiful as slate, nonetheless copper had been important, and there were probably other small mines about the place. Further south there was even a silver mine near Aberystwyth, although Stella thought it unlikely that one of those would be either big enough or anonymous enough for what she was looking for.

It didn't take much of an internet trawl to come up with answers, and straight away Stella could see that this was going to take some refining down.

"Come on," she told herself sternly, "you're a history graduate! You know how to do this. It might be a while since you had to do stuff like this, but you haven't forgotten that much," and Ivan grunted his agreement from his duvet on the floor beneath her desk. "Thanks for the vote of confidence," she said, bending down to give him an affectionate scruff of the ears, "but you're not the one with your paws on the keypad! This may take some time."

Going and fetching her Ordnance Survey maps of the region, she was very grateful that one of the websites had broken the lists of names down into regions. That made the locations a lot easier to find, and the first one she really looked at closely also jogged her memory.

"Workers, Ivan, they needed workers!"

She was on her hands and knees on the floor, that being the only surface large enough for her to spread the maps out on, and Ivan had wormed his way forwards to put his whiskery chin on the edge of the map of Snowdonia she was looking at.

"Look at this," Stella said, tapping the map at the town which had given its name to one of those regions, and Ivan huffed companionably even though he hadn't a clue what she was talking about. "Bethesda – a biblical name. I bet the chapels had a stranglehold on those poor folk. But looking at this list, there must have been little mines all up that valley with mining villages attached to every one of them. No buses running back and forth in the early days, you'd have had to walk to work, so people must have lived close by or they'd never have got there."

She sighed and sat back on her heels.

"I think we can discount any of these mines where the towns still exist, though, don't you? I know they're hardly major places, but there must still be enough people around to start asking questions. And anyway, places like Bethesda are on main routes through the mountains – this is the main A5, for God's sake, you couldn't do much of anything clandestine there, could you? Even these days, when a lot of people go abroad for their holidays, Ivan, there're still a significant number of families pouring out of Birmingham and Manchester to the seaside around there every summer, never mind the day-trippers. No, whatever I'm looking for, it isn't here."

Recognising that she was getting tired and probably wasn't going to achieve anything more productive for the day, Stella folded the maps back up, but made sure she'd bookmarked the one website so that she could find it easily again. She had a feeling that she'd be working her way through its lists, and if some of the groups of mines could be easily dismissed, there would be others where she'd be tracking down every one. Those would be the remoter ones, the ones where she'd probably be scouring every grid square of the map for some clue as to where they'd been. Oh well, it was certainly going to give her something different to do over the half term.

What she wasn't expecting was to get a phone call back from Soapy at nine o'clock that night.

"You're not an early to bed person these days, are you?" he asked first.

"Not that early, and only when I'm at work," Stella declared, becoming slightly worried by his grim tone of voice. "That was quick. I wasn't expecting you to ring me back for at least a day or two."

"And I didn't think I would be, either."

"Oh dear, that doesn't sound good."

"It isn't." She heard Soapy taking a swig of a drink and wondered whether she ought to have a bracing one ready herself.

"So," he began, "I thought I'd start with my old lot. I stayed up late because they're hours ahead of us out there, and it was probably going to be easiest to catch them before they went out for the day."

"Gosh, I'd forgotten the time difference."

"I hadn't. Too many phone calls home while I was away. And I was reckoning on early morning patrols going out, so I knew the lads would be up early local time.

"Well I kept it simple. Just said I was trying to track down Dav, and was he out there with them? Made sure I didn't say anything that would arouse anyone's suspicions, anything they might go to someone higher up over."

Stella swallowed hard. "I'm not going to like this, am I?"

Soapy grunted. "Oh, this bit's pretty much as we expected. I sent out a couple of texts and made one call, and all of them confirmed that the whole of Dav's platoon never went out with the rest of the lads. I just said we had a family party coming up and Cath wanted to invite Dav, and I got very natural responses, all along the lines of, 'no, mate, he's not out here, left him and the others back at base.'"

"So they think they're at Lichfield?" Stella gasped.

"It very much sounded like it. And my mate, Mick, who was the one I called, would have been the first to drop a hint if he'd known anything. As it was, I had to cover my tracks a bit by giving him some guff about Dav having said he might have another assignment, and that's why we hadn't invited him – Mick – 'cause we knew he was out of the country, but wondered if Dav might be around. It's a good job I didn't Skype him because he'd have seen I was lying through my teeth. Mick knows me too well."

Heaving a big sigh, Stella said, "Well having seen Ade's postcard we kind of knew that, but it's really good to have it confirmed by people who have no idea why we're asking. ...What's the bit I'm not going to like?"

"Well you rang Wendy, didn't you? So you know about Andy."

"Oh God, yes! That's just awful."

"Well I've tried every other bloke in Dav's platoon I have a contact number for, and I can't raise any of them. Not one!"

"Oh no! Oh crap!"

"And if they're here in the UK, not Afghanistan, then that makes it all the weirder, doesn't it? I'm afraid I ducked out of ringing the wives. But then again, Wendy said that after speaking to you she felt for the first time that there was something she could do, and I thought it might be better to let her carry on. Aside from that, she'll have a bond with any other recent widows she discovers. I'm not so good with knowing what to say under those circumstances."

"It's tricky," Stella agreed. "The reason I rang Wendy was partly because Andy and Dav were close, but also because she was one of the few wives who wasn't hostile towards me by the end. Most of them I just wouldn't know what to say to either – and of course, since my day, several of them are probably divorced and it's a new woman on the scene who doesn't even know my name."

Soapy grunted his agreement. "I don't like it that I was getting 'number unobtainable' for all of them, though. If any of them have voicemail – and I know some of them do – then I ought to have been able to leave a message. But either that facility has been switched off, or the 'mail box' is full up because they haven't been able to pick up those messages already in there."

"*Humph*! I may be being overly suspicious, but I think the first is more likely. I have lots of messages about supply teaching coming through to my voicemail, and I can tell you that these days there's quite a capacity on most providers. There'd have to be a huge number of calls from frantic family members to fill one up like that. And every single one of them? No, that's not remotely possible. And that makes me think about Ade's lad, too. Why not send his dad a text? Why have to go through all the subterfuge of that postcard?"

"Jesus!" Soapy gulped. "Didn't think of that! But you're right, if he'd had his phone on him it would be the simplest of things to just send a quick text message. An actual call you might not risk – too easily overheard and too long – but a text? No, that's fast and silent. Bugger! That means that their phones are probably disconnected and sitting in some safe place, and the lads were told to turn the voicemail off before they handed them over. Fuck it, this gets worse and worse the deeper you go!"

"I haven't heard back from Bob and Ade yet, but then I didn't expect to. They were primarily chasing that captain, and maybe he wasn't on their ward today? God forbid, but the whole platoon might be strung out in threes and fours across other wards, depending on how bad they are."

"No," Soapy immediately dismissed, "not that many, and for all the reasons we talked about before. No, what I'm worried about is those who weren't wounded enough to be taken to hospital. You've said all those lads you saw had physical injuries that would necessitate some serious surgical treatment. But as I sat around waiting to make those calls last night I got to wondering – when did the psychological trauma set in? Was it straight away? Or was it delayed?"

"Oh Lordy, I see where you're going with this. If it was delayed, or at least not immediately apparent when they were evacuating the ones who were bleeding, then they might have just been shipped back to wherever they were staying…"

"…And if that colonel was already shitting bricks over the lads blabbing on the wards…"

"…Then they might not have sent the rest somewhere for treatment but be trying to deal with it themselves! Oh Soapy, I don't like the thought of that. Some gung-ho, upper-class, twit issuing orders to them to forget it is probably the last thing any of them need, if they're starting to get as befuddled as the lads we've seen."

Soapy grunted his agreement. "And the longer it goes on, the harder it would be for the top man at wherever it is to eat humble pie and admit he's out of his depth. If the whole thing is sliding into a right royal fuck-up, you just know that the higher-ups will be looking for a scapegoat, and the man on the spot may be all too aware that he's likely to be it. Further up the chain they might get their knuckles rapped at some later hearing, but it won't be their heads that roll, and the mentality is all too often that they think they'll come out of it better if they're seen to have acted decisively – and that means having booted out someone beneath them at speed. That local man will know it'll be him, and again, he'll be working on trying to salvage something so that he comes out with at least an honourable discharge. It's pretty callous, but it's human nature. And you have to allow alternatively, that he might be totally out of his depth and be repeatedly calling for help, but getting no sensible response from his superiors who don't appreciate just how serious things are. It wouldn't be the first time that's happened!"

Stella could feel her insides tying themselves in knots again. The thought of Dav and his friends being in that depth of trouble tore at her terribly.

"Didn't anyone give any hint at all as to where the others were going?" she asked despairingly, knowing that the answer would almost certainly be no.

Soapy heaved a sigh. "No, not a thing. I suspect that if you pressed them when you next saw them they'd say that they thought the lads had been lucky/unfortunate enough to have been selected for another training exercise, depending on how you see it. Lucky, in the sense that they're not dodging bullets in Kandahar. Unfortunate, in that most of the time if some new idea is being tried out, it usually turns out to be of bugger-all use in the field. You know the sort of thing – looks great on a computer screen but takes no account of the random human factor."

"And we agreed not to give the lads still in cause for concern, in case them asking questions backfires on us …I know …but this is turning into a nightmare of far greater proportions than I imagined a couple of days ago."

"I know what you mean. Cock-ups of this magnitude don't happen that often, and I'm more used to thinking of something like this happening out in the field. A patrol lost because the wrong GPS coordinates were given them and they strayed into dangers they weren't prepared for – that kind of thing. Oh I know there have been accidents on rifle ranges and the like, but in a strange way you have to expect that at some time something like that's going to happen when you're using live ammo. The advantages of knowing how live ammo behaves are huge, and with the best will in the world you can never make something like that one hundred percent foolproof. But this? This is off on a whole other planet as far as I can see! Where the hell are they?"

And so Stella told him of her idea about the mines.

"That's a damned good thought," Soapy agreed when she'd finished, "but potentially we're looking at checking nearly half of Wales for abandoned mines. That's like looking for the right flea on a gypsy's dog!"

Chapter 8

Tuesday

It was a shock to get up the next morning and realise that it was Tuesday and her half term was already almost halfway through. If she was going to accomplish anything before she went back to teaching then it had to be soon. Dare she turn down any offers of supply work that came in at the back end of the week? It inevitably happened then; someone picking up a bug whilst on holiday or twisting an ankle in some sport they normally had no time to do. No, she told herself firmly, there were still her bills to pay, and she wouldn't be doing Dav any favours by getting into debt. After all, where else was he going to go if he needed somewhere to convalesce? She couldn't imagine his ex-wife being any too keen on having him around after the acrimonious divorce, and the accusations Dav had justifiably thrown at her.

Hopefully nobody had ever told Dav that it had been Toby whom Alison had been screwing with nightly fervour, and her hoping he would take her in once she had ditched Dav. But while Alison herself had had enough sense of self preservation not to name names (or had that been Toby warning her of the dire consequences if she did?), she certainly hadn't spared poor Dav the gory details. Pretty understandably he had been vitriolic in his condemnation of her, finally seeing the side of her that had long had everyone else wondering what on earth he saw in her.

"That cow Alison won't give a damn about him," Stella told Ivan as she brewed up some fresh coffee. This was her holiday treat, since normally she was flying out of the door in too much of a hurry to brew up the real thing. She was lucky if she managed to grab a portable mug of instant on the way out on most mornings. "Time to start looking at those maps again! We have to find him, Ivan!"

Yet she had barely settled down once more in the dining room which doubled as her office when the phone rang. Carefully stepping over the carpet of maps, Stella grabbed the phone and was surprised to hear Wendy on the other end of the line.

"Wow! I didn't expect to hear from you so soon!"

Sounding like an echo of Soapy, Wendy said sourly, "I wish I wasn't ringing you back." Then she seemed to take a deep breath before saying, "But first I want to thank you, Stella. Not just for me but for the four other wives and partners in the same predicament."

"*Four*? Holy crap on a cracker, Wendy! Four!"

"Yep! Five of us. All sitting at home crying our eyes out wondering how our men could get killed on a bloody training exercise. Tom Bailey was one, and Jane says she's sorry she's never been in touch with you. She says she had her doubts about Toby for years, but then after you'd gone and he was worse, not better, she started to think that you'd been very hard done by."

Stella remembered Jane alright. She'd not held back from telling Stella what she thought of her, and in truth it was a bit two-faced to be shifting the blame to where it always should have gone – onto Toby – at this late stage. Stella could have done with a couple of good friends all those years ago. But then Tom Bailey had been a decent bloke, and if he was dead then neither he nor Jane deserved that.

"Your silence is telling," Wendy said with a dry wisp of a laugh. "Yes, I remember how Jane spoke to you, too. There never was any call for that. But she's in shreds, Stella. Whatever she's like to other women, she adored that big daft lump of a husband of hers, and they managed to knock out five kids – the youngest is only six, so she's in a pretty rough spot now."

"Blimey, widowed in her early forties and with a late-arrival kid! No, I wouldn't have wished that on her, even at her worst," Stella admitted. "So go on, who else have the army done the dirty on?"

"Stuey."

"What? Stuart Bogdanovic?" It was an exotic surname for a lad who couldn't have got more Worcester if he'd tried. "Oh no, he was a good lad and I always liked his Fiona."

"Yes he was, and so were Mark Goodfellow and Ed Martin. You probably don't remember them because they came either just before or just after you left, after all this time I can't remember which. But what's really struck me, Stella, is how these are all men who had been in a long time. These weren't lads who'd only signed up in the last year or three. Every one of them was coming towards the end of their lengthy service, and from talking to their other halves, none of them were planning to re-sign-up. Mark had had his first marriage fail because of foreign postings and didn't want his second to go the same way, and Ed was planning to get wed when he came out, because he'd seen enough go down the pan to not want to risk his own marriage."

Stella was doing some rapid calculations. "So all men at least in their thirties and with a good deal of know-how between them. Oh, I don't like the sound of this at all."

"No, neither do I. Talking to Jane and then to Stuey's Fi, I've begun to wonder whether the whole idea was that once this stint was over, that they'd be offered an early release? You know, to get them out of the way before they got back into the barracks and started chatting to the other blokes? Let's face it, while none of them would blab to a civilian – and what they had to say possibly wouldn't mean much anyway – there's no way that that colonel could control whether they started having a few bevies with the lads and someone started telling tales, not realising what they were letting slip."

Stella felt her blood running cold. "God, that's callous, but I'm totally with you! It makes a terrible kind of sense, doesn't it? You want to run some very hush-hush tests, and you don't want anyone else in the army to know what they were, or what the outcomes were, so who better to use than a bunch of lads who were already halfway out anyway?"

"They must have scoured the whole bloody army to find a platoon like ours," Wendy said bitterly. "How many others could have had that kind of number of experienced men all due to leave?"

"What about the rest, though?" Stella suddenly thought. "I mean, we're talking about five of you with confirmed losses. Then there's the five in the hospital. But as Bob and Ade said to me, there're twenty-seven men in a platoon plus their officer – their lieutenant. Where the hell are the rest of them, then? Where are the other seventeen? There might be a couple in another ward, but as Bob pointed out, the whole platoon can't be in the hospital without a lot of questions getting asked, so where are they? You can't just 'disappear' that number of men off the army's payroll without questions being asked, surely?"

Wendy gave a snort of disgust. "Well that's where it starts getting really interesting! Fi says that the last time she spoke to Stuey, he said that three of his mates had been transferred out and not been replaced."

"Not replaced? Does that mean that they went wherever it was under strength?"

"It sounded very much like it. And once she'd pulled herself together a bit more, Fi was spitting bullets like me. She says that Stuey was told that his buddies were being sent to another platoon which had had men retire out of, and which they wanted bringing up to full strength before heading out to Kandahar. So when I got to Ed's Lucy, I made a point of dropping a hint into the conversation. Sure enough, one of Ed's mates got shifted to another squad to make up their numbers, too. By my reckoning, Stella, there might have been as many as six or eight lads who hadn't been in that long who got reassigned. It wouldn't be hard to do, after all. It's not as though they were being re-cap-badged to a different regiment, just shifted around internally, and that can happen for all sorts of reasons, even something as innocuous as promotion."

"The sneaky bastards!" Stella breathed. "You're right, the other blokes wouldn't think it worth commenting on that. When Soapy texted them or spoke to Mick, they'd naturally be thinking of those members of the platoon whom they knew were still in the UK, not the ones who'd just changed platoons in what must have seemed like a perfectly normal shift. And Soapy was in a different platoon, so I always knew he wouldn't know everyone in Dav's well enough to have all their phone numbers – the ones he did were always going to be the old hands, the ones who'd been around for years."

"And of course, he was right. He wouldn't be able to contact any of them because they're the very same ones who've disappeared off to this unknown place."

"So the younger, newest men are where everyone expects them to be, and the older guys are assumed to be marking time until they leave, or are like Ade's Tom, and are someone who gets shifted around because they have special skills. God, Wendy, what have they been dragged into?"

"I was hoping you'd be able to tell me."

So Stella relayed on what Soapy had told her and her own theory of the mine. "I know half of it is speculation," she apologised at the end, "but it's all we've got to go on so far."

"Well it sounds convincing to me," Wendy declared. "And I'll tell you something else, their own second lieutenant, who they'd had for a couple of years, made full lieutenant and got moved on just before everyone flew out. He's out dodging bullets in Afghanistan, too. Whoever is with those lads of ours is either a total newcomer, or someone they don't know well. Their own captain flew out too, so he's not the one making the excuses to that colonel.

"It was only after we put the phone down before that I thought of that, and at first I just thought, 'oh, Stella won't know him, of course, 'cause he came after she left,' as the reason why you hadn't recognised his voice. But then I remembered that Captain Bryce's wife was fuming that he wouldn't be present when their second kid is born because of being out there. I'm actually glad about that, because I always thought he was a decent sort, and it didn't sound like him to be so careless of the men."

"I'm glad too," Stella agreed. "I'd hate to think that someone who personally knew all of these blokes could just abandon them to their fate. But this is an awful lot of manoeuvring, isn't it? Someone's gone to an incredible amount of trouble to make sure this group of men are totally isolated, and that nobody's likely to ask questions about them. That makes me think that whatever's happened has really caught them on the hop. They weren't remotely expecting to have to deal with this number of casualties, for a start off, because they haven't got their story even halfway straight."

Wendy paused, then said cautiously, "Don't think I'm daft, will you, but what if they really *weren't* with the army? You said that your new friend Ade's son said that. So what if the army has done its preparation and covering its tracks, then sent our lads off to work with some outside contractor, or whoever they are, expecting them to have done the same amount of work?"

"Jeez!" Stella breathed. "No, I don't think you're daft, Wendy! I think you just made the most sense of this of all of us. Some loony boffin from Porton Down, or somewhere else maybe, comes up with one of their ideas, they approach another approved contractor to get it tested, and they in turn get in touch with the army saying that they need some lads to test this new magic 'thingy', only they never thought it might go wrong – never even considered the possibility. I've met a few scientific types when I was at uni, and honestly, Wendy, some of them aren't on this planet! One very highly thought of professor, who did really ground breaking research, didn't realise that you actually had to *empty* the vacuum cleaner!"

"Eh?"

"Truly, Wendy! I was earning some extra cash by doing some office temping in the Chemistry department, and Prof dropped his vacuum off in our office for the odd-jobs chap to have a look at because it wasn't working. Well Simon came up with his tools during his lunch hour to have a go at fixing it, and he was having a right game getting the bag off it. When he did, it exploded all over us! It was that rammed full!"

She laughed at the memory. "God knows where Prof thought all the crap went to – outer space, probably! There were the six of us hanging out of the office window, laughing ourselves silly in between coughing ourselves near inside out. Did it ever cause a mess! But my point is, this Prof was a genius – the real thing – but he hadn't a clue about real life. He was so up in the stars with his theoretical stuff that the nuts and bolts of making something work in a practical sense were way beneath him, not because he was a snob, but because his brain just couldn't come down to that level.

"Well what if a group of total eggheads like that came up with something? You or I would say that someone with both feet firmly on the ground would need to be in charge of the actual physical tests. But what if someone's palm got greased to push tests forward? The way the government's been going for the last decade or so, with everything being put out to tender for the rock bottom price, sooner or later something was bound to go wrong."

"Oh!" Wendy gasped, with Stella all the way. "And this thing's been brought forward too fast and with no proper supervision? Oh my God, Stella! You can just see it happening, can't you? A bunch of civil servants who never get out of their offices, taking the word of some intermediary that everything's in place, when whoever that is doesn't really have a clue…"

"…and the boffins close to wetting their knickers with excitement that they get to play with their new toy…!"

"...with nobody stopping to think what might be needed in the way of medical care or equipment if it all goes wrong!"

They both sat in silence for a moment, too horrified by the implications to speak and yet knowing that it made the most sense of what had up until now been such a puzzle.

"I tell you something else," Stella finally said. "Where do they often take new armaments to try them out? Old quarries! They're deep, and usually well away from habitation. The MOD must have dozens of them on their books. But if you wanted to be really Secret Squirrel about something – if you were worried about some eager nerd of a kid flying his drone overhead at just the wrong time – where else would you go?"

Wendy gasped. "An old mine! You were right!"

Now Stella's mind was running at speed. "Are you getting back in touch with any of the women you talked to?"

"Fi and I are meeting for a coffee this afternoon. That's why I thought I'd ring you this morning."

"Great. Can you get her thinking, too? Anything to do with Wales. Anything Stuey might have let slip, any hint he might have dropped that meant nothing at the time, but in the light of what we're thinking might now seem significant."

"I'll definitely be asking! Do you want to join us?"

"Where are you meeting?"

"The Costa's in Malvern, so not far from you, only over the hill."

"Can I say maybe? It's just that I think I need to ring Soapy and tell him what you've said, and then ring Bob, too. They deserve to know, and if one of them comes up with anything worth chasing, I'm going to join them. I'm on holiday for only a few more days, and I can't tell you why, Wendy, but all my senses are screaming at me that time is of the essence. It won't bring back Andy or Stuey, but it might make all the difference to the lads who are still missing."

"No problem. If you make it we'll be glad to see you, but if we don't we'll take it as a good sign that you've got something to chase."

As soon as she'd put the phone down from Wendy's call, Stella decided that she'd ring Bob first. She still had time to catch him before he went out for afternoon visiting hours, but if Soapy kept her talking then she might miss him until the evening, and that nagging sense of time told her not to do that.

He picked up almost straight away, but Stella could hear instantly that something was wrong.

"What's happened, Bob?"

She was sure she could hear crying in the background.

"The lad they called Flynn ...his real name was Errol ...the one who kept having the convulsions? ...He died yesterday evening."

"Oh no! Oh God, I'm so sorry to hear that!"

She heard Bob walking away from the sounds of crying and a door being shut, then Bob spoke more normally.

"Jane's been in a terrible state ever since. Our Josh is okay, and so is Ade's Tom, but the other lad, Craig Biggins, had his first seizure last night."

Stella felt sick. "Oh no! You think he's going the same way as Errol?"

Bob's voice was thick with emotion. "Hard not to worry about that, isn't it? And although we've been reassured by the doctors, Jane's still worried half out of her mind that if he can suddenly start convulsing, how long could it be before Josh or Tom start?"

"Bloody hell! Oh, Bob, I'm so sorry! I'll leave you in peace."

"Don't you dare! It's only the hope that I can do something that's keeping me going at the moment. So come on, spill the beans, what did you ring up to tell me?"

By the time Stella had finished Bob was swearing softly but fluently.

"The absolute bastards!" he growled. "But I think you're right, it's the one thing that makes sense. The army would be crapping itself, because there are bound to be questions asked as to how they let our lads go off on this thing without checking further. It certainly explains why that colonel was in such a tizzy – he must have watched the whole thing unravelling in front of him like an old army sweater and with no way of stopping it. If there were no precautions put in place there'd have been nothing he could use. Doesn't excuse him not doing right by the men, mind you, but then if he's out of the army and associated with whoever it is, he might not actually be a serving soldier."

"You think he might have been offered a post with some research facility and he's just hanging on to his old title?" Stella wondered.

"I'd rather think that than of him still serving," Bob declared. "Maybe he was a naughty boy and got told that if he left then it wouldn't go any further? Not exactly a dishonourable discharge, but nonetheless shunting him off sideways into a civilian liaison role to avoid any scandal."

"But what would he have done to get off with that?"

"Sexual impropriety would be my guess. Given that everyone on active service is an adult, there's always the grey area of what's consenting and what isn't. It's always hard to prove that someone was put in a place where they felt they had no choice but to comply – tends to be one man's word against another, you see. But if there'd been more than one complaint over the years, there'd come a point when those higher up could start seeing the colonel as a liability, someone who would sooner rather than later bring the army into disrepute. But that's a guess. I could be far from the mark."

"I'll be sure to run that past Soapy when I call him. He's bound to have a take on that, what with being in so recently."

There was the sound of another phone ringing.

"Hang on a tick, Stella, that's the house phone. I'd better get it in case it's the hospital."

As she heard Bob suddenly exclaim, "What?" Stella's heart sank. Please God let that not be news that Josh had been taken ill. But then she heard Bob calling to Jane and someone else, "It's okay, just a call for me."

It was only moments, though, before Bob was back on his mobile with Stella.

"How fast can you get up here?" he demanded.

"If I leave now? Within the hour, I suppose?"

"Then get your skates on girl! I'm heading for the hospital now. That was Ade! He's spotted a sandy-haired bloke doing the rounds of the beds. Thinks it's that bloody captain! But you're the one who can identify him – so get up here before Ade starts pounding some civilian into mincemeat!"

Chapter 9

Tuesday

It was a wonder that Stella never got a speeding ticket as she forced every drop of speed out of her old Renault bombing up the M5. Cursing every slow driver and trucker who got in her way, she tore into the hospital car park in record time and was relieved to find a space close to the entrance for once. Leaving Ivan in the car, for there had been no time to take him next door when Dai would want her to stop for a chat, she opened all of the windows a crack and ran inside.

No-one would steal her car, of that she was sure, because the only thing Ivan got possessive of was his car. In the house he was the most useless watch-dog ever, and while he was more than fond of his food, Stella had never had a problem taking things like bones off him. But anyone who stuck their fingers in through those windows would be likely to go away with a few missing, and Ivan certainly gave them warning that he was going to snap. No child was going to inadvertently come to harm, but God help any aspiring car thief!

She moved as fast as she dared through the hospital itself and up to the ward, sliding to a halt as she saw Ade and Bob marching purposefully out of it in the wake of a tall, sandy-haired man whom she was sure was the captain. Slipping in behind them she hissed,

"That's him, I'm sure of it! Where's he off to?"

"No bloody idea," Ade growled, "but he's been flitting back and forth between our lads' ward and somewhere else for the last hour. It's like he doesn't know where to be for the best. The first time he went out I thought he was maybe just going to the loo, and the second that he'd had a bad curry the night before. But this is the fifth time he's done this. I would have followed him before, but the doctors appeared and we wanted answers about Craig and the chances of our lads taking bad like him."

"Did you get any?" Stella asked hopefully, but Ade and Bob (who had got there well ahead of Stella, being local and only a few minutes' drive away, and had been with Ade by this stage) both shook their heads.

"They're as bloody mystified as us," Bob declared. "They can't understand why the medication isn't working. On the plus side, though, apparently both Errol and Craig have this strange marker in their blood, but neither of our lads nor your ex have any sign of it. And it seems it's been there ever since they got brought in, it didn't just come on, so that's given us some hope. Haematology has been doing its collective nut trying to work out what it is, we were told, but their best guess so far is that it's from something those two ingested, so it's unlikely to be transferable."

"Thank God for that!"

Ade grimaced. "Oh yes! But now I want to know what that sneaky sod's up to. Look, he's going into that ward!"

The three of them slowed down and peered into the ward. It had every appearance of being another military ward – something that was not a given when Selly Oak catered to the general population of southern Birmingham and simply had a military wing, even then sometimes having civilian patients on some of those wards if they required similar treatments.

"This looks like more of a mixed ward, though," Stella observed. "That old chap in the first bed can't possibly be a serving soldier, not at his age."

"Probably did in the past," Ade postulated, "'cause he's the right age to have served right at the end of World War Two or out in Korea. At the very least he'd have done National Service. I wonder if that's why he's in here? Some old injury giving him gip?"

"Maybe," Bob agreed, "But look at the stuff he's wired up to. I'm no doctor, but that looks just like what my dad was plugged into after he had his heart attack." He looked about him and then nudged the other two. "Look! Cardiac Ward! It says so on that sign over there."

Stella shrugged out of her jacket. "Here, hold that for me, Bob. I'll sneak in as if I'm another visitor and see if I can see who that captain went to. I'll be less obvious than you two. Most of the afternoon visitors are women or old men — you two'll stand out like sore thumbs, and if he sees me elsewhere I'll look different with my jacket back on."

Just to add to the effect, Stella grabbed one of the elastic hair ties from her pocket and pulled her hair back into it. She only had collar length hair, but sometimes up on the hills with Ivan it was easier to tie it back than have it whipping in her face, and today she was glad that she always had ties in her pockets. Now she looked a short-haired woman in a green flowery top instead of a long-haired one in a long stone-coloured jacket, and she modified her usual stride to something more girly as she entered the ward.

Smiling at some of the other patients, she scrutinised the line of beds on either side. One bed had the screens pulled around it, and she could see the forms of nurses brushing against the material as they tended to someone.

"Such a shame," an elderly voice came from beside her, and she turned to see the old man nodding towards the enclosed bed. "Only a young bloke, too. No age to be going with a heart attack."

Sliding into the chair by his bed, Stella took a chance. "Look, I know this is going to sound a bit weird, but have you seen a tall, sandy-haired chap coming in and out of here? Might be saying he's a captain in the army?"

"Oh him!" the old man said with a sniff. "Funny fella he is! Sometimes he goes to the lad down there who's in trouble – that's where he is now. Other times he goes to that other younger chap in the fifth bed on the far side. He can't be a relative to be visiting both of them, can he? Who is he?"

"That's what we'd like to know! There are three of us with family in the military ward down the corridor, and we've been given a right load of old eyewash about what kind of accident they've been in. That sneaky captain – if that's what he is – has been in and out to our lads, and we think he's something to do with the army as well, but he's never in uniform, and he seems to be deliberately avoiding the families who might ask awkward questions. He only seems to talk to the ones he knows he can bullshit."

"Is he?" The old chap seemed to perk up a bit, probably bored stiff lying in his bed all day and glad of something of interest to be happening. "They've said I'll be in here for a day or two more – I've got to go across to the Queen Elizabeth to have my stents fitted and they haven't got a bed for me yet – I'll keep an eye on him."

"That'd be great! What's your name?"

"Dennis."

"Lovely to meet you, Dennis. So does that bloke only come to visit those two?"

"There was a third lad, but he went home the day before yesterday. Funny thing was, that captain chappie didn't seem happy about it at all. I heard him arguing with the doctors over it. He seemed to want them to keep the lad in longer – well I say 'lad', they all look young when you get to my age. He was probably thirty-something. Of course the doctors got a bit shirty with him about that. Told him that beds on these wards are at a premium. I'm only here because my wife's not well enough to have me home while I'm waiting, or I'd have been sent away too, because there's nothing they can do for me until I can have the stent put in."

He paused and then said, "And that's a funny thing too. Talking to the others in here, we're all heading down one of two paths. It's either having stents fitted or by-pass surgery. But the lad over the way isn't having either of those. I'm sure he said that they've told him that his attack was brought on by extreme stress, and that once he's had time to recover that he ought to be alright. I'll get him chatting tonight. The last time we spoke he seemed a bit off with the fairies."

"How do you mean? Was it the drugs they're giving him?" Stella was hoping like mad that this poor soul wasn't heading down the same route as Errol. But Dennis was immediately shaking his head.

"Oh no, not like that. It was the way he was talking about stuff. Said he'd seen things he never expected to see. Well I'm afraid I might have been a bit brusque, 'cause I said I'd been in the army too, and what had he expected when he signed up? And he said it wasn't that sort of stuff, though he'd been out to Afghanistan and seen some horrors of war out there. He said this had been some hush-hush assignment, and that it was there that he'd seen something absolutely horrific – and it must have been bad, because just the memory of it set his machines beeping like a swarm of mad wasps. The nurses came running in and told him he had to calm down. I felt a bit bad about that. After all, I'd prodded him."

Stella decided that she ought to tell Dennis something of what they knew in that case, and told him about the lads in the other ward, though not of her suspicions of some kind of testing that had gone wrong. That was in part because she didn't want to prime Dennis to see something that wasn't there. He was a useful control sample for them if he could come up with something which pointed the same way without prompting.

Dennis harrumphed as she finished. "It's always the poor bleedin' squaddies who get the shitty end of the stick," he said cynically. "They sent us out to Korea in bloody tropical gear. Some tit saw 'Far East' and assumed we'd be sweating our socks off in a jungle somewhere, not freezing to death halfway up a snow-covered mountain in a Korean winter. So I'm not surprised someone's ballsed up with these lads. ...Hang on a tick, he's coming back!"

Stella ducked her face away as if she was going to put something in Dennis' bedside locker as the captain strode past, but she heard Dennis' soft chuckle of,

"Well someone's pissed on his chips! Face like bloody thunder!"

"Can you have that chat with the lad across the way?" Stella asked him as she straightened up and realised that the captain had fully left the ward. "I'd better scarper. I've left my two new mates outside and they're both ex-army dads who're running out of patience. Things might get interesting if I can't hold them back a bit!"

She hurried out of the ward, just pausing to check that the captain wasn't simply at the nurse's office or talking to a doctor outside.

What she wasn't expecting to see was the captain bracketed by Bob and Ade, both of them clearly looking for a confrontation.

"Bollocks!" she heard Bob say brutally. "Don't give me that shit! We want some answers, matey, and you're going to give them to us!"

"Look, I can't do that!" the captain was saying firmly, but Stella could see in his eyes that he was worried. "You know the Official Secrets Act. You know I can't tell you."

"Bugger the Official Secrets Act!" Ade snapped. "If this was a war situation I'd be bloody upset, but I'd accept it. Bob and I have both seen action. We know what it means and what can happen. But this isn't it, is it? Where have our lads been? Don't give us some old flannel, 'cause we know bloody well it wasn't Afghanistan. We've got eyes in our heads, you know! They're lying there like a couple of sodding lilies and surrounded by lads who look like they've been dunked in gravy! Doesn't take a fucking genius to work out they haven't been in the same place!"

Stella thought that for all his anger, Ade had so far kept some measure of control, because although he was pushing hard, he hadn't let any of their suspicions slip. The captain foolishly didn't take enough notice, though.

"I still can't tell you," he said waspishly, and made as if to shove Ade out of the way.

Bob's arm was around his neck like a striking snake, muscled forearm and biceps squeezing either side of the captain's throat with his hand clasping his other arm which was braced against the captain's back. It was a very effective choke hold and the captain began to go red in the face.

"Nothing to see here," Ade said firmly to a bunch of visitors who were passing and gasped at the sight. "Troublesome patient. Keep moving!"

"Now I'm going to ask you again," Bob hissed savagely in the captain's ear. "Where the fucking hell have our lads been?"

Something about the way Bob had the captain held was being particularly effective, or Bob was a lot stronger and more practiced at this than he seemed, because Stella could see the captain pulling hard on Bob's arm, and also trying to push him backwards to get him off balance. But Bob had positioned himself better than that, with a concrete pillar to brace himself against, and his captive was well and truly caught unless the captain could try a more effective tactic and things were to develop into a full brawl.

Ade went and stood very close to them, effectively blocking most people's view of what Bob was doing, and Stella took her cue from him and moved herself into the remaining gap. She wasn't big enough to hide as much as Ade, but she could still do her bit.

"I'm going to ask you again," Ade said sternly. "Where were our lads? Is it that you *can't* tell us because you honestly don't know where they've been? Or because you've got some senior officer dancing on your nads telling you not to let something slip?"

Again, very clever, Stella thought, hinting at the colonel without letting on that they actually knew. And she was sure she'd seen a hint of panic in the captain's eyes when Ade had said that. He'd covered it well a second later, but it had been there.

"What's your name?" Stella demanded, and that really seemed to throw the captain."

"*Gnmph?*" was the strangled question back.

She looked him in the eye, not having to fake her own anger as the thought of Dav came to her once more. "Well you're not Captain Bryce, are you? Or did you not expect us to know who's our lads' regular officer of your rank? He's out with the rest of the lads, isn't he! And you lot shoved their most recent lieutenant off elsewhere too."

"You can't possibly…"

"Oh I bloody can, you stupid man! Or do you think that us wives never pick up the phone to one another? Bryce's wife is right furious that she's going to give birth without him there. That's the trouble with you snooty officers – you don't bother thinking about the family things, do you? That one wife might call on another for help and tell them why!" *There, that's rattled you*, Stella thought with savage glee. *Nothing that isn't wholly explainable but something else you've missed!*

The captain had stopped struggling now and was starting to look genuinely worried.

"What's your name, matey?" Bob snarled in his ear. "Are you even a real captain, or just the captain of the local Boys' Brigade who works for a military contractor?"

"I'm a commissioned officer!" he spluttered back indignantly.

"Who with?"

"The Mercians, of course!"

Ade leaned in a little closer. "Then why all the Secret Squirrel stuff, eh? Why aren't our lads out with the rest of them? Your story doesn't add up, pal!"

The captain groaned. "Oh God!"

"He's not here," Bob growled, "and he's not about to turn up any time soon, either! So your best bet for getting out of here without me twisting your head off is to start talking!"

"I can't!" gargled the captain, now a definite shade of puce as Bob tightened his hold.

"Uh-oh!" Ade suddenly said in warning. "Security heading this way!"

Bob let the captain go with a shove and a wagged finger of warning. "You might have got off this time, sunshine, but we're watching you!"

The captain was already moving away, rubbing his neck, but he stopped in shock as Bob's last riposte over his shoulder as they moved off was,

"One way or the other we're going to find out about Wales."

His colour rapidly changing from puce to white, the captain called after them, "Wales? What do you mean?"

Hurrying around the corner into the next corridor, Stella retrieved her jacket from Ade and shook her hair loose again, even as Ade was saying,

"That shook him! For a second there I thought you'd blown it mentioning Wales, but didn't he go a funny colour when you did! That shite-hawk knows something more than he's letting on!"

Bob sniffed disgustedly. "And what's the betting he's going to call for back-up?"

"I'm on it!" Stella declared, already breaking into a trot as she headed for the exit. "He won't do it in here now, will he? He'll go outside to phone!"

She ran for the stairs and took them two at a time, startling other visitors at her mad dash, but she got outside ahead of the captain and went and retrieved Ivan from the car. Nothing suspicious about someone getting the dog out for a pee, she thought, and gave her hair another ruffle so that it fell further forward over her face.

Sure enough, as she allowed Ivan to sniff at every blade of grass close to the entrance, she saw the captain come hurrying out, mobile phone in hand.

"Right, Ivan, my lovely, time for you to play your part," Stella told the big white dog softly, and gave him a gentle tug to move in the direction of the captain.

Completely focused on making the call, and no doubt assuming that security would be keeping Bob and Ade busy for now, the captain didn't even look Stella's way. Striding off towards where a few pathetic plants were doing their best to fight the exhaust fumes and provide a colourful border to the car park, he was almost hunched over the phone as he punched in the numbers and then jammed it to his ear while it no doubt rang out to some distant office.

"Sir? ...It's Hardy ...What do you mean, 'why am I calling you?' You said to contact you in the event of something going wrong. Well it has! ...No, I couldn't have controlled it! And having just nearly had my head torn off by a father who's clearly served, I'm getting pretty pissed off with being the one who's eternally in the firing line!" He ripped the phone away from his ear and made a very rude gesture at it even as Stella could hear the tinny sounds of a voice, though she couldn't tell what was being said.

"No, *sir*! And you'd better listen to me for once!" he continued acidly. "They might be only the families but they're starting to put two and two together, and they're coming up with some worryingly accurate conclusions. ...No, I can't put them off! Who do you think I'm dealing with here? These two fathers are former regiment themselves. They're not some misguided pair of civvies! They know how things work and they're not so daft as to not be able to tell that something's very wrong."

He threw his head back and rolled his eyes heavenwards at something the person on the other end was saying. "Christ, sir! The wife of one of them says she talked to Captain Bryce's wife. How do you stop that sort of thing? You can't, can you? So they know that while all the other lads are out with him where everyone thinks they are, that these few have been somewhere else. I can't say anything to counter that without them openly laughing in my face, and trying to would only create even more suspicion."

He spun on his heels in his frustration, coming right back at Stella who was only a few paces behind him.

Ivan saved the day by choosing to deposit the remains of his dinner just at the right moment, allowing Stella to cover herself by both ducking down with the plastic poop-bag on her hand and saying, "Good boy!" to him as she did so, every bit the responsible dog owner and seemingly utterly disinterested in the captain and his phone argument.

The captain stamped past her, totally oblivious to her and Ivan, and then paused by the next tree, allowing Stella to edge a bit closer again. If he turned she could haul Ivan over to the other side of the stunted shrubs as if making for a car, making it worth the risk of being spotted, but she did fluff her hair up a bit again to look less like the woman who'd been in his face only minutes ago.

"Oh, I'm over reacting, am I?" she heard him say. "Then how come one of them asked what had happened in Wales? And don't you dare say that I should have silenced the lads better. I warned you this would happen, and if you drag me into a court-martial I shall say so!"

Stella saw him pursing his lips and then pulling a face at what was being said to him.

"That won't work," he then said in the flat voice of a man at the end of his tether, too stressed to argue any more. "Oh, I'll do it since you're ordering me to, but I'm telling you now, it won't work. These are parents worried sick about their sons, and given that one of them has died despite the best efforts of the doctors, and now another's about to go the same way, you can't blame them.

"And I'm telling you this for the record now as well, I don't like being ordered to lie to them. Not about something like this. I've had enough. I don't care what the cost. We should have come clean from the start. That way at least the families would have been compensated in a proper manner, and there'd have been no more accusations to be thrown at us other than what's happened being such a shambles. But the longer this goes on, sir, the worse it's getting! It's going to come out whether you like it or not, and the more we seem to be covering things up, the worse we're going to seem. God help us if one of the tabloid newspapers gets a hold of this and starts campaigning for answers on the families' behalf, because egg on our faces will be the least of our worries!"

Chapter 10

Tuesday

Stella followed the captain as he shoved his phone back into his back pocket and stormed off towards the road. He unlocked a nondescript grey Nissan, and then she saw him get in and lean his head on the steering wheel in what looked very like despair.

Taking a chance, she chivvied Ivan back to her own car, shoved him in, and then got behind the wheel, pulling out of the car park and around to where she could see the captain and his car. He was still there, and for a horrible moment she wondered whether they had pushed him too far. However much she wanted Dav back, it wasn't at the price of pushing some poor soul into a breakdown, but she'd barely pulled into a gap in front of someone's drive – praying that an irate householder wouldn't come out and demand that she move on – before she saw a puff from the Nissan's exhaust and then moments later the captain pulling out.

Dumping her own mobile onto the seat, and then connecting it up so that she could use the hands-free as she waited at one of the major traffic lights, she pulled up Bob's number and waited while it rang out. When he answered she said,

"It's Stella, and I'm on the road following the captain."

"Bloody hell, girl, you be careful!"

"I will, but Bob, I'm not sure he's the bad guy we think he is. At worst he's been caught in between a rock and a hard place, I reckon." She told Bob what she'd seen and heard him relaying the information on to Ade at intervals.

"So why are you following him?" she heard Ade say, having been put on speaker so that both of them could now talk to her.

"Because I thought it might be useful to see where he goes. For a start off, it's going to be telling whether he goes back to Lichfield, or at least to one of the married quarters, isn't it? I mean, if he does that then he's had the dirty done on him as much as our guys have. He's just another lowly minion caught in the same trap, because captains come ten-a-penny compared to those who give the real orders, don't they? As a serving officer they'd have him over a barrel — especially if he's got family. What the hell do you do if you're shot out of the army at speed without even the time to arrange to rent a house, unless you're lucky enough to have parents you can go to?

"I know how that feels, guys. It happened to me when I broke up with Toby. One minute I was living in married quarters, the next I was effectively homeless, because there was no home of our own for me to get in a settlement. All that saved me was being able to go early into student accommodation, and they made an exception in my case because of my particular circumstances — I mean Toby having been violent towards me, not just coming out of the services."

Belatedly she realised that she hadn't told Bob and Ade that when she heard their sharp intakes of breath. Bugger! Oh well, no going back now. That was another genie she couldn't shove back into its bottle.

"Don't smother the little shit on my account," she said in what she hoped were breezy tones. "I've had my revenge on him in other ways — like leaving him with the delightful prospect of having to stick with his current wife while he convalesces."

"*Hmph!*" Bob grunted, implying that he thought Toby had got off lightly, while Ade said,

"Nevertheless, Stella, you didn't tell us that."

"But that's why I want to find Dav so much," Stella remonstrated with them. "He was the one who stood up for me back at the time. I'm not doing any of this for Toby. He's way beyond the point where I'd do anything for him. But Dav was a total gent every step of the way, so can we focus on that, please?"

"Point taken," Ade conceded. "Okay, so you think it'll be telling if you can see where this captain goes to?"

"Yes I do! Well don't you? I mean, if he pulls up in front of some swanky new detached house with all mod cons, he's not going to have bought that without being dirty unless he's been saving every scrap of money he earns, or he's got a wife who's in some kind of high-paid professional job herself, is he? He's a youngish bloke for his rank. He's not some forty-something who's been shoving money into an account for years, and we know how much you have to put down for mortgages these days. Serving army men aren't a good investment from a bank's point of view – they'd have wanted a hefty deposit – so an old fixer of a house is one thing, but something swanky is going to really stand out."

"I see where you're going with this," Bob agreed, "but be really careful, Stella. This bloke is acting like he's right on the edge. It could mean he'll lash out at you. If he thinks you're some reporter who's going to drag him through the muck, I mean. Or he recognises you as the woman who was with us. He might feel really threatened by you in ways you're not anticipating."

"Oh, I'll be careful, don't you worry," Stella reassured them. "If it's any reassurance, he looks at the moment like he's heading towards Lichfield. That could mean he's possibly another victim, albeit in a different way."

She rang off and concentrated on her driving, making sure she stayed way back once they got onto the A38 dual carriageway going towards Lichfield. It was easy to hang well back on the busy road, periodically ducking out of sight behind big trucks on stretches where she knew it was unlikely he would turn off. If she lost him here then it would confirm that he was dirty, because they were into expensive commuter country now – the homes of people who worked in England's second city but who could afford to live that bit farther out in pleasanter surroundings than the inner city.

Yet they passed those turn offs and went on into Lichfield itself, moving towards the more ordinary housing, and into streets of modern mass development housing, making Stella glad of her old Victorian terrace. At least she couldn't hear her neighbours flushing the loo, and going by the similar homes belonging to some of her teacher acquaintances, these were modern semis and terraces where the walls in between were about as soundproof as tissue paper. If the captain was making a packet on the suffering of others he surely wouldn't be living here.

As he turned off the Western Bypass and then into one of the warren of residential streets, Stella hung further and further back. He could be being very clever, of course, and was taking her on a wild goose chase, but Stella thought not, and so she finally parked up, and leaving Ivan on guard duty once again, she set off on foot. She'd memorised the number plate, and now began a very careful wander along the streets looking for his car. It took four wrong turns into four cul-de-sacs, because this estate road seemed to feed a whole string of these short no-through-roads, but then she turned into one and immediately stopped, because his car was only three houses in.

There were no drives to these terraced houses, just pathways to the front doors through pocket handkerchiefs of front gardens – all tiny patches of lawns carefully tended in a desperate attempt at pride in houses you could do very little to make individual. But the danger for Stella was that the lounge windows were far too close to the actual road, and nothing would look stranger to his neighbours than her ducking down behind cars to creep closer. Yet this wasn't a great problem in her eyes. She'd got what she'd hoped for – a clue as to the captain's financial situation – and that was looking more and more as though he was someone caught in the middle, not the instigator of the problem. That didn't mean he didn't know more than he was telling, though; just that in all conscience they ought to be a bit more careful about the accusations they threw at him.

She hurried back to the car and got out of there fast, but not before making a note of the address and taking a quick photo of the street so that she could show Ade and Bob. And if the captain had been careless about being followed, she wasn't. She didn't know Lichfield well and so she followed signs for the famous cathedral, stopping several times as if looking to find somewhere to park near it, or checking on her route. Satisfied that there were no repeated sightings of particular cars behind her, she finally got onto the main roads back into Birmingham again. There was no easy way back home without going that way, anyway, and she thought it might not be a bad idea to go and check on Toby, given that the evening visiting times would be coming up by the time she got back in the vicinity of the hospital. Bob struck her as the kind of man who would have a thing or two to say to someone who had hurt a woman, and she wanted to make sure that in his distraught state he hadn't worked out his frustrations on Toby.

Toby turned out to be fine, but glad to see Stella.

"You rattled a few cages this afternoon," he said cheerily, as she pulled up a chair to beside his bed. "That captain bloke took off like a scalded cat after your mates had a word with him. They came back in here and told their lads, who told me. Tom says he went white when you mentioned Wales – although I can't say that I remember much of that. You've really put the wind up him!"

"We felt we needed to," Stella replied, suddenly feeling utterly drained by the day and strangely relieved that Bob and Ade hadn't come and told Toby what they thought of him. "Don't suppose you have any news for me?"

"Like what? Not much to see here."

"Oh don't be an arse, Toby. I meant like *you* remembering something."

"You okay, Stell'?"

"No I'm bloody not! Instead of having a much needed rest from tearing across three counties to different schools for the week – a situation you left me having to deal with because I need to be self-sufficient – I'm running around like a mad thing trying to find your old best mate! I'm knackered, Toby! You think teaching is a doddle, but it isn't. I never have time to build any rapport with the kids because I'm never anywhere long enough.

"And the fallout from you and you not being able to keep your fists to yourself, is that I don't settle into anywhere well anymore. I'm better keeping my escape routes open, but that's sodding exhausting when on any week I can be in Gloucester for three days and then Hereford for two, and all the time having to drive back and forth to Malvern. I can't move closer to any one school since I'm not in any of them for long enough, and all because thanks to you, I can't stand having people creeping into my life anymore!

"I don't have your stresses – my life's never in danger – but my days are very long sometimes, and I need my respite weeks. I'm often out of the house at seven o'clock and not back until twelve hours later and with marking still to do. That's no joke! And don't you forget that the only reason I'm doing this right now is because one of us needs to pay Dav back for the shit you heaped upon him – or do you choose to forget his divorce like you do ours?"

Toby lay there staring at her open-mouthed. "Jeez, Stell', I didn't realise you felt like that!"

"Really? *Really*? How did you expect me to feel? ...You've never actually thought about that, have you? Not until now. Not until I scuppered your plans for you to come weaselling back to me, because you and Seedy aren't getting carpet burns on your bums from shagging on every available surface every day, and twice at weekends!"

He gulped, staring at her wide-eyed. For a moment she thought he was going to start his usual bluster, but he didn't, closing his mouth with a snap and turning to stare at the wall as he went red with embarrassment.

"I'm sorry," he finally said thickly, and Stella realised to her shock that he was close to tears. "I'm really sorry, Stell'. You're right, I've never considered how much damage I did to you. It's a bit late in the day for me to be saying this, but I am sorry. Truly." He sniffed and then reached for a tissue, blowing his nose noisily before adding, "And I'm really glad you're trying to help Dav. I was a shit mate to him."

"Yes, you bloody were! Has he ever found out that it was you who was rogering Alison up hill and down dale?"

Toby shook his head, looking down at the sheets in shame.

"And where's Alison, now, eh? I bet you don't even know, do you? You led her up the garden path with all your stupid false promises, just like you always do, and then when you'd made your conquest, but her life was in tatters, you moved on and never looked back. Well think on this: has anyone told *her* Dav is missing? I bet not. As an ex, she'll no more be on a Families' Officer's list than I am. I know I couldn't stand her, but I wouldn't want her to learn that he's dead by some post in a newspaper – even she deserves better than that."

"Oh bloody hell!" Toby was looking genuinely queasy as the realisation crashed in on him. "Err...no, I have no idea where she went to. I know she changed her phone number, but that's all."

"God, you're a right bloody prince!" Stella said in disgust. "So come on, then, Prince Not-so-charming, is there anything you can tell me that might remotely help? Anything else you've remembered while lying here?"

There was an embarrassing silence for a moment, but then Toby blinked and said cautiously,

"I'm not sure if it's helpful or not, but I think I have a vague memory of helicopter rotors."

"Like you were in one?"

"Yeah, but not fully awake, if that makes sense? I just have this ...well it's more of a feeling really, that I was maybe in a chopper and being flown somewhere, but that I'd kind of come to for a moment and then went under again. So I don't think I even properly opened my eyes, I was just 'aware'. I'm not sure where that fits in with the ambulance bit, though."

Stella leaned her arms on the bed and tried to wriggle the tension kinks out of her neck as she said, "Well that actually makes a bit of sense. Bob was the one who picked up on the fact that you were unlikely to be ambulanced all of the way. He thought that unless you were really off the grid, that you'd have been taken to somewhere like the field hospital at Llandudno first. But that given the severity of some of the lads' wounds, that you'd more likely have been choppered into here."

Toby gave a grunt of disgust and shook his head. "Bloody hell, why didn't I think of that? He's right, of course they would. God, Stell', it's like my head got stuffed with porridge! Ever since I woke up here it's as though I'm having to drag every thought out through thick gloop. It's getting better, thank heavens, but there're whole patches that feel like my memories have just vanished into some sort of mental quicksand – they're under there somewhere, but God knows when I'll be able to get to them again." He paused, then said worriedly, "But if getting them back means I'll have the nightmares Craig over there is having, maybe I don't want them back *that* much."

"What does he have them about? Can he tell you?"

Toby wrinkled his nose. "To be honest the poor sod's a bit out of it most of the time, but when he's in the throes of one of them he keeps screaming, 'get her away from me! Make her go away!'"

"Who's she?"

"Buggered if I know. I think I'd remember if there'd been any women with us."

"*Hmph*! Yes, you would! Nose like a damned bloodhound for any woman – even half dead."

"Gee thanks, Stell'! Don't pull any punches, will you."

"Sorry. I didn't mean it come out like that. I never wished anything like this on you, not even when I hated you the most." That made Toby blink. Evidently it had never crossed his mind that Stella might feel like that. "But no, I get what you mean, any women would have to have been involved in this directly, because you wouldn't have been running across lab technicians and the like."

Mollified, Toby expanded, "He sometimes refers to her as the 'queen', but I don't think he means Her Maj' – not the actual queen. ...And he said something – it was a bit scrambled, mind – about her being dark, but again, I don't think he meant some African Amazon of a woman."

"Dark as in evil, you mean?"

"That's the impression I got, but I couldn't be any more specific because this was all coming out of him in a jumble. You know what it's like when people talk in their sleep, it's all a string of words, and some of them make sense and others don't."

Stella sat back and huffed out a long breath, her brow creased in a puzzled frown. "Well that's a weird piece in the jigsaw if ever there was one."

"Isn't it! And there might be more coming, because God help him, Craig's getting worse by the night – and it is always the night when he gets in that state. He sleeps most of the day now, but he's okay then. It's at night that he gets in a right state, and that's when he has the seizures, right after he's got deep into one of his nightmares."

"Poor chap! ...But Errol – or Flynn as you lot seemed to call him – he had seizures during the day, didn't he? I mean, I saw him having one, or at least all the nurses piling in to help him."

"Yes he did. But by that stage he was a lot worse than Craig is. He was where Craig is now when they first brought him in …No, no I can't say that, 'cause I don't remember that. When I first remember really waking up in here, that's what brought me round, hearing Flynn screaming his head off."

"Any thoughts, feelings, about when that might have been? You've been in here a bit over two weeks, Toby, but how many of those days can you remember?"

His face screwed up in concentration. "I reckon… I *think*… I must have been here about four or five days before I was really aware of what was going on."

"And how fast did Flynn deteriorate?"

"Into the seizures, you mean? Oh, I think he was already having more than one a night even then. I know I heard the doctors saying they were worried about his heart giving out, because he was that bad."

"Oh crap!"

"Yep, he was in a really bad way, Stell'. I think we all knew he wasn't going to make it. The doctors were just too perplexed all the time. They kept stuffing drugs into him and then looking shocked when they didn't even touch whatever was wrong with him. You just know in your heart that's a bad sign."

"And what about Craig?" Stella was beginning to think she would be having nightmares of her own about this tonight.

"I'd say his chances are fifty-fifty. I don't think the doc's are any the wiser about what the root of the problem is, but they're trying him on some of the concoctions they finally found seemed to slow things down for Flynn, and I don't think he's got any worse even if he's not improving. Your mate's lad, Tom, said this morning once the nurses were out of the way, that he'd heard them all conferring in the night, and they were saying that if they can keep him at least stable, there's a hope that whatever it is in his blood might break down naturally. Seems it had gone wild in Flynn. Something about strange crystals in his blood, although God knows what that means, and the doc's don't seem any closer to understanding that either."

The bell rang for the end of visiting time.

"I'd better go," Stella said with a sigh. "Poor Ivan's been cooped up in the car all day. I need to get home and feed him and at least take him for a short walk."

She had just got up and pulled her jacket on when Toby reached out and grabbed her hand.

"Stell'? I know this is too little and too late, but I'm sorry, okay? About us. I …I never thought you saw it as me actually …you know …hitting you." Stella's eyebrows shot up and he hurried on, "I was so used to the horseplay amongst the blokes, see? It gets a bit hairy. Not full on fights, but I've had the odd black eye from mucking about, and so have the others. I never thought you'd …well…"

"…Be frightened by you punching me in the back? Or knocking me down the stairs?"

His eyes went wide. "No! No, I never meant to do *that*! I just meant it as a bit of a shove …a…a…"

"A *what*, Toby? That's been the trouble all along, hasn't it? You treat women just the way you treat the other blokes, but it's not funny when someone who's half a head taller than you and nearly double your weight starts lashing out. It doesn't matter if it's in play or not, it hurts – really hurts. You never fully accepted that I genuinely needed to go to A&E that night, but I did. You broke my bloody ribs!

"That was when I got truly scared of you, that night when instead of coming and picking me up and taking me to hospital, you just told me to stop putting it on and fucked off to the pub." He'd been flinching at her words, but for the first time Stella thought he probably took in and understood just what he'd done to her, and decided to try just one last time to get through to him.

"While you're lying here tonight, think back on all those times when you thought I was just being stupid, or hysterical, and try and see them instead as me being genuinely hurt and frightened. Then you might begin to grasp why I will never, ever allow you back through the door of my home. I can never trust you again, Toby. Love or hate has nothing to do with it now. I would never get a wink of sleep even knowing that you were in the next bedroom. And that's because you have no comprehension of when it's appropriate to use all those things you've been taught in the army, and when it isn't.

"Oh you'd start out with good intentions, if what you've been saying to me about really being sorry is true. But the worst of the times when we were together weren't the ones when we rowed. I was braced for you to start waving your fists around then. It was when we were having a laugh. When we were fooling around. You'd just flip. One minute you'd be tickling me and it was silly but fine, and then next you'd have me in a choke hold or were really landing punches.

"I think you had some kind of PTSD long before this, Toby, and you need help. Because I think the only reason you didn't get like that with Seedy was because you worked your stress out through sex. She's such a nympho, she could cope with having it anytime, anywhere. So as soon as you started kicking off, instead of it turning into a fight, she could rip her knickers off and arouse you in another way so that it turned into something else. In a way, you were addicted to sex.

"But you might find that's not an option for you after all of this. So while you're in here, if you want to do me a favour, if you want to do something to prove to me that you really have changed, ask to see a psychiatrist. Ask for some help while you're in the right place to get it. I can't help you, but they just might."

Chapter 11

Wednesday

It wasn't until the next morning that Stella realised that neither Bob nor Ade had been in the hospital the previous evening. Perhaps they were giving it time for things to calm down? After all, they wouldn't want to be barred from going in to see their sons. Tomorrow with luck there'd be a different security team on, and by the time the ones who'd seen them came back around, they'd have hopefully forgotten about them, given that they hadn't actually had to intervene or write any reports on the matter.

She'd woken up with a ferocious headache, realising that it was probably dehydration since she'd hardly had time to grab anything after her morning coffee yesterday. So she started with her largest mug and green tea, taking it to sit out on her tiny square of a back patio in the unexpected burst of morning sunshine. Ivan was pursuing his ball around the tiny garden, dropping furry hints that he would really like to get out on the hills today.

"Yes, we'll go," Stella told him, ruffling his ears. "You were a clever boy distracting that captain yesterday, so we'll go straight after I've had breakfast."

Mollified, he went and found his rag toy and began shredding bits off it in a patch of sunshine on what passed for the lawn, no longer exactly level after his bone burying efforts.

"If only my life was as uncomplicated," Stella sighed, as she couldn't help but laugh at his antics.

But what had what Toby told her meant regarding Craig's nightmares? Where on earth did this 'queen' fit in? Who could she possibly be? With a second mug of green tea, her headache had lifted enough for her to start thinking straight again, and she was trawling her mind to wonder where he might have seen such an image. A quick look at the TV guide confirmed what she'd suspected, that this wasn't just him watching a scary movie on the screen by his bed, and in his state of mind, it preying on him once he went to sleep. Anyway, those sorts of nightmares didn't usually last for more than the one night. No, this sounded – however bizarrely – as though it was something he'd actually seen. But what could it be?

Queen? Queen of what? The only thing which came to mind was a queen bee. Had he been stung by something? Maybe not a bee but some other insect? She went and retrieved her laptop and began searching. Hornets sounded a bit more like something that would give you nightmares, especially once she had found a piece which said that hornets could release an attack pheromone which could mobilise the whole nest. That sounded really nasty. But was that the case for the English versions or just the more exotic tropical ones? She didn't know and it wasn't easy to tell from what she was reading.

Then another thought kicked in and she realised that surely the hospital would have noticed if someone was covered in multiple stings? The sting of hornets apparently released something called acetylcholine, an organic chemical which affected the nervous system. But sitting back from her reading, Stella knew that something as straightforward as that wouldn't have had the hospital baffled. A fellow teacher had once got bitten by a horsefly, which had been far nastier than she would have thought possible, and yet it had been a fairly simple matter to treat it. Something the local doctor could do, let alone the hospital. No, whatever kind of 'queen' poor tormented Craig had been screaming about, it seemed very unlikely that it was an insect one.

Feeling frustrated and drained, Stella grabbed Ivan's lead and took him out. What had started as a promising morning soon clouded up, and with heavy dark clouds blowing in from over the Brecon Beacons with the promise of rain to come, Stella took Ivan home and decided to work on the maps once more. It was only once she'd spread them all out again that she realised that she'd never called Soapy the day before. Events had overtaken her, and so with a sigh of frustration at this dotting about, she went and made the call.

At least talking to him made her feel better, though, and by the time she'd relayed all of her news it had helped her to sort it out in her own mind.

"So what the hell this 'queen' means I do not know," she concluded. "It could just be that the poor sod's tripping out of his mind on whatever meds they've got him on, but for no reason I can explain, I don't think it's that."

"No, I do see what you mean," Soapy agreed. "You'd think if it was having that much of an adverse effect that they'd have stopped giving it to him in a hurry, not be standing there scratching their heads. There'd have to be an awfully urgent medical reason for them to carry on, and you've said that in other ways they seem to have got him stabilised, so they wouldn't be wanting to do anything that actually brought on these seizures, would they?"

"Exactly!" Stella exclaimed with relief, glad that she wasn't the only one who could see no logic in this.

"Well I wouldn't be worrying too much about that," Soapy consoled her. "It might well turn out to be just the ramblings of a very disturbed mind. We've all got junk hidden away in the depths that might surface under pressure. I'm rather more interested in this Captain Hardy. He sounds as though he's really between a rock and a hard place and he knows it. That talk of speaking out if it comes to a court-martial …that's fighting talk! That's the kind of thing you say when you know your career is down the shitter anyway. You don't say that to a superior lightly, not least in case they were undecided about dragging you in front of a hearing and that settles it for them."

"I was starting to feel sorry for him by the time I'd tracked him home," Stella confessed. "It was a ghastly little rabbit-hutch of a house. I know mine's a terrace just the same and needs some stuff fixing on it, but at least it's built of good old fashioned solid bricks and local stone, and I'm in a lovely spot up here on the hillside. His house had that sort of lost look you get when someone only goes home to sleep. No sign of kids, and I'd be surprised if he's married. There was no sign of the kind of things a woman might do, like some ornament or a vase of flowers in the front window. It looked positively drab compared to his neighbours. They at least seemed to be trying to stamp some sort of individuality on the place. The place looked depressed, and I'm wondering if he isn't too."

"You might be closer to the truth than you think," Soapy agreed. "I'll reach out and see if I can find anything out about him. Shame we don't have a first name for him. That would have allowed me to make out

I was an old mate of his, or had at least served with him, but it's not an impossible task. I'll see what I can do."

"And I'm going to get back to tracking down mines," Stella said with a sigh, as the first rain hit the front room window in a squally burst.

She poured over the maps for the rest of the morning and on into the afternoon, hunting down mine after mine on the large scale maps, and blessing the fact that the UK had the Ordnance Survey, where every contour line and detail on the landscape was mapped out – European maps had nothing like the same detail on them. They weren't the latest versions of the maps, however. She couldn't afford to update them at today's prices, but for what she was looking for that didn't matter. Things hadn't changed that much since these had been her dad's cherished collection. He'd handed the whole lot over to her as a graduation present, already knowing that he only had a few months left before the lung cancer took him.

"I want you to have them," he had told her firmly. "I know Evelyn," his by then live-in lady friend, "thinks they're just so much old junk to be chucked out. She'll look after the furniture you don't want or don't have room for, but the maps she'll have out in a skip before you can sneeze. But you'll love them like I did. Use them, kid. Get out and have some fun! Be like Bilbo Baggins, setting foot out of your door and never knowing where the path might take you!"

Her dad had been so relieved to see her away from Toby by then, and Stella wondered what he would think of all this. He'd probably have been down on his knees beside her, she thought, because whatever he'd thought of Toby by the end, he'd liked Dav, and he loved any excuse to go exploring maps.

"So come on, Dad," she said, raising her eyes heavenwards. "Give me a hand here. Where should I be looking?"

The afternoon drew on, with her finally giving in – despite normally trying to be frugal with her electricity bills during these lighter months – and putting all the lights on to see what she was doing, as the rain made the summer's day prematurely dark. The search proved to be somewhat easier than she'd first anticipated, though, as the more northerly groups of slate mines and quarries were all too close to habitation, she felt. And it did come down to slate mines, she'd realised very early on. The huge coal mines of South Wales weren't even a consideration, being too recently closed and still too closely monitored, and also close to major clusters of towns.

It had to be further north if anonymity had been a prime requirement, not to mention that Harlech postal mark on the card – nobody would post something there from southern Wales. And the copper mines hadn't sounded very promising either – too few in the wrong places, and too many of them had been open cast mines. Whatever she was looking for, it was something underground she felt with a certainty she couldn't quite explain.

The Bethesda group she'd already discounted, but the Dyffryn Conwy group got crossed off almost as fast for being on the well-traversed north Welsh coast. Too many tourists who might wander in, as well as locals. But other smaller groups also ruled themselves out. Llanfair-ym-Mault as the name of a group didn't mean anything to her until a look at her road atlas index showed her that it was the proper Welsh name for Builth Wells, on the face of it just another small market town. But Stella knew that the Royal Welsh Show was held at the showground there in July, and various other events went on there through the year, because it was a good place for farmers from all over central Wales to get to.

"Not a cat in hell's chance they'd risk anything too close to there," she told Ivan, who had once again come to help by anchoring a map corner with his nose. "No, the Builth area wouldn't be it."

And so it went on until she had only two groups left, Corris and Mawddach, and she wasn't wholly convinced of Mawddach. The lower reaches of the River Mawddach valley covered the towns of Dolgellau and Barmouth, and the latter was a popular seaside resort. On the other hand, the upper reaches of the river were a lot less traversed by walkers and tourists than the slopes of Snowdon to its north, despite being stunning countryside.

Yet walkers were also a consideration for the Corris group, whose territory (as best she could tell) started just on the other side of the great central Welsh mountain of Cadair Idris. She herself had hiked up Cadair, and she knew how many others regularly took to its slopes. It had been popular with the regiment's families too, its steeper slopes giving the men enough of a challenge, while still allowing the wives and children pleasant walking on the easier stretches.

"I reckon Toby would have known and remembered Cadair," she said to Ivan, sitting back on her heels and contemplating the sheets of clear plastic she had placed over the precious maps, so that she could mark places without harming the originals. Some schools still used overhead projectors, the ones who didn't have wealthy parents' associations to help provide the digital replacements, and she always made sure she had some of the now old-fashioned clear sheets they used in her school bag.

Now she was blessing the fact that she'd laid in a stock of them, just in case her regular stationers stopped carrying them as unwanted items in the computer age. And with judicious use of whiteboard pens which wiped off, she'd already cleaned and reused several of them. However, she was now thinking it might be time to get the permanent markers out and mark the prime candidates.

If Cadair Idris itself was out, other spots weren't. The ones not far from the main Dolgellau-Machynlleth road she similarly discounted, but climbing up the Afon Dulas valley there were three mines which were more remote. Aberllefenni was a small hamlet, and Cymerau and then Ratgoed up towards the top of the valley were even more remote, and there were a handful more like them. They would bear investigating she thought, but if she was going to do that then she ought to go tomorrow. That would at least give her the whole weekend to do any further investigating needed.

She looked up at the clock. Five o'clock. Should she traipse up to the hospital again? Inwardly she was groaning at the prospect, especially since she hardly had anything new to say to Toby, and she could call Bob or Ade, but then remembered Dennis in the other ward. She hadn't seen him yesterday evening, and he might just have something for her, but she needed to get up there in that case. If a bed had come up at the cardiac unit up the road she might have missed him already, but he was her best chance of making something of this tangle about what had been seen. The lad in the other bed to him was at least coherent over that, which was more than any of the others were.

"Sod it," she sighed. "Micro dinner again," and vowed to call in somewhere and at least get some salad to take with her tomorrow.

It wasn't a pleasant drive, with the wipers and headlights on all the way up the M5, but she got there in one piece and headed for the cardiac ward. Hurrying in she turned to Dennis' bed and to her horror saw a completely different man lying there. Damn it, she was too late! Instead of arguing the toss with Toby last night, she should have at least stuck her head around the door here.

"He got sent across this morning," a voice said from behind her, and she turned to see the pale soldier giving her a tilt of the head to come across to him.

Pulling up a chair, she was mightily relieved to hear him say, "Dennis said I should talk to you if you came back."

God bless Dennis!

"I'm Toby Donaldson's ex-wife, Stella Fox," she introduced herself, holding out her hand, and was pleased when he took it with a wan smile.

"Karl Wright. Blimey, you're a bit different to the current model," he said with the best he could summon in the way of a cheeky grin.

"Very different!" Stella smiled back, "But I'm also a friend of Dafydd Jirel, and it's him I'm worried about."

"The serg'? Shit! What do you mean, worried?"

"Were you in Dav's squad?"

"Yes!"

Stella groaned inwardly. How should she break the news to this man? The last thing she wanted was for him to have another heart attack.

"Look, I don't know quite how to say this, but Dav is missing – not dead, mind you – or at least as far as we know."

"Oh Christ! What do you mean, missing?"

She took his hand, hoping that it would comfort him in some small way. "Okay, just take it easy and keep breathing! The thing is, some of the wives have had notifications that their husbands didn't make it."

"Oh no! Who?"

"Stuey Bogdanovic, Tom Bailey, Ed Martin, Mark Goodfellow, and my old friend Andy Hunter."

He went even paler. "They never told me. I kept asking, you know, because I had this memory of seeing two or three lads on the ground covered in blood and not moving, but he wouldn't tell me. Just kept going on about how I mustn't say anything to anyone."

"Was that Captain Hardy?"

"Yes, I think so. It's all a bit hazy, but I think he was there."

"Where, Karl? Where were you?" Stella realised she was holding her breath in anticipation; this could be the clue they needed.

"In the underground place. In the cavern."

"And where was that? Was that where Captain Hardy was with you?"

He frowned, concentrating. "No, I don't remember him being down there with us. But he was that one who gave us orders at that place, that I do recall. ...He wasn't there when it all went wrong, though."

Very softly Stella prompted him, "What went wrong?" but she felt his pulse start to race. "Steady on! Just go back a step. What about this cavern, then?"

That seemed to work, and after a deep, ragged breath, Karl said, "We were testing something for the boffins. We had to go and put these things like claymore mines on the walls, and then we'd back off. I mean back right up to the surface. And they'd set them off, but they weren't actual explosives I don't think. Somebody said they were some sort of sonic wave. Well they didn't seem to be doing a fat lot. I can't see what all the hush-hush is about, frankly. We'd go back down a day later, 'cause they were expecting rock falls, you see. Couldn't go straight back down in case something was unstable. Well it never was, or at least not until that last time."

Stella felt him shivering again and decided to back-track a bit once more. "So you'd been there a while by the sound of it? Getting a bit bored?"

She got another watery smile for that. "Weren't half! We were stuck in this big old house and the boffins were off in some other old buildings, but they wouldn't even let us out for a run on the hills – not that we had a clue where we were. Tom confirmed we were in Wales. He managed to sneak out one time, you see. Said he'd spoken to a farmer. God, I hope he's okay."

"He is! He's in a ward just down the corridor, a bit knocked about, and he can't remember a lot about anything, but he's getting better. His dad is one of the people, like me, who's trying to find out what the hell went on. Him and Josh's dad."

Relief washed over Karl's face. "Great. So it's not all bad news, then?"

"No, not at all. But we – the families, that is – feel that we're being lied to big time. There's something very fishy going on that isn't adding up. For a start off, all the wives of those lads who died all thought their husband was the only one, and that they'd been killed in some accident on a training exercise. They're all really angry at being lied to now they've got to talk to one another."

"Training exercise? What a load of bollocks!"

"Just what we thought. Why would you try and cover it up like that? And the thing is, Karl, there are a couple of lads on the other ward who aren't doing so well, Flynn and Craig." She wasn't going to tell him that Flynn was dead, or how he'd died, for fear of really upsetting him. "And the doctors are baffled as to what's making them so ill. That's why we want to know so badly what happened out there – wherever that was. Ade, Tom's dad, got a postcard from Tom hinting heavily that you guys were in trouble, and the postmark on that was Wales, so we've got that far. But you seem to be the only one to date who has anything like a clear memory of even bits of it."

"I wish I bloody didn't!" was Karl's heartfelt response.

"I can see that. But can you go back to this place you were at and tell me a bit more about that, do you think?"

He took a deep breath. "I can do that …just don't ask me to talk about the queen!" and he gave a great shudder.

Chapter 12

Wednesday

For a moment Stella was dumbstruck. There it was again, that reference to a queen of some sort. Yet Karl's reaction told her that she shouldn't ask about it yet, at least not until she'd got more of the normal sort of information out of him, and maybe not even then if it was that traumatic.

"We'd be grateful for anything you can tell us," she said soothingly instead.

Karl stared up at the ceiling for a moment, and Stella guessed he was trying to sort his chaotic thoughts into some sort of order.

"It was all very odd right from the start," he began. "We got bussed out there, but at Hereford we got transferred onto one with all of its windows blacked out. So the only thing you could see was out of the front past the driver. And it was a fair run, I remember that – in fact I've no idea why we went via Hereford at all, unless it was to deliberately confuse us. We were all getting a bit pissed off with it, to tell the truth. I mean, we all signed the bloody Official Secrets Act – that should have been enough. But even when Dav and Andy went and started quizzing the driver, all he could say was that he'd been told to deliver us to this place and not stop on the way."

He stopped and thought a bit more, then added, "I'll tell you something else, too. Dav said the driver had a sat' nav' and it was taking us by all the minor roads.

You know, like it had been programmed in for him, and that he had no more idea of where he was going than we did. So all we ever saw were the old-fashioned white signs to places that were probably a couple of farms and some cottages. Not a major road sign in sight. And by the time you've passed the tenth sign to Llan-something-or-other, or Ty-what's-its-name, you can't remember any of them properly – and we swore that was deliberate.

"It was Dav, even back then, who said he was sure we were in mid Wales. He always did have the sense of direction of a homing pigeon. So when we piled out and found ourselves in some kind of disused industrial place, he said he thought the big mountain that was just about poking through the clouds occasionally was Cadair Idris, but he couldn't tell which side of it we were on. Typical bloody Wales, it pissed down every day, and the clouds hang so low in those steep valleys you can't tell where the hell the sun is. Not that we got outside much to see it anyway."

This was pure gold to Stella. So her deductions had been spot on! "Tell me more about this industrial place, then."

"An old slate mine, we realised once we got sent down it. Must have been disused for half a century or more, 'cause you could tell that the roofs had been off most of the buildings for a long time, and someone had had temporary tin roofs put on. God did it make a racket when you got a good downpour! Even the big house had tarpaulin over part of the roof, and inside you could see where the water had run down the walls from it leaking."

"Do you think it was a big site originally?"

Karl shook his head without even having to think about it. "Naaah. Reckon it was always a very local affair, that one. But I tell you something else. The caverns they sent us down into weren't wholly mined. I never thought you'd be able to tell the difference, but you can. When we first went down it was into the old mines. And they had roughly squared off walls on the tunnels, and even in the caverns it was easy to see where the miners had found good quality slate, and then it had petered out and they'd moved on to another stretch.

"That was where we did the first tests. They sent us down with this old boy whose dad used to work the mine. Heaven knows where they found him or where he went home to at night. It's not as though there were any locals. In the entire time we were there, we never once got let out to go and visit a local pub. By the time we'd been there a month we were all crawling the walls.

"I remember Ed being really pissed off because they took his Kindle off him. It wasn't one of the up to date ones that you can use like a tablet to do internet search on and the like, just a basic one, so there was no need for that. Ed was always the big reader amongst us, and not just the popular stuff, either. He had philosophy and all sorts tucked away on that thing. He was going nuts not having a book to read – really got to him that did. ...In fact most of us wondered why on earth Ed was in the army at all, because he was a bright bloke. He'd even done an Open University degree. Not your average squaddie at all. It was him who started to make sense of what we sa... what we saw."

Stella saw him shiver and his monitor started to beep a bit more anxiously too.

"It's okay," she said soothingly. "You're never going to have to go back there again. Easy does it. Let's get back to what you were talking about before. You say they took Ed's kindle off him, but we suspect that they took your mobile phones off everyone, is that right?"

It created the right kind of distraction and the monitor settled down to a steadier beep. "Yes they did," he said with a roll of his eyes. "At first we thought it was massive over-kill. Just the army being its usual overcautious, sign-in-triplicate, self. After a while, though – and it didn't take long – we started thinking that it was in case we started making calls back to base at the very least. You know, the 'what the hell is going on?' kind of conversations."

"What made you all so suspicious?"

"The way everyone else was behaving for a start off. I mean, we knew we wouldn't have understood one word in ten the boffins said to us. That's pretty much a given. You just nod and smile at the daft bastards, and hope to God they aren't going to get you killed along the way. But they were totally segregated from us – and that took some doing in a place that small, I can tell you.

"They got their breakfasts after us, so that bloody Captain Hardy could make sure we were all back in the house and accounted for before they went into what served as our mess hut, even though we were catering for ourselves, no cooks there. And then at night the same thing happened again, and they had some static caravans to sleep in across the other side of the place. In between, we had the doings to make ourselves coffee or tea, and the biscuits weren't in short supply – which was a damned good thing because we went through them like locusts out of sheer boredom. Between that and the lack of exercise we were well on the way to becoming fat little piggies."

"So you never got out at all?"

"Not off the site, no. Toby and Dav cornered Hardy and demanded that we at least be allowed to run around within the compound just to keep us halfway fit, and he reluctantly agreed, but only when he gave the say so. And the funny thing was, that always came when there was ten-tenths cloud low over the hills and we didn't stand a chance of locating ourselves by any landmarks."

"Couldn't you see anything out of the windows of the house?"

"Not a lot. The glass was very old and going cloudy – you know, the way old wine glasses go – and most of them had the muck of ages caked onto the outside. Your Toby set us to cleaning the ground floor ones and Hardy did his nut. Really screamed his head off at Toby and the lads he'd detailed as the work party to do the outside. Told them to get back inside and never try anything like that again. Well you know what Toby's like, he got right in Hardy's face and told him that he thought he was a total wanker who'd lost the plot. Hardy threatened him with disciplinary action and Toby just laughed at him. Said what the fuck could be worse than being *imprisoned* in this shit hole?

"He used that word, 'imprisoned', you know. Said that we were in effect being held and punished for something, without the proper channels having been gone through. And for some reason that really put the shits up Hardy. He completely backed down, and we saw him scurrying off to the radio shack, which was the only place where we suspected there was any contact with the outside world. That was when we started thinking that everything wasn't exactly kosher with the setup.

"I mean, why would Toby threatening to tell the big cheeses back at base make the slightest difference? Surely they ought to know where we were and what we were doing? But that night we had a big powwow after lights out, all of us, and we all agreed that something was definitely not right.

"So Dav decided that we ought to launch a night raid on the radio shack…"

"…What? Dav? Law-abiding Dav…?"

"…Yeah. Gives you some idea of how worried we were, doesn't it! And we did it, you know, we got in there. Bloody hell, it was locked up tighter than a virgin at a used-car salesman's conference! Double padlocks, extra passwords on the computers, the bloody lot! Not that it did us any good, the computers were there but there wasn't any way to connect them to anything, even if we'd been able to get any of them to start up fully. There wasn't even a phone socket that we could see, not one. We couldn't send an email, make a phone call, nothing!"

"That's an insane amount of security. Do you think the boffins took the internet hub away with them each night?"

"That was the first thing we thought of, too, but we searched the hut from top to bottom, and we came to the conclusion that the boffins had been as cut off from the outside world as we had. And that worried us even more. If we'd been doing a genuine testing, surely they should have been sending the results of each test back to their base – wherever that was?"

"You'd think so, wouldn't you?"

Karl suddenly gave a brittle laugh. "I wouldn't have believed it, you know, but it's helping, telling you this stuff. Sodding Hardy's been all over me every day nearly, threatening me with all sorts of stuff if I said a word. I've been wondering why that would matter so much? And bless her, my old mum wouldn't understand it even if I'd told her. She's desperate to get me home and fill me up with her homemade steak-and-kidney pies, but if Hardy's said that I mustn't talk about something she'd be totally overawed and go running out of the room if I tried."

Stella decided to offer something back in return. "Bob, Ade and I have been saying that you lads haven't been done right by," she said, praying that this wouldn't set him off stressing again. "One of the first things we were asking ourselves was how fast you lot got help. Whether there was a delay, and from what you've said, there must have been. If Hardy was the only one with contact with the outside, and you were otherwise that cut off from the world, there couldn't have been any provision for care in case of an accident. For God's sake, you were down in an old mine. What if there'd been a roof fall, for instance? There doesn't seem to have been even a thought about something like that, much less a disaster with the testing. We thought that was why Hardy was so antsy. He knew he was on a sticky wicket right from the off."

"Jeez!" Karl gulped, "I never thought of it like that, but you're right. There was never anything more than the usual first aid kits about the place. ...Bloody hell, that was what Toby and Dav meant when they said that it looked like either a rushed job – some test that was being hurried through before the funding got pulled or something – or one that hadn't been properly sanctioned!"

Stella nodded. "And we're coming more and more to the conclusion that somebody told the MOD a load of old bull. That whoever they are wanted to test their 'thing', and let the MOD's contacts believe that it was set up properly with all the proper precautions in place. Only they weren't."

"That makes a lot of sense. ...And that's jogged something loose. I couldn't swear to this in court or anything, but I'm sure I remember them – the boffins, that is — saying that they thought they had something that would replace landmines. Something that wouldn't cause so much suffering amongst the ordinary people when an army moved out, and didn't clear an area behind them. I remember that because Toby, ever the cynic, said that it wouldn't make a wet fart's difference to the poor buggers out in some third world country getting a leg blown off, because all the mercenaries and terrorists had warehouses full of old stock to work through at bargain basement prices. Fancy new technology wouldn't be on their shopping lists with the price they'd have to pay for it."

"And he was right," Stella said with a sigh, thinking it was such a shame that Toby wasted his talents when he could come up with insightful thoughts like that. Why did he have to be such a dickhead most of the time? He had the potential to be so much more if only he'd put a bit of effort into it.

And that reminded her for the first time in years of why she'd been so drawn to him back when they'd been younger. He'd seemed like someone who had such a bright future, someone who drew you in with his enthusiasm and fire. When had that all faded? She couldn't pin point any exact moment, but she thought now that maybe it had come about when he'd found that the world wouldn't just fall into his lap the way things had at home. In a nutshell, Toby hadn't coped with growing up and the inevitable disappointments that came with the real adult world. Such a waste.

"So it was supposed to be some sort of anti-personnel weapon, was it?" she asked.

"That's the impression we got. Except that it didn't seem to be working. We weren't sent down every day, you know. It was about every third or fourth day, and Hardy told us that was because the boffins were making fine adjustments, but as time went on we began to think that they were making it up as they went along, because nothing improved. I mean, we'd have understood it if it hadn't worked one time, then had closed an entire tunnel off the next time. That would have at least been understandable. But it never seemed to do a damned thing."

"Did you ever see the boffins' reactions?"

Karl shook his head. "No, we didn't, and there were only five of them on the site by the end. We reckoned there were about eight to start with, but at least three or four seemed to suddenly disappear. Not that it was easy to tell when we never saw them close up, and when we did see them across the compound they were in identical white lab coats.

"We thought the missing ones might have gone back to where they came from, and that was why Hardy was going round like a snake had bitten his arse. You know, failed tests laid at his feet and that sort of stuff, or worse, complaints made higher up the ranks. But in the last days we started to change that to wondering whether they had left at all or had come to grief somewhere?"

"Why did you think that?"

"Because Andy decided to take three of the lads and go and have a squint at the boffins' quarters one day when they all seemed to be in their main hut – something knocked up out of what we thought might have been an old workshop in the days of the mine. One of those lads, Tufty, had a bit of a dark past – no lock he couldn't get past! And we'd been watching the boffins like hawks. They didn't seem to be exactly thriving either. So we wondered whether we'd been totally wrong to think that they were living with all mod cons while we got the shitty end of the stick.

"So Andy and the lads went off and came back looking right shaken. They said that there were lockers full of stuff for nine men. One looked like it hadn't been touched in weeks, but three others looked as though their mates had tried to force their way in. ...And there was a letter! It seemed to be the start of one to someone's wife."

"Oh crap, a bereavement letter?"

"Andy said it started off like that, but that there were loads of scribbling outs, as though whoever was writing it was having a terrible time trying to sort out what to say. And then we recalled that Hardy had said that the boffins needed to go down and see things for themselves. Some bollocks about whether it was the right sort of rock. We all said that surely that ought to have been sorted out before we started? I mean, you go down an old slate mine, you expect to find slate, right? So if that wasn't right, why were we there in the first place?"

"It sounds very fishy," Stella agreed.

"It was. And we realised that it was after that that we saw fewer of them about."

"Did you have any clue as to what had happened?"

"Yes and no. The next time we went down there we got directed into a side tunnel we'd always ignored until then. We'd never been told to go that way before. Funny thing was, the old boy – the old local – he'd always said *never* to go that way. Said it was dangerous."

"And where was he in all of this?"

"That was another funny thing. He took us down the first couple of times and then we never saw him again. We hadn't seen that as odd then, because on those times we did nothing more than familiarise ourselves with the tunnels. No tests or anything."

"So he wouldn't have seen anything he shouldn't have in terms of security," Stella said, nodding thoughtfully.

"Exactly! And because of that we just accepted it that he wasn't around once we started carting stuff down below and setting timers and primers. But once we got sent down into that new stretch of tunnels we began to think that the old boy knew a thing or two."

"Oh?"

Karl gave a shiver. "You didn't have to go far down that old mine tunnel before you came to what even we could tell were natural caves. They had those stalac-thingys…"

"Stalactites?"

"Yes. And the caverns weren't all chipped away at, they had projecting bits and odd cracks and crevasses. They were big too. One was enormous! You had to watch your step because you came into it well up on the one side – you know, actually came out of the tunnel and found ourselves about a third of the way up the cavern wall, with a bloody great drop in front of us. The walls weren't a straight drop, mind, but you'd have gone one hell of a purler if you'd missed your footing. God knows how far the floor fell away from it on the far side from us, but Brian chucked a rock down there and it seemed ages before we heard it splash into water.

"There was an old metal walkway around the side of it from the mining days, and our first task was to make that properly safe. That took a good week because we asked for bits of kit and they seemed to take days to come – like welding gear – and we had to rope up well to get out on the old bits in case it all fell apart under us. …Who hadn't anticipated we'd need that, eh? Surely in an old mine you'd expect to have to make repairs, if only to something like the winding gear? We had to traipse up and down long flights of steps and ladders instead of a lift, and I know the mine went out of use in the 1950s by the look of some of the stuff we found, but those weren't the Dark Ages – they had pit lifts even then!"

He paused and gave another shudder. "What's horrible is that we actually relished getting that old walkway back to being usable – we were *that* bloody bored! The chance to do something on a daily basis, however basic and manual, was such a blessed relief. God! If only we'd known what it would lead to!"

"Can you tell me?" Stella asked cagily. "Don't give yourself another heart attack for pity's sake! Did you do another test?"

Karl screwed his eyes up, but his monitor said he was coping although its beeps weren't quite as regular as they had been. "Yes, we did one at the mouth of another natural cavern. It looked as though the miners had expanded a natural crack in the rocks leading between them into a proper tunnel, and this time you came out on the floor of the next cavern, so there was solid rock beneath your feet."

"And did that work any better than the previous ones with the tests?"

"Not that we could see. Seemed another total bloody failure in our eyes. Nothing was different when we went down to check it for the boffins the day after the next. And they were so disappointed, although Dav reckoned a couple of them looked more relieved than anything."

He took a ragged breath and now the monitor began to beep more erratically. "Then we went down again to set another set of those weird devices." He gulped convulsively. "The minute you got to the big cavern it felt different. ...Can't explain it any other way than to say that you could feel a presence down there, and it wasn't good. Normally there was always somebody goofing about making ghost noises or doing imitations of Gollum, but not that day.

"And then we got to the other cavern. ...We'd just put the boxes down on the ground ...and we heard them ... heard voices." His face crumpled and he began to sob. "Oh Christ!"

Stella instinctively got up and wrapped her arms around him to hug him, and with his voice muffled in her jacket she heard him sob,

"They told us to go. ...Said we didn't belong there. Andy was at the front ...started shouting for us to get back. ...I was at the back. ...Heard Tom Bailey in the middle getting on the radio to Hardy telling him we were coming back up, and then Hardy's voice blares back saying we must carry on. ...That fucking braying voice of his echoed round and round the walls ...and then *she* came. ...Their queen came!" and he broke down completely.

Chapter 13

Wednesday

There was the sound of feet and two nurses came hurrying in, clearly having been alerted by Karl's monitor going off, and Stella gratefully stepped back to allow them to take over. She was very relieved to hear him saying to them, though,

"It's okay …I'm okay. …No, I'm not in any pain. …No I was just talking …it helped. …It's really helped."

And then she turned to see the tall West Indian nursing sister she'd met on her first visit standing behind her.

"He was one of my ex's men," she explained, although that was stretching it a bit since Karl hadn't actually been in Toby's squad. "I just popped in to say hello."

The sister smiled at her. "It's alright. Actually, I'm glad he got to talk to someone. His mum's done not'in' but cry over him. I know he's her chil', but it ain't helpful for him, all dat weepin' an' wailin'!"

Stella had to smother a smile at the way the sister's accent had got broader in her disgust. At home she was probably one of those earth-mothers who swept everyone in the family under her wing, dispensing food and sensible advice in liberal quantities to anyone who needed it.

"I'll come and chat to him again as long as I'm not going to get thrown off the ward," Stella offered, and got a beaming smile in return. That was probably helped, though, by the way the other nurses had already got Karl soothed and resting with no harm done. But it prompted Stella to be bold.

As both she and the sister walked out of the ward she dared to ask, "Do you deal with all the military cases, then?"

"I'm an army nursin' sister," was the proud reply, "but I'm normally on the other ward. I'm just coverin' here tonight."

"Then can I ask you something? I know Captain Hardy's been around threatening the lads with all sorts…"

"…Has he now! I won't have that with *my* patients!"

"Oh yes. Toby and Karl, and Tom and Josh. They've all been told to not speak of how they got wounded, and the worst of it is, they don't know why. But the two dads I got chatting to said they're worried that these lads didn't get help soon enough. I mean, it's not like they had to be brought back like the ones from Afghanistan. They were in the UK! But Karl was just telling me that Hardy was the only one with communication to the outside world at this testing area they seem to have been at, and that he wasn't even with them when everything went wrong. So how long did it take before they got medical help?"

The sister had stopped in her tracks and was staring at Stella, her expression getting darker with every word Stella spoke, and for a second Stella thought she was in for a right telling off. But it was quite the reverse.

"They didn't bloody tell us dat!" the sister fumed. "An' him comin' all high and mighty wid us too! *Phfaah*! No wonder we been havin' trouble gettin' the meds to work! We been thinkin' that we got them straight away and they had triage on site!"

"I don't think that happened," Stella confessed. "Something happened underground according to what Karl just told me, and how on earth they got out I do not know. My guess would be that they helped one another."

The sister had started marching off, not so much the frigate in full sail as an aircraft carrier armed, dangerous, and ready to strike; and Stella trotted in her wake, determined not to miss out on what was going to happen next.

The sister steamed onto Toby's ward and made a beeline for her records, and even as Stella pulled up beside her, she saw the sister had grabbed Tom, Josh, Toby and Craig's files and had the four of them spread out across the nurses' desk. Her finger was moving from one to another, clearly comparing something she understood far better than Stella, and she obviously wasn't happy with what she was seeing. As Stella sidled up to her she turned and said,

"We knew the wounds weren't fresh when they got here – we could tell that from the clotting, for a start off – but we thought they'd been treated pretty quickly with field dressings." She shook her head angrily. "These boys we get in from overseas, they need special care, but they get the basics right away. So we assumed that these boys had too. Dis," and she stabbed at the records with a furious finger, "dis you do as soon as possible. It's standard procedure. So when we see dis," and she stabbed at what looked like the name of a drug, "we assume it was given …well, within a certain time scale, you understand?"

"I do."

"So when we saw it wasn't working – as we thought – we carried on from there. But we didn't expect it to have been given not so long before we got them here!

Maybe even too early for it have started fully working yet! Or at least, not long ago compared to when the wounds and the other damage was done …that a long time had elapsed between damage and treatment. *Phfaah!*'

She straightened up and stared Stella in the eye. "How long do you think they were left before they got help?"

"I honestly don't know," Stella admitted. "But Toby said he thought he'd been in an ambulance. Well I didn't think anything of that, but the dads of these two lads have been in the forces, and they reckoned that they'd have been choppered in from anywhere remote. And that led us to start wondering where on earth the ambulance would have fitted into the story?"

The sister returned to the records, flipping through each one. "Well they all came here by military air ambulance."

"Oh that doesn't sound good, then," Stella groaned. "That sounds very much as though they got taken to somewhere else before the chopper came to pick them up, doesn't it?"

"And your man is certain of dis?" The fury and the stronger accent were rising again.

"Let's go and ask him?" Stella suggested, and together they bore down on Toby's bed, their approach causing him to give them worried glances.

"Toby, we need you to think really hard about this," Stella said firmly. "Are you absolutely sure about what you told me about the ambulance ride? You couldn't have been mistaken? Not some other time you got hurt?"

"Err, yes, I think so. And I've never been in an ambulance otherwise. Why? Is it important?"

"Yes it is! I've been talking to the sister here, and it could be that bloody Captain Hardy gave them the wrong information when you arrived. If you'd been in trouble for far longer than the doctors and nurses here were led to believe, then that could account for why some of the treatment has been less effective than they expected it to be."

Toby gasped. "Oh shit! That is bad!"

"It is," the sister said sternly. "We thought the," and she reeled off the names of two drugs which meant nothing to Stella and Toby, "had been properly administered and hadn't worked." She struggled to get her fury under control. "All of you were hallucinating 'orribly when you came in. All screamin' your heads off when you were even half conscious, and then passin' out again. And we weren't sure whether that was 'cause of stress, or somethin' you'd been exposed to. But we couldn't get nothin' sensible out of that captain or his colonel!"

"I bet you'll be making a complaint about that?" Stella guessed.

"Already been done!" the sister said with a satisfied sharp nod of her head. "We don't like bein' messed about with like *dat*. Not just Dr Chen but Mr Iraklidis, the consultant, too! A very sharp letter got sent by him, and he went and told the hospital administrators that he was sendin' it as well. You don't mess with Mr Iraklidis!"

"Good for him," Stella said, hoping she was showing the right kind of awe. Inside, though, she was less awed than whooping with delight. So had that been the reason why the colonel had been all over Captain Hardy like a rash? Had the shit already started to hit the fan even before Bob, Ade and herself had started asking questions? That made a lot more sense, and it explained the colonel's worry if someone above him had received the consultant's letter and started asking what the hell it was all about.

"We're goin' to have to ask you a lot more questions about what you remember," the sister was saying to Toby, "and it's goin' to fall most on you, those two boys over there, and Karl in the other ward. Your friend," and she nodded towards where Craig's bed once again had the screen's drawn around it, "and the boy in the other ward aren't up to it. So what you tell us could well make the difference as to whether we can save their lives."

Stella thought she had never seen Toby look so serious as when he replied. "We'll do our very best, sister, I promise you."

The sister then disappeared with speed behind the screens and they could hear her telling the nurses to stop giving something immediately and just do something else while she went and found a doctor. Moments later she came past them like a rocket on rails and vanished off the ward.

"I think I'm going to make my escape," Stella said quietly.

"But I've hardly seen you," Toby protested. "You've got to tell me what's going on! How did you light such a spark under her tail?"

"I went to see Karl Wright in the cardiac ward. He's a bit more with it than the rest of you. It was what he told me that started this."

"Like what?"

"Like about you lot all being down in some natural cavern beyond the slate workings, and something going horribly wrong. I haven't got time to tell you all about it because I need to get home. I've got an early start tomorrow because I'm going to head into Wales for a look around."

"Don't go alone!"

"Toby?"

"I mean it. Look, your new mates were just here. You only missed them by seconds. Go and see if one of them will go with you. I really don't like the idea of you stumbling across something by yourself."

"You could have told me they were here sooner."

"When? You and the sister came flying over and kept firing questions at me."

"Okay, point taken. Well I'm going to run, and see if I can catch up with them."

She hurried out of the ward, hoping both to catch Bob and Ade, and not wanting to get caught up in some lengthy argument over how come she had got suspicious over treatment times, something to which she could contribute virtually nothing beyond what she'd already said. Out in the car park she looked around and spotted Bob and Ade lounging on the bonnet of her car, grinning like pair of naughty schoolboys.

"You really need to get a more inconspicuous car if you're going to do much of this Sherlock Holmes stuff," Bob chuckled as she reached them. "We eyeballed it half a car park away."

"Very funny," she riposted with wafting hand movements. "Get your bums off my car while I've still got some suspension left!"

"That's not nice," Ade said with a mock huff. "I think she's saying we're porky, Bob."

"Well neither of you look exactly half starved," Stella threw back, laughing with them.

"So what have you been up to, young Stella?" Ade demanded. "You came scuttling out of there all furtive-like. Don't keep us in suspense."

By the time Stella had finished, the pair of them were agreeing with her assessment of the consultant's lighting a fire considerably higher up the tree than the colonel as the cause of his berating Hardy.

"Poor sod," Ade sympathised, "he really was caught in the crossfire."

"Oh don't feel too sorry for him," Stella protested. "Don't forget that he had the only means of communicating with the wider world at wherever they were, and his tardiness could be a substantial chunk of why two more lads are dead. You didn't see the sister. She was spitting fury, not just because they'd been told a cock and bull story, but because it directly affected the way they'd started treating our guys. I got the very strong impression that they might have tackled the problems very differently if they'd been told the truth right from the start."

"But he might have radioed it in and it was those on the other end who dragged their feet," Ade pointed out.

"*Hmph*, I was thinking about that when I went for a walk last night," Bob said, clearly not convinced. "I didn't know these details, of course, but …well to be honest, Jane and I hadn't been getting on so well before this happened to our Josh, and we'd agreed to a trial separation. And while we can still pull together where he's concerned, there's only so much of each other's company we can cope with at the moment without the shouting starting again. There was another row brewing last night, so I thought I'd just remove myself. I might not have been easy to live with when I came out of the army, but I'm not such a bonehead that I don't see how much of a toll this has taken on Jane.

"So I decided to go for a long walk, and I'm getting into my stride and I start thinking. It's very peaceful walking late at night on a week night once the pubs have turned out, you know, you don't see a soul. I wasn't heading for anywhere in particular and so that allowed my mind just wander, and that's when I started wondering why someone hadn't called in the rescue right from the start? For God's sake, it's not as though the army doesn't have a presence in Wales. My old lot are always yomping over the Brecon Beacons! It wouldn't have been such a big ask to get them to turn out to help a bunch of the regular lads who'd been in a bad accident. If anyone can keep their traps shut it's them."

"Old lot?" Ade asked with a quirk of his eyebrows as Stella said,

"I thought you were with the Mercians?"

Bob looked suddenly guilty. "Ah ...about that. Erm, yes, I did start out with the Mercians, but I didn't finish with them."

"Based in Hereford, were you?" Ade said with a grin starting to spread across his face.

"What's significant about Hereford?" Stella asked suspiciously, realising she had missed something.

"SAS," Ade said with a wink and nod towards Bob. "The Hereford Hooligans. I thought you nabbed Hardy a bit smartish, no wonder he couldn't break your hold on him."

"That's why Jane insisted that we move back up closer to her family once it was clear I was on my way out," Bob explained. "She wanted to get away from the culture of the regiment. By that time she'd had enough of being part of the tight family it creates.

"But for me it was torture, because I didn't want to leave. I'd have found it a lot easier to cope if I could have still gone and had a few beers with the lads every now and then, or we could have gone round to the ones I'd always thought of as 'our' friends for the odd summer barbecue. It was a nasty shock to hear Jane saying that she'd never liked more than half of them, and had only put up with them for my sake. She made it sound like so much of our marriage had been a sacrifice on her part, and that it was only fair that now we went to live where she wanted. But coming back here to Birmingham didn't make things better, they just deepened the cracks."

"Oh Bob, I'm so sorry," Stella sympathised.

Ade was also nodding thoughtfully. "It was different for me," he said. "I'd had more than enough by the time I came out. I'd been ready to leave for the last two years – couldn't wait to get out. But I've known blokes like you, who took to the life like ducks to water, and every last one of them struggled in civvy street. And I came out when I was younger than you, and needing to find a job pretty sharpish, so I got to make friends with other blokes both at work and through things like our kids' activities. And we'd both always lived around here, so there were still folks about who I'd known since I was a kid."

"I grew up on a shitty slum street in old Ladywood that isn't even there anymore," Bob confessed. "The bulldozers went in a year after I left. I hated the place so much, and mum's tosser of a boyfriend, I joined up as a cadet at sixteen and never went back. Nothing like Jane's accountant dad and his flash house in Harborne, and that's what Jane wanted to get back to, but all I feel is the walls closing in on me."

"Hence the late night walk," Stella said, understanding more why he'd taken it.

"Yes."

Ade nodded, "And why you thought of your old mates and wondered why nobody thought to ask for their help. It'd only be a hop and a skip in a chopper from their barracks to mid Wales. And because you lot go off on your own so much, I'm guessing that your medics are a cut above the normal too?"

Bob nodded. "You see why it just didn't make sense? Whether it was a rock-fall that did the damage, or something giving way and collapsing down there, it makes less difference to the outcome than the question of how and when the alarm was raised. Hardy should have called for help straight away. So assuming he did and that he's not that much of an arsehole that he thought about his career over the men, *someone* took that call. And that somebody should have acted faster – and I'm still not happy that when that help didn't come soon enough, that he didn't think to make calls elsewhere.

"Even if it was only at that stage that others discovered that whoever was running the whole operation had lied through their teeth about what safety measures were in place, the army's not without resources, for God's sake! We're bloody trained to react fast. There are firing ranges and MOD places all over Wales where there was bound to be *somebody* they could call on. There's even the RAF Rescue place up on Anglesey which isn't that far away as the crow flies. But at the bottom line – if you were doing something so far off the radar that you daren't call on any of them…"

"…Then the Secret Squirrels to cap all Secret Squirrels were also not that far away," Ade finished for him. "Holy crap, Bob, they must have been up to something very dodgy – rather than properly 'secret' – if they couldn't ask for them. Something you wouldn't want a squad of Andy McNabs and Chris Ryans to come asking questions about sounds more like it was downright illegal."

Bob harrumphed. "I think someone, or more likely some company, lied through their teeth to get this weapon tested. And I think it must have been to the extent of falsifying reports and lab tests. It's the only thing that makes any sense. Maybe using a 'cut and paste' technique with bits of genuine information from real tests, so that each piece was correct in its own way, but just didn't apply as a whole to the thing they were selling as a new piece of technology to the MOD. And that means that they must in part be developers of that technology, or they wouldn't have had the information to bugger about with in the first place."

"And do you think 'selling' is maybe closer to the truth than you thought?" Stella wondered. "Only listening to you now, the one thing that leaps to mind is that some miserable sods saw a way to make big money by quite literally *selling* something to the army with false credentials, and being far, far away by the time it was found out it was just worthless junk. Arms deals involve eye-watering sums of money – even I know that. So was some cabal of business men thinking they could scurry off to the tropics with a few cool million each on the back of this?"

"Jeez!" Ade gulped. "Now there's a motive if ever there was one. Blimey, Stella, you could well be right."

Yet they never got any further with that conversation, because two security men came around the corner of the building with two other men, and one of them called out,

"That's them over there!"

"Oh you've got to be joking," Bob muttered under his breath. "Don't tell me those two jobs-worth's are still fretting over our little scuffle?"

But it was one of the other two men who then called, "Stay where you are, please sirs! Police!"

"What the fuck?" Bob breathed, as Ade groaned,

"You've got to be joking!"

When the foursome came level with them, the one plain-clothed policeman turned to the security men. "Now you're sure these are the two men?" They both nodded. "Alright then, you can go, thank you. We'll take it from here."

His companion looked them up and down and asked, "Can I have your names, please?"

"What's this all about, Officer...?" Ade asked politely in return.

"It's DC Mortimer, and I need to ask you where you were last night?"

"Good heavens, in connection with what?" Stella interrupted.

"The serious assault on a Captain Hardy. I believe you two know the victim and had an altercation with him at the hospital yesterday?"

"We asked him some questions, yes," Ade protested, stepping forwards so that he was the one most in the detectives' view. "Wouldn't you if you thought he was responsible for your son lying in that hospital bed?"

He was doing the indignant father bit very well, but Stella knew it was because he'd instantly realised that Bob wouldn't have an alibi if he'd been out walking on his own. Backing him up, Stella now stepped forward and added,

"And if you think we're just making that up – about him being responsible for those lads in there – you just ask the consultant, Mr Iraklidis. Him and Dr Chen and the ward sister! When I just left they were all fit to tear a strip off Hardy when he dares to show his face again. They're launching a full enquiry into this, you know."

The second detective sighed. "I'm afraid Captain Hardy won't be showing his face again. He's dead. The only question now is whether it was manslaughter or murder."

All three of them gawped at the detectives in horror.

"What do you mean, dead?" Ade demanded. "When?"

"Last night, sir. So which one of you was it that had their arm around his throat yesterday?"

"That was me!" Ade said belligerently. "And I had good cause with the way he spoke to me! But do your best if you can to pin that on me, because I was in the Weoley Castle Working Men's club right up to closing time, and there's a whole crowd who saw me there too!"

"I'm afraid I'll still have to ask you to come down to the station with us," the detective said. "And I'll need a contact number for you two, too."

Stella immediately rattled off her home and mobile numbers, getting a surprised look from the detective.

"Yes, it's a Malvern address," she snapped, linking her arm through Bob's proprietorially to drop the hint that he'd been there too, "and while you're at it, take a look at this car because it was parked outside all night, or do you think the neighbours wouldn't notice this?"

"Alright, no need to take offence," the detective reprimanded her.

"Offence? Don't you think we've all got enough on our plates with worrying that our lads might be the next to develop these weird symptoms that the hospital doesn't know how to treat?" Stella bit back. "There are more families than just us who had cause to hate the sight of Hardy, but that doesn't mean that any of us wanted him dead!" She wasn't having to fake the tears she was barely holding back over that. She'd never known anyone who'd been murdered before.

"I think you'd better take your wife home," the other detective said to Bob, who didn't correct him, and then to Ade, "Come on then, sir. The sooner we get your statement taken, the sooner you can go home too."

But as they walked away with Ade stomping off in front, Bob and Stella heard the older one say to his mate, "I reckon we're barking right up the wrong tree here. That was genuine shock over Hardy's death, they aren't the ones."

Chapter 14

Wednesday

As Ade vanished from view, Bob put an arm around Stella's shoulder.

"You're shaking," he said gently.

"I've never known a murder victim before!" And she found herself weeping as he hugged her properly. "Bloody hell, Bob, whatever he was, he didn't deserve that!"

"No, and that settles it. There's no way I'm letting you go wandering off into the wilds on your own. We could be dealing with some very dangerous people."

As Stella pulled away from him to unlock her car and grab the box of tissues she had in there, Bob pulled out his mobile and punched in a number.

"Hi Jane, it's me. Look, love, there's been something else happen. ...No, not to Josh. Nothing like that. But Ade and me were just coming out and the coppers caught up with us. Apparently that Captain Hardy got murdered last night. ...I know, terrible isn't it? ...We thought that. But the thing is, I'm going to drive Stella home. She was with us when they started throwing accusations around to see if any of us would rise to the bait as the ones who did it, and she's shaken up. ...Oh for fuck's sake, Jane! Just stop it, will you? She lives all the way out at Malvern – that's why I'm not letting her drive home! Or do you want her to get smashed up on the motorway because she's crying too hard to see where she's going?"

Stella saw him taking the phone away from his ear and pulling a face at the tirade that was coming back at him. When there was a gap he snapped back at his wife,

"Yes, but *you're* not alone, are you? You've got your mum *and* your dopey brother and his wife, let alone our two girls! That bloody barn of your dad's is like your family hotel! But she's living alone and has nobody." Another string of screeches came back at him.

"Do you know what?" he fumed. "Since you've blackened both our names when we haven't even done anything, I'm coming by and getting my grab-bag. Then tomorrow I'm going to head off into Wales and see what I can find. I'm not going to spend the next few days having you lot chuck accusations at me, and sitting at Josh's bedside giving me black looks – you don't grasp how that upsets him, you know. ...Don't know my own son? You don't bloody know *me*!" and he snapped the phone shut angrily.

"Sorry you had to hear that, Stella. Come on, shift over to the passenger side and let me drive. Can I have your sofa for the night? Then we can both go hunting tomorrow."

Bob began to expertly navigate the side roads around the hospital, obviously knowing exactly where he was going, and Stella gave him a while to calm down before she asked,

"Are you sure about this, Bob? I could drive, you know, and she sounds very upset."

With a huge sigh, Bob replied, "Sometimes it feels like Jane was born upset." Then added, "No, that's unfair, she wasn't always like this." He gave another sigh. "She blames me for Josh going into the army – that's another of my sins I'll never be forgiven for, it seems. She just never got that he's a chip off the old block where that's concerned. He didn't go in to prove something to me, or because he felt he had to match up to me. He went because I took him through some of the basics once I was based at home more regularly – used to take him out on runs and things – and he took to it like a duck to water, couldn't get enough of it. The apprenticeship his college seemed to keep pushing him towards just bored him silly, and Jane's constant badgering him to get bits of what were meaningless paper to him, so that he could join her brother in the family firm, felt like a hangman's noose looming over him. He told me all this without any pushing, and I agreed that he'd be happier in the army – maybe not a career bloke like me, but at least doing one stretch in there while he was young enough to enjoy all the physical stuff and get to see a bit of the world."

"And they do have excellent apprenticeships," Stella agreed. "Some of the kids I've taught have really found their feet in the army and come out as very well qualified mechanics and things."

Bob gave her a wry grin. "You can see it. Jane never could. I think we've had it, me and her. We'd had a blazing row the day I met you, because Jane said that that was it, Josh was coming out of the army whether he liked it or not. I said that it was up to him – he's a grown man now. But it ended up with the whole family screaming in my face and telling me not to encourage him, and how they'd never forgive me if I did."

"How old is he?" Stella asked, somewhat aghast.

"Twenty-six!" Bob laughed. "Not exactly a child. I got Jane knocked up when we were barely out of our teens and her dad did the shot-gun wedding thing. Our two girls are younger than Josh by some way, yet they always treat him as though he doesn't know a thing, doesn't know what's good for him."

"Have they taken their cue from how their mom treats you?" Stella dared to suggest, and got a surprised glance across at her from Bob.

"That's very perceptive. You know I never thought of it like that, but yes, that's the way Jane talks to me in front of the kids. It's her way of having a row without the shouting."

"Then maybe Josh signing up was in part a way to get away from all that passive aggressive stuff? Some sergeant bawling in your face might be a lot easier to handle — you know what you're dealing with there — than all that dancing on eggshells. Few teenage lads I've come across cope with emotional confrontations. They're way behind the girls in that respect."

Bob said nothing for a moment, but Stella could see the surprise on his face and guessed that he'd never thought that Josh might be running away from his mum and sisters, who were all trying to rule his life for him.

"We made him get his A-levels," Bob said, still slightly bemused, "but I was at base in the armoury by then, not actually going off on stuff but marking time until my retirement. Now you've said that, it's come back to me that it was during that time that Jane really started going on about coming back to Birmingham. And then her dad died, and her mum was living in this vast house with just drippy James and his even dafter wife; and Jane said it would solve all of our problems because we wouldn't have to buy a house at Birmingham prices. But I know for a fact that Josh didn't want to move to there, and looking back on it, he made sure he went into the army before we left." He shook his head. "How did I not make those connections?"

"Perhaps because you were having such a hard time dealing with leaving the army, and dealing with the different family members yourself?"

"Do you know, I think you're right. ...Anyway, here we are. Looks like the bloody Addams Family's mansion, doesn't it?"

They had pulled up outside of one of a long, tree-lined street of huge detached Victorian houses, all very gothic with pointed attic windows and finials, and buildings to the side which had obviously once been stables.

"Stay there," Bob warned her, "you don't need to get involved in any of this."

As he walked towards the front door a security light came on and bathed the front in stark white light, making the place look all the more forbidding. It allowed Stella to see that it was double-fronted, and that the front rooms must be huge going by the size of the two grand bay windows either side of the ornate stained-glass doorway. Bob seemed to slip inside almost furtively, and he reappeared a few minutes later like he'd just burgled his own home, lugging a large holdall, which he took round and deposited in the car boot.

He then took his keys, negotiated the three parked cars on the drive, and went and opened one of the double doors to the former stables, and once he'd put the light on, Stella could see that it was now used as a garage. A very smart red sports car was in there, alongside what she was sure was a Jaguar, neither of which she could imagine Bob driving. He went right to the back of the garage and disappeared from view. Then a light came on up above, and Stella realised that there was a room above it, no doubt originally for the groom. She could see Bob's shadow moving about, and then the light went out and shortly afterwards Bob emerged again, locking the garage door behind him and with two large holdalls this time.

"Just in case stuff," he said to her with a wink as he got back behind the steering wheel, then more solemnly, "I hate to ask a favour of you like this, but after we get back, is there anywhere secure you could store this stuff for me? I can't explain why, but I've just got this funny feeling that I shouldn't be leaving my old army stuff there anymore. It's really not the sort of thing that should get slung into the landfill site where God knows who could pick it up."

"You think Jane would do such a thing?"

"I think her bloody brother James would!"

"Is he the Jag' driver by any chance?"

"Oh you saw that, did you? Yes, the Jag's his, and the Lotus is 'Mummy's'." He pointed to a newish top of the range Mercedes on the drive. "That's Jane's, bought with what 'Daddy' left her. The Clio and the Fiat 500 are Sophie and Debbie's cars. I wasn't allowed to bring my battered old Land-Rover with us – 'lowers the tone of the neighbourhood, don't you know, darling.' That's what her mum said," and he rolled his eyes in disgust. "I've never even *seen* the bloody neighbours, much less talked to them, so that's a load of crap, and somehow in these last hellish years I never seemed to be able to get to a point where I had a car of my own – I was always borrowing Deb or Soph's. ...Got a decent mountain bike, but that's not exactly the machine for locking up your valuables in."

"No, I can see that," Stella said sympathetically. "And there's no problem with storing stuff at my place. I've got a spare bedroom at the back of the house that no-one ever comes to use – so you won't need the sofa, there's a brand new bed in there that's never been slept on yet."

Inside, though, she was amazed that Bob had stuck this awful situation out for so long. Maybe his situation wasn't so different to what hers had been, with the biggest problem being where to go if you left? She could well imagine that Bob was sensible enough to not just take off when he couldn't cope, and then find himself sleeping rough on the streets, as far too many unfortunate ex-servicemen seemed to. And if he'd left the army already into his forties, and with no job where he could prove consistent income, getting a mortgage would have been next to impossible. Even renting a place could be horrifically expensive, as Stella knew to her cost.

The only way she'd got out of the eternal trap of paying such high rents that she couldn't afford to save for a deposit had been her dad dying, and Evelyn declaring that she wouldn't stay in his house for anything. It had turned out that Evelyn had long had a house of her own, and somewhat flasher than Stella's dad's, which she'd been renting out and getting a nice little nest-egg from, and his will had made Stella sole beneficiary. She hadn't been able to bring herself to live in the house he'd shared with Evelyn, and anyway it had been in totally the wrong place for her work, but it had been easy to sell for a good price. Certainly enough to pay for most of her house straight up, and the essential repairs needed that had been the cause of it going for a song in the first place, but which had put so many prospective buyers off it. Yet clearly Bob was going to get no such rescue package, and that made Stella feel very sorry for him.

As Droitwich and then the northern turn off for Worcester flashed by on the motorway, Stella dared to ask,

"What about a job, then? What have you been doing since you left the army?"

Bob's sigh seemed to come up from the soles of his boots. "That's been another problem. There was no need for me to work in terms of having enough to live off. With us shacked up in the family mansion back there, we had no mortgage to pay or rent to find, so it was easy enough to live off my army pension. Jane has always worked in an accountant's office, even when we lived in Hereford, so she's just slotted into a job in the family firm, just a bit higher up the tree. Seems to bloody love it! Totters off to work in her Merc' and her high heels and suit. She never seems as happy as when she shuts the door on me and gets to forget I exist.

"But me, I couldn't settle. Didn't help that I had no idea what I would even *want* to do. The army was that, always had been. I've subcontracted myself out to a building company as a demolitions expert, because with all the urban regeneration going on, they need someone who can bring an old factory or a warehouse down without flattening the block. But there's only so much of that work out there, and I can't turn my hand to being a brickie or anything else like that."

"You sound like you were bored stiff?"

"I was! And that didn't help with things between me and Jane. She's now precisely where she's always wanted to be, whereas I couldn't see any future for me at all aside from house husband – and I'm sure as hell not cut out for that!"

Stella giggled. "No, I don't see you doing the washing up in a floral apron!"

"Wash your mouth out, young woman!" but at least Bob was laughing too.

They got to her house just as the late sunset was putting on its best show, which with Stella's house facing westwards, gave her a grandstand view.

"Oh this is lovely!" Bob enthused, as the sunset washed the distant Black Mountains and Brecon Beacons in amber and purple.

"It's why I bought this house after Dad died," Stella admitted. "Anywhere in the area would have done for work, but the view and the peace and quiet sold it to me."

"That I can believe." He stood just gazing at the view and drawing in the fresh air like a starving man being given freshly baked bread. Stella could see the tension draining out of him in the way his shoulders relaxed and what she'd taken for a habitual frown disappearing.

Letting him savour the view, Stella went and let Ivan out, and the big dog bounded up to Bob, stuffing his wet nose into Bob's hand in greeting.

"Hello big fella!" Bob responded, immediately bending down and ruffling Ivan ears, which brought on little grunts of happiness from Ivan.

"You're honoured," Stella said, laughing as Ivan collapsed on the floor to roll over for belly rubs. "He normally doesn't like men much. He's not nasty, just wary, but he obviously feels safe with you."

"He's a rescue?"

"Yes, hauled off a travellers' site somewhere, all skin and bone with half his ear missing and a broken tail – that's why the end bit doesn't wag with the rest of it."

"Poor old fella!" Bob said, obliging Ivan with more rubs when he stopped and got patted with a large paw to continue. "I hate people who are cruel to animals!"

And that, Stella thought, was as good a reason as any to trust Bob in her house. Ivan wouldn't have let him over the doorstep if he'd sensed anything untoward about him. Toby and Ivan had only crossed paths once, and it was the only time Stella had ever known Ivan really bare his teeth and mean it – and that hadn't even been here on his home territory but in a park.

"Come on, let's get you two inside. Ivan! Dinner time!"

Like a shot, Ivan flew into the house, and they heard his excited yip coming from deep inside.

"That's him barking at the kitchen cupboard where his tins of meat and kibble are," Stella explained, "Like I need reminding!"

Once Ivan was lying on his squashy bed, full and contented, and Bob had been shown to the spare room at the back and lugged his bags up, Stella made them a hot drink each and showed Bob her maps.

"Thank God! A woman who knows what a real map is for and doesn't just use a sat' nav'!" was his first response.

"My dad's old collection," Stella explained.

Bob looked at her quizzically. "You've spoken several times about your dad, but not your mum. Were you two just very close or what?"

"Oh. No, it's because Mum got killed when I was tiny. I have no memory of her at all," she hastily added to fend off any expression of sympathy. "I've never missed her because I never knew her. It was my dad's parents who helped bring me up, and that's because Mum's folk thought Dad was to blame for her death. He wasn't. They'd lost a baby not long before and Mum took it very hard. Quite a late miscarriage, I understand. But Dad still had to go out to work, so he couldn't be with her all the time.

"On the day it happened, he'd taken me to his mum's as he'd been doing for a week or so, because he was getting worried that Mum wasn't looking after me when he wasn't there to prompt her. He went off to work, and the next thing he knew the police were there saying that she'd been run over. It seems she just walked out in front of this great big truck. It wasn't the driver's fault. The coroner said she took her own life while the balance of her mind was disturbed. These days we'd probably call it post-natal depression combined with grief. But it really put Dad off having another relationship all the time I was growing up – he couldn't face the risk of going through that again."

"Blimey, no, I can imagine that," Bob said. "That certainly explains why you were so close."

"And these maps were part of that. Dad was big into hiking in his single days. Went all over the UK by catching buses or trains and then starting walking. So when I was little we used to come here to the Malverns from Worcester for walks, and then as I got bigger and able to walk for longer, we ventured farther afield."

She grinned at Bob. "You might not believe it, but I've got my own tent and stuff stored away under the stairs. Ivan and I have done our share of rough camping," then laughed at Bob's stunned expression.

"Okay," he said cautiously, "so you're not going to be the novice I thought you'd be at this. Come on then, show me where you were going to go tomorrow."

Stella tapped the map that covered the Dolgellau area. "See this valley here? Well there are disused slate mines here, here, and here. But there are also a couple just over that ridge where all the Forestry Commission forests are, and they're here and here as best I can tell. They must have been worked out before the others, because there's nothing to say that there was a mine there. It's just that the names correspond with those on the list of disused mines and they're in the right area. That, to me, makes them ideal candidates for what went on."

"Right, we'll start with them, then!" Bob said decisively. "Six o'clock too early a start for you?"

"Not at all. See you bright and early!"

Chapter 15

Thursday – Friday

With the early summer dawn it was already bright and sunny when Stella and Bob got up and began packing her car.

"Ivan goes on the back seat," Stella explained, as Bob hauled his bags back out. "He gets a bit car sick on long runs if he can't look forwards."

She had been adamant that Ivan should come with them, explaining to Bob that while a couple tramping the hills might look questionable, somehow once you put a dog into the mix, everyone accepted that you were just going for a walk.

"You'll find Ivan is our greatest asset when it comes to anonymity," she had told him. "I've had a lot of experience of that. A woman on her own seems to be fair bait for every know-it-all bloke out on the hills, but with a big dog beside you it's amazing how invisible you become. It wasn't the reason why I adopted him, of course, but it's been a definite unexpected bonus. You've heard of crazy cat ladies? Well 'gone to the dogs' ladies are just as undesirable, it seems."

"Then there are some very strange blokes out there," Bob said with a bemused shake of his head.

"Not exactly strange," Stella qualified. "It's just that once you've got to the wrong side of thirty, the ones who haven't been snapped up, or who already haven't coped with living with at least one woman, often seem to be the ones who are looking for a surrogate mum.

Someone who they can have the whole attention of, and who'll look after them. Sharing with a big daft lump like Ivan is way too much to ask, it seems, and I've found it a very good barometer for sussing out the ones I'd even want to be friends with, much less anything more."

"Jeez! And these are the people I've been fighting to protect!" Bob said in disgust. "No wonder I've had such a hard time adapting to life outside of the army!"

Certainly Stella had never got packed up and ready to go in such a short space of time, but then she'd never had such a willing companion before. Within the hour they were pulling away from Stella's house, not only with the car packed, but with a couple of flasks and a quantity of sandwiches to see them through the day until they could find a pub for an evening meal.

Stella took the first turn behind the wheel. Bob said that he was insured to drive other cars, and today when she was feeling less shocked and alert she wasn't so keen to just hand over the keys. She still didn't want to risk a bump in the heavier trafficked area close to home when he wasn't actively a named driver on her policy – somehow she thought that Bob might take things rather more briskly than she would! Once they were deep into Wales on quieter roads she would be glad to have a break, but to start with she set off on the A44 heading for Leominster.

"You might as well carry on on this road beyond Leominster," Bob advised. "You could go up towards Ludlow and then across, but it's six of one and half a dozen of the other, and there are often accidents on the Ludlow bypass or up by Craven Arms."

And so they drove on, only heading north towards Newtown once they were deep into Wales. They had agreed to make for Machynlleth and then go into Dolgellau to find a B&B for the night before they started searching. They had the camping gear with them, but as Stella said,

"Better to look the normal holiday makers to start off with. If we stumble across something dodgy, it will put off anyone who decides to follow us if we go back to a proper place and then just amble down to the local pub. We can always start camping once we know where we want to investigate more closely."

With both of them having been to Dolgellau before, it wasn't hard to find the way there and to agree on somewhere to stay, discovering a friendly farmhouse B&B just outside of the town which was prepared to accommodate Ivan in a room as well. They took the rooms for three nights in order to seem like folk there for a long weekend – there was nothing remotely remarkable in coming for a Thursday through to Sunday morning stay.

"Right," said Bob, "we need to go back the way we've come as far as Corris and then turn off east up this tiny road here."

They had spread the map out on the bed in Stella's room as they prepared to go out again, having told their curious landlady that they were old friends from uni who'd come for the walking, and no, they didn't want a double room, thank you. He'd been much amused at Stella's invention of him as having been a mature industrial archaeology student, given how hopeless he'd been at history at school, but the landlady had swallowed the bait, even telling them where they might want to go and look at stuff.

"There's a good museum in Corris where you can have a look in a mine," she'd told them helpfully, and they'd smiled and made noises of appreciation at her kindness, never letting on that they had very different intentions.

They found their way into Corris easily enough, and onto the small road which led up into the hills. These were rounded, tree-covered hills rather than the stark mountain landscape of Snowdonia, and for once Wales was showing itself in its best light on a bright sunny day, rather than the more usual rain driving in off the Atlantic via Ireland. Open fields were punctuated by mixed woodland, and then they came upon the sign for a Forestry Commission car park and walks, and could see the serried ranks of the dark conifer plantation off to their right.

"Useful to know that there's a proper place for walkers," Bob noted. "Might be a good place to lure any unwanted followers we pick up."

That hadn't occurred to Stella, and it made her glad that Bob was with her. She'd only been thinking of looking around, not of what might happen if anyone saw her and took violent exception to her being there, even if she was on land where the public had every right to be.

As they got up to the tiny hamlet of Aberllefenni, it was possible to see the old slate quarries, huge scars on the landscape even now, and though they got out and had a brief walk around, it was blindingly clear that this wasn't the sort of thing they were looking for at all.

"This is way too public," Stella said, and Bob agreed.

She was glad that Bob had taken over driving as they continued up the valley, and the road got narrower and the sides of the valley steeper. She was a confident driver, but the thought of having to turn the car around on something this tight, and with a steep drop to the small river beside it, was something she'd rather not have to do, especially if it was at speed. It wasn't much farther on to Cymerau where they found somewhere to pull in once more, but again all the indicators were that this had been an open cast mine or quarry.

"There's nothing here to indicate that there was ever anything underground," Bob said as they stood by the car scanning the landscape. "I can't see anything that looks like it might ever have been winding gear."

"Do we carry on to Ratgoed?" Stella asked. "Ivan could do with a walk, and it looks on the map like it's a fairly clear track up the valley – not exactly arduous. The car should be fine here."

Bob nodded. "Why not? We might as well get a feel for the place." He looked down at the map. "Ratgoed quarry, or whatever it was, looks like it's now hidden by the Forestry plantation, but we'll be able to tell very easily if anyone's been around there, I would think."

They both already had their walking boots on, and so they swung off up the road, Stella impressing Bob with the way she settled into a steady pace without any signs of struggling to keep up. Ivan was trustworthy off the lead with no livestock around, and so it was uncannily easy to fall into the feeling that this was just a very pleasant day out. It had been a very long time since Stella had enjoyed the simple pleasure of walking with someone. Toby had all too often made it into a show of superiority after they'd been married, and the rare times Stella had gone out with colleagues who professed to enjoy walking, she had found them too fond of dissecting work as they walked, rather than enjoying the scenery. It was bliss to walk with someone who felt no need to make small talk, and had she known it, Bob was thinking exactly the same.

Bringing Jane and the kids out into the countryside had become a kind of torture. Jane always wanted him to pay attention to her, somehow thinking that if she played the girly girl that Bob would enjoy playing the macho man. Instead, he had wanted to show the kids some of the things they would have otherwise walked straight past, but by the time he had helped Jane over obstacles she could have easily negotiated on her own if she'd taken his advice and worn sensible shoes, the girls were usually bored stiff and Josh was racing ahead to stay out of earshot of the inevitable rows.

Sophie and Debbie had soon reached a point where they would complain all the way home that there'd been nothing to see, because there had been no shops to peruse, encouraged by Jane who had made quite the dramatic performances of 'soothing' them with promises of 'proper days out' to the retail hells of Birmingham's Bull Ring Centre, or the other huge Midlands mall of Merry Hill — or Merry Hell, as Bob thought of it. Those days had been exquisite torment for Bob and Josh, and they had learned to opt out of them in far less dramatic fashion than the girls' performances in the countryside. But as he swung along, sucking in the clear air and feeling it cleanse his thoughts along the way, Bob thought that Stella had seen things with remarkable clarity regarding Josh. If Jane had driven a wedge in between Bob and his daughters, she had also driven one between herself and her son.

As Stella exclaimed in delight, "Oh look! A sparrowhawk!" and pointed skywards, he could have damned near wept with relief. Not since his time in the army had he had a friend he could share such simple pleasures with, and it only highlighted how far apart he and Jane had drifted. Time to make a clean break of it, he vowed, discovering a new resolve on the matter. He wasn't doing any of the family any favours by hanging on in that gothic monstrosity of a house which had never been his home.

That Stella then didn't scream and dissolve into hysterics when the sparrowhawk stooped from on high and took a small bird in mid air, severing its head in the process which dropped to the ground right by them, and spattering blood onto their boots, further impressed Bob. Her stern command to Ivan to leave it, and it being obeyed, had her rise to near goddess status in his eyes. Good grief, what sort of five-star fuck-wit had Toby been to let a woman like this go? It was all he could do to remind himself that they were here for a very serious purpose. *Don't go getting distracted*, he told himself firmly, *she may not want any bloke's advances after what she's been through.*

So it was probably a good thing that having got back to the car and driven into Dolgellau once more, that they went into a busy local where any hint of a romantic dinner was firmly quashed. Being surrounded by local farmers and workers on a raucous Thursday night, it was all they could do to get food ordered and to drink their beers without getting jostled, and they made an early night of it but deciding on an early start on Friday. With the landlady primed for when they would want breakfast, they went to their separate rooms, neither knowing that the other was thinking very similar thoughts.

"It's great being out with Bob, isn't it?" Stella said to Ivan as he curled up on his blanket beside her bed, "But Dav could be in dire danger!" Ivan's tail beat a tattoo on the floor. "Yes, I know you like Bob." The tail thumped on the floor again. "But you liked Dav too." Ivan's ears went down and he gave her his most mournful look. "So we'll find Dav first, okay?" Ivan gave a huff, turned and trampled his bed in several successive circles, then settled down while still cocking an eye Stella's way, as if to say, 'don't miss your chance, though!'

When they got up the next morning it was as though the weather had predicted their intentions. Yesterday had been the breathing space, the time to just tick the box that the three least likely quarries were indeed off their list. Today would be a day for much more determined searching, and the slate-grey clouds looming low over the hills echoed their steely resolve not to waste time.

With Stella map-reading and Bob driving, they set off again back towards Corris, but this time they were going a bit further south before they turned off eastwards again.

"In a four-wheel-drive we might get over that ridge from Aberllefenni," Bob had said sagely, "but those are tracks, not roads, and we'd most likely wreck your car if we tried. Better carry on and turn down this B-road road just before Machynlleth, and then come back north-eastwards along that as far as we can, before we turn off onto the tracks."

"We're still going to be on foot from this little hamlet of Pant y Celyn, though," Stella added. "But it's the only way we'll reach Chwarel Coch. The fact that it's called a quarry probably means that it's open cast, and not what we want, but it's this neighbouring spot higher up that I was wondering about, Mynydd Cwm-goch. That red reference – the 'goch' bit – makes me wonder whether, although these are listed as slate mines, there might not have been some copper found there?"

"I think that's good deducing," Bob agreed, and they set off braced for at least a three mile hike up to the first spot, and to spend probably the whole day on the hills.

As a result, once they'd tucked the car away tight into a hedge where it would be out of any farmer's way, they both picked up rucksacks. Stella's had both food and drinks for them, plus a couple of water bottles for Ivan and his portable bowl, while Bob had waterproofs for them both incase the weather closed in, and some other stuff he wouldn't show Stella. That all by itself made her a little nervous. Bob wasn't the sort to worry needlessly, so if he had items like knives in there souvenired from his army times, that meant he was anticipating real trouble.

In one way it was a good thing the weather wasn't as sunny as yesterday, because the climb soon got pretty steep, and they were both working hard to keep up the pace.

"God, I've become a soft old sod!" Bob said in disgust, as they stopped for their first break and swigs at their water bottles. "My old mates would be taking the piss out of me something chronic if they could see me puffing and panting over a little slope like this."

"Well there aren't any of these hills in Birmingham," Stella consoled him, "so it would have been a bit hard to stay in practice there."

Putting his bottle back in the pack's side pocket, Bob nodded. "Granted, and although I got the bike out whenever I could, I'm already feeling muscles that haven't been used in a while. You might need a crane to get me out of bed tomorrow if they stiffen up!"

Despite his protestations, though, he still led them at a brisk pace, never taking Stella faster than she could cope, but nonetheless moving them on with great purpose. They had been following the twisting trail of what was probably a logging road at first, as it snaked up the valley side, but then they came out onto open heath. Now Stella was glad that she had Bob with her, because he struck off confidently across the open countryside, leaving the rough track veering away to their left, in a way that she would never have risked doing on her own. Part of that was just being sensible, because Stella knew that as a lone walker, something as simple as a twisted ankle could spell real trouble, and so it was better to stick to somewhere where you could be easily found. But because of that, she'd also got out of regular practice at striking out with just a compass point to aim for, and there was part of her that was relishing the renewed adventure.

After another short steep uphill, they once again found themselves heading into a conifer plantation, and following the line of a small craggy cliff on their right.

"Here we are, Chwarel Coch!" Bob declared triumphantly as they rounded the end of the crag. "Well that looks like nobody's touched it in decades."

"Yes, it does, doesn't it," Stella agreed, "but it's so hard to tell even if you look at the satellite images on Google Maps, because they overlay things like the tracks, and that makes even paths look deceptively like proper roads. I thought this looked the less likely of the two, but in one way I think it's much more promising that it generally looks so deserted round here."

She turned and looked around her. "These trees look like they're a slightly more recent planting than some of the others, but they still have to be a good ten years old, wouldn't you say? So I doubt even the Forestry people have been up here in a while. All this is in the in-between stage of being past the planting and thinning out stage, but still a good way away from being ready for felling."

"Yes it is nicely anonymous at the moment," Bob agreed, throwing a large stick for Ivan which he'd had dropped at his feet with an excited yip. "Ivan isn't going to suddenly run out of steam is he? He's a big lad to have to sling across my shoulders to carry back down to the car!"

Stella laughed. "No, he's good for a few miles yet, but I wouldn't throw that stick too many times even so."

With Ivan proudly towing another stick so large that the one end dragged on the ground, they set off again on the hunt for Mynydd Cwm-goch. This time they were heading into the darker woods in an altogether older stretch of plantation, following the course of a tiny river. They crossed another small ridge and then dropped down into another tight valley, and a mile up its course they found the old mine.

"Now this is more what I expected," Bob declared with satisfaction.

Various pieces of heavily rusted chunks of metal lay strewn across the open area, most of which Stella couldn't even begin to guess the uses for, except for some big, rusty-toothed cogs which had possibly come from a winch. A lonely tall chimney still pointed skywards from the one building of any substance left standing, but a collection of low, crumbled walls spoke of there once being several other buildings on the site, albeit all of them small and very roughly constructed. And there across the clearing, like some medieval manuscript's depiction of a Hell-mouth, was the dark, square maw of the entrance to the mine itself.

"That's not even blocked off!" Stella gasped. "God, I wonder how many sheep they lose in a year if they get in there?"

"Not many. Sheep are cannier than to go into places like that. We're more likely to find the remains of some fox's den inside."

Bob was already fishing two solid-looking flashlights out of his pack and a rope. "Don't laugh at me, but I want you roped to me. I've had a bit more experience of scrambling over loose rocks and things that might give way, and of breaking my fall. I don't want to lose you if something gives way when we go in and have a look."

He expected to have more of an argument about that from her, but now that she was confronted with an actual mine, Stella felt more than a little nervous about going in. For no reason that she could sensibly describe, she had a really bad feeling about the place that she couldn't shake off. It wasn't that she was claustrophobic. She wasn't exactly keen on small places, but she was far more worried by the kind of crushing crowds you found in shopping malls at Christmas – there really was only so much of that she could take. But generally she wasn't bothered by more natural cramped spaces, or maybe that was it? This wasn't in any way natural, and it both looked and felt like some suppurating scar across what had previously been a beautiful spot.

"Right, are you ready?" Bob asked her. Ivan had been tied by his lead to one of the huge cogs so that he wouldn't follow them in, and he was already whiffling pitifully, not happy about being left behind. "You be a good lad and guard the packs, Ivan! We'll be back soon!"

"Good boy, stay!" Stella commanded, and bracing herself for what they might find, she followed Bob into the darkness.

Chapter 16

Friday

As soon as they were into the darkness, Bob put his flashlight on and Stella followed suit. To her surprise she saw that there were the remains of a narrow gauge railway beneath their feet, at first just a single track, and then some yards deeper inside, it forked into two and diverged off into each of two tunnels.

"We'll start with the left-hand one," Bob said, putting a chalk mark on the wall with an arrow pointing back towards the opening, which had already vanished around a bend. On a brighter day they would have seen the change in light back there, but today it had already disappeared, and he had no intention of getting lost down here.

They tramped on a short way, discovering nothing but a few discarded remains of teenagers' picnics, the result, no doubt, of youngsters feeling very daring at venturing into such places but not being either daft enough or brave enough to go any deeper. But beyond there, what was also clear was that nobody else had been down here. Pieces of rust broke off the rails when Bob gave them a kick, confirming that it was unlikely that a group of men as big as the platoon could ever have passed this way without leaving more evidence of their passage.

They went back and ventured down the other tunnel, which took a little longer since it in turn branched into two ways, but the net result was the same.

Some chunks of slate had crumbled off the tunnel walls to lie undisturbed, and in one place a substantial pool of water had collected in a hollow, rotting the railway sleepers over the intervening decades of disuse, and reducing the rails to sheared-off rusty spikes, which was the point when they turned back. Even before they got to the outside they could hear Ivan's piteous whining, and when they came into site he promptly tied himself in knots with his lead in his excitement at seeing them again.

"Calm down, you big daft fur-ball," Stella remonstrated with him as she tried to disentangle him. "Good grief! We were only gone for a few minutes!" No sooner had she unwrapped one large furry paw then he entangled another by spinning around. In the end it was easiest to just let him off so that he stepped out of it, but unlike normal, he didn't then go bounding off to do his usual trick of coming zooming back in and buzzing her in his excitement. Instead he stuck to Stella like glue, making her say to Bob,

"I don't know what it is about this place, but Ivan really doesn't like it. Something here is genuinely distressing him. It wasn't just about being tied up while we were away."

She half expected Bob to just laugh it off, and was pleased when instead he bent down and made a fuss of Ivan saying, "What is it, old chap? What can you sense that we can't see, eh?" He straightened up and began leading the way out of the small cwm to begin the return walk to the car, but said, "I don't discount his instincts lightly. Dogs are much better than us at picking up when a place is dangerous, especially when it's natural dangers. He can probably sense that the old mine is unstable or something."

However, Stella couldn't shake the thought that there was something decidedly creepy about the place that nothing to do with it just being disused. For no reason she could explain, she had the strong feeling that they had been watched when they were inside that old mine. Yet glancing around her now, she didn't have the same feeling.

No, it wasn't the valley. Whatever it was it wasn't up here, out in the daylight, not even with the clouds lowering and beginning to brush the distant top of Cadair Idris, with detached wisps of them coming down to dangle over the trees like the stuff you strung over the Christmas tree to imitate snow. That was just weather. It wasn't even really threatening rain here just yet, but something back in that mine had definitely been menacing, and as she turned back to give it just one last glance, she could have sworn that she saw the hint of a figure at the mine's mouth. Nothing substantial. Something as wispy as those clouds, but the sensation of its presence was considerably stronger than what was visible.

And just at that moment Ivan gave another worried little whine.

"Yes, I know, lad, I feel it too! Let's get out of here!" and they hurried after Bob.

They got back as far as Chwarel Coch, and then Bob stopped for them to eat their lunch while there was a comfortable patch of sunshine breaking through the clouds. Emboldened by the normality of strong tea along with cheese and pickle sandwiches, Stella gave Ivan his bit of cheese and then ventured to say,

"Please don't think me some dopey girl, Bob, but I looked back as we left the old mine, and ...well, I think I saw something. I know it was probably a trick of the light and you're going to tell me not to bother about it, but it really creeped me out."

Bob didn't burst out laughing as she expected, but instead regarded her seriously. "So you felt it too?" he asked instead.

"Blimey, I expected you to laugh at me!"

But he shook his head. "When you've been in some of the wilder parts of the world you learn that not everything can be explained away with science. Some of the isolated tribes I've come across in remote areas have a connection with nature that we can't even get close to, for instance. And I strongly believe that even here in the Western world our survival instincts are stronger than we allow for, if only we'd learn how to listen to them a bit better."

He sat back and looked at her, then seemed to make his mind up about something. "I've never even told Jane about this, you know, but just before we were about to ship out for Afghanistan — that was going to be my first experience of what it was like out there when I was still with the Mercians — there were some real Roma people passing through the outskirts of Lichfield. Not just scruffy travelers, mind you, but the real thing and just the one extended family. They're increasingly rare, but you can always tell the difference, because instead of having a filthy mess left behind as with the travellers, you hardly know they've even been there. Well our platoon had been out on a run and spotted them, and the old lady — probably the old grandma — she calls out to us, telling us to come back and she'll read us our fortunes."

He was staring off into the distance as if seeing that long past time. "Well we all thought it would be a laugh to go back, so we got permission and went off. We thought it would be some cheap trick with shadows and lights, see? But all there is is the old lady sitting off to one side, all on her own by the camp fire, and the rest of us wait over with the rest of her family and we go over one at a time.

"The strangest thing, though, was when we compared what we'd been told. It wasn't the usual bollocks at all – none of, 'you're going to meet a beautiful woman and live in a mansion' crap – and to two of the lads she just said, 'You go out and enjoy yourself, son.' It made no sense at the time, but those two lads never made it back. There's no earthly way that old lady could have known that, but I swear by all I hold sacred that what I'm telling you is true."

He sucked in a deep breath. "So if you say you felt something weird back there, I believe you, because I did too."

That wasn't what Stella had expected at all, and she was lost for words. So much so that Bob had to prompt her by asking,

"So what did you see?"

She thought hard for a second. "It was tall and vaguely human, but something about it just wasn't right. I can't put it better than that. ...If you pushed me, I would say that it was too tall and too slender."

"That fits with something I could have sworn I thought I saw just out of the corner of my eye while we were down there," Bob now admitted. "I didn't say anything to you because when I looked properly there was nothing there, and it was creepy enough down there without me putting the breeze up you with talk of strange things."

"Thank you for that, because I had the horrible sensation of being watched by something down there as it was. If I'd thought you were picking up on it too I'd have been really freaked out!"

However Bob then beat her to it by saying, "But I'm awfully glad you felt that too because I thought it was just me!"

"And Ivan!" Stella added. "I reckon that's why he was in such a tizzy over us going down there."

Bob leaned over and gave the big white dog an ear ruffle. "I guess we should take a bit more notice of you, lad." Then stood up and stretched, and looking over at the oncoming clouds, said, "I think we'd better get moving. That rain's coming in faster than I thought, and I have no desire to be stuck on this bloody hill with the clouds around my ears. I've had enough creepy experiences for one day."

They made it back to the car just as it went from fine drizzle to full rain, but that also settled any plans for the rest of the day. Hikes over the hills weren't going to be on the cards in these conditions, not with it looking like it had set in for the rest of the afternoon.

"Shall we try the museum?" Stella suggested. "It might just give us a hint of what we're looking for?"

And so they drove back to Corris and managed to grab the last two places on the final tour of the day. They hadn't been expecting to actually go down into the mine on the trip, but the available places were on the two hour version, and so they got kitted up and joined in with the family of four who had already booked in. The two young boys were very excited at the outset, but as the trip went on it became clear that the youngest one – who had only just reached the minimum age to come down – was becoming increasingly scared that they might never get out again. Consequently the family were very glad for Bob to take over watching the older, just pre-teen lad so that the younger one could hang onto his dad, and that allowed Stella and the mum to bring up the rear making small talk.

"That was interesting," Bob admitted after they'd emerged and rescued Ivan from the confines of the car for a comfort break.

The old Victorian mine had been like a time capsule, allowing them to see the lives of the men who had delved for whole days at a time in the dark, with only feeble lights to guide them.

"I don't know about you, though," Stella said thoughtfully, "but I got no sensation of the kind we got back up at the other mine."

"No, I noticed that. I suppose you could say that it was because it was a sanitised tourist experience, but I think it was more than that."

"Yes, we're far lower down the mountain here, aren't we? That was much more what it must be like going down a coal mine. But before, we were going into the heart of the hill rather than deeper into the floor of the valley. Do you think that makes a difference?"

"Who knows?"

They returned to Dolgellau and managed to get in to the pub before the Friday evening rush for food started. Both of them were ravenous, and they gladly tucked into homemade chicken and mushroom pies and chips. It was as they were relaxing and enjoying a second pint of beer, being within walking distance of the B&B, that the first strange thing happened.

Perhaps because of the unaccustomed exercise, Stella found herself dozing as the pub warmed up and it got increasingly stuffy inside, but it was too wet for them to go and sit outside. The general hum of voices was having a soporific effect on her, and so she wasn't really sure at first whether she was just overhearing someone else in the pub speaking.

"Don't delve to deep!" the voice said, as though issuing a warning.

She blinked and scrubbed her eyes.

Bob caught her doing it and grinned at her. "It's getting to me too. Let's finish these drinks and get back to the B&B. We can open a window and plan what we're going to do tomorrow."

"Good idea," Stella said, but they still had half a pint left each, so they weren't going immediately. It was too noisy for them to be able to talk freely, though, and so once again they settled into companionable silence and Stella's eyelids began to close despite her best intentions.

This time, when the voice came there was a face with it. Stern with high cheekbones and slanted eyes, it nonetheless lacked any real colour and seemed to float ethereally, its outline wavering, but there was no mistaking the warning in its words this time.

"Do not delve into the deeps!" it snapped so fiercely that Stella involuntarily let out a squeak of surprise, then opened her eyes to see several of the locals suddenly staring at her.

"Something just bloody bit me!" she excused herself by saying sheepishly, blushing furiously and made a show of rubbing her neck.

"The wet brings them out," a friendly lad with a mop of Celtic flame-coloured hair, and a swath of freckles across his nose, said with a laugh. "Buggers eat me alive in this weather!"

Bob gave her an odd look but she made furtive shushing gestures, and he took the hint that she didn't want to talk about it here. Once they were walking back, though, and away from being overheard, she told him what had happened, ending with, "That damned mine must have got to me more than I thought."

"Do you want to carry on?" Bob asked cautiously.

"God, yes! Dav is still out there somewhere – hopefully still alive, but if not then I still want to know."

"So we'd better plan what we're going to do tomorrow, then, always providing that the rain lets up a bit."

With the maps once more spread out over Stella's bed since hers was the larger of the two rooms, and with the window open a crack and bringing some much needed fresh air in, they felt more able to think things through logically.

"So were there any other areas round where we've been that you still want to look at?" Bob wondered. "I'm having to defer to you here because you've done so much more looking at these lists than me."

However Stella shook her head. "No. All the others on that group's list I've discounted for one reason or another, but the whole reason why I wanted to stay here in Dolgellau, rather than down in Machynlleth, is because I've got some north of here that look like contenders."

She pointed on the map to a river valley which snaked its way northwards from the town, its mouth being to the west at Barmouth so that she was taking her finger upstream along the river's course. "This is the Mawddach River after which the group of mines is named, and as you'd guess, most of the old mines are here in the valley. Some of them like Peniarth down here by Tywyn, and Bryn-y-gwyn just up the road from us here, are almost on top of substantial towns.

"Well it won't be any of them, but there's this area up in what's marked as the Coed-y-Brenin Forest – that name translates as the King's Wood, you know, and so it struck me that a lot of that is going to be undisturbed land. I'm not suggesting that there are unmarked mines actually within the modern forest boundary, but do you think that in the past miners might have been allowed to dig so far and then no farther?"

"Hmmm, you mean there might be a mine around there that got closed rather earlier than the others, if it had reached the extent to which it was allowed to excavate before it reached forbidden land? Yes, that would be a possibility."

"So there are these two names," Stella said sitting back with a sigh, "and I can't actually find either mine specifically. But I've been working on the assumption that when these old colliers named the mine groups, that they went from the ridge on one side of a valley and across it to the ridge on the other, in essence following line of sight. That's why some of the mines in the Mawddach group are geographically closer to some of the Corris group than others within the Corris group were to them. The separation is definitely topographical in a boots-on-the-ground sort of way, not the way we often make political boundaries nowadays.

"So if these two mines are in the Mawddach group, then they must be up on the hillside one way or the other where they were within view of the valley. Or at least back then they were. You have to remember that the Forestry Commission was invented after World War One, when the government realised how much a shortage of timber could have cost the war effort."

"I'm with you. These mines would most likely be Victorian, so decades before a lot of the forests got planted. And that in turns means that just because all we can see now is a great block of pine trees, doesn't mean that in the past it wasn't visible." He paused but continued thoughtfully. "But there is a modern consideration we have to take into account. Look at how many patches of land on this bit of the map have the red outline of National Trust land around them – especially lower in the valley. Given that we're looking for a very dodgy operation, I don't think they would have risked doing it on Trust land. You'd never know when some warden might turn up to keep an eye on the place. I know they're hardly armed and dangerous, but one of them going missing would create quite a fuss."

"No, point taken. If one went missing having stumbled across something, I'd presume that there'd be some kind of record at his office of where he was going that day, and before you could sneeze, the place would be crawling with mountain rescue folk."

"Exactly. At some point they were always going to be taking a chance with this, because nowhere in the UK is that far from civilisation, except some of the wilds of Scotland. And while they seem to have had no scruples about lying to the MOD, nor of having a criminally negligent attitude towards the men, given that discovery would mean prosecution for those behind this scam, I reckon they'd be pretty careful in the choice of location."

Stella retrieved the piece of paper on which she'd written the names of the two mines, which had somehow ended up under Ivan on the floor.

"I'd been hoping that the names would give me a clue when I began searching," she confessed, "but Blaen-y-mynach just translates as 'front of the mountain'." She waved a frustrated hand at the map. "Which bloody mountain? We've got enough to take our pick of! ...The only clue I could find which fitted the area as well, was this valley which climbs up into the mountains on the western side of the Mawddach."

"But it's not in the Mawddach," Bob pointed out. "It's a separate valley running parallel to it."

"Bear with me! Look at the names of these places, which going by how scattered they are, are presumably small farms. How many 'Blaen's do you see? More than elsewhere. But once you get up to the top of the valley, beyond that little lake, you're almost on the ridge between it and the Mawddach, and most telling of all, there isn't another group to the west of there."

"Ah! So nobody to claim it?"

"That's right. I suspect the terrain between there and the coastline from Barmouth right up until you get closer to Harlech, was just too rough for any kind of industrial operation. And look at how close the contour lines are on the map at the coast. Those are some very steep slopes compared to down around the other side of the river. The slate probably does run through geologically, but the cost of getting it out would have been so high it wouldn't have been economically viable."

Bob was nodding as they scrutinised the map further. "I think you're right. By the time you've discounted the National Trust areas, and those that are going to be heaving with tourists, it has to be the western side of the Mawddach we're looking at, and regarding this Blaen-y-mynach mine, up on the ridge is about the best contender. How many miles can you do in a day, Stella? Because we'll have to leave your car down on the roadside, and it has to be four miles on the map before you even get to the top of that valley, and on the ground with those steep slopes it's going to feel more like six. I know we're heading for mid-summer now, and we've got the long light evenings meaning we can take plenty of long breaks without getting stuck in the dark, but even so, it's going be a very long day."

Stella nodded and looked down at Ivan. "And we have to consider him, too. I wouldn't leave him with a stranger or stick him in a kennels, even if we could find one."

"No, and his instincts have been pretty useful, too. I agree, Ivan is part of the team. So in that case I think we're looking at camping overnight. We could ask the landlady if we can leave some stuff here since we've paid for the rooms – that way we won't be leaving a car filled with stuff by the roadside. Are you up for that? What about work? Will you need to zap back to Malvern on Sunday?"

Stella picked up her mobile and logged in to her emails. "Nothing as yet. But then it's always this last half-term of the year where I get very little work. It's kind of silly season for the younger students; the A-level kids have pretty much finished; and even the ones two years below who are doing their GCSEs are rather bombed out from exams, but aren't in a position to start A-levels until they know for sure that they've got through. So, yes, it looks as though I'm free for the next couple of days, at least."

"Great, so we'll get the tents out!"

"Oooh, hang on a tick! I've got voicemail. I wonder if it's Ade?"

Stella went and put her phone down on the windowsill where she had the best signal and then, putting it on speaker phone, she connected to the message.

"Hi guys!" they heard Ade's cheerful voice say. "I'm guessing you're out of signal, but I just thought I'd let you know that everything's fine here. The coppers aren't looking at us anymore – partly because they have another lead, it seems. And whatever you said to that nurse, Stella, it's really had an effect! They took the lads off all meds for a day on Thursday and gave them something to help flush things through their systems, and then later today — that's Friday — they started all of them on something else and it's looking good. Tom and Josh are set to make a full recovery, and things are even starting to look a bit better for Craig — and that's just within three or four hours of changing things. Thought you'd want to know, let me know what's going on! I'm in suspense here!"

The grin lighting up Bob's face was enough to tell Stella that he was delighted at his son's progress, and so while he went and made a call to his family, Stella rang Ade and brought him up to date with their lack of progress.

"So did the police not want to talk to Bob, after all?" she was able to ask now that Bob was in his own room.

"No, it was the weirdest thing," Ade's slightly crackling voice came over the phone. "They took my statement, and it was blindingly obvious that it couldn't have been me that did for Hardy, but that DC Mortimer was muttering something about still needing a statement from you and Bob. Then the other one, Finch, comes in and whispers something to him and they both go tearing out. A couple of minutes later some nice WPC comes in and says I'm free to go, and when I ask her what's going on, she says that they have new evidence and a new suspect."

"Blimey! I wonder what that's all about?"

"No idea, but I'll be keeping an ear open! Good luck with the camping!"

Chapter 17

Saturday

Stella had been intending to relish the night in a proper bed, knowing that Bob's idea of camping might be considerably more basic than hers, but in the depths of the night she was woken by a scream. What was that? It wasn't a fox's scream, that she knew having heard enough of them at home, though they could sound very like humans at time. Then another one came. Given that their two guest rooms adjoined one another in a little annex off the main farm building, that had to be from Bob. Ivan, too, was sitting up and whining, his nose pointing directly towards where Bob's bed was on the other side of the wall.

Hoping like mad that the farmer wouldn't see her flitting around in just her skimpy summer pyjamas, Stella opened her door and went to tap on Bob's.

"Are you alright in there?" she called softly, but got no reply. "Bob?"

Damn it, she was going to have to nip outside and see if she could see in through the window, which at least was an option with the rooms being on the ground floor.

"You stay!" she told Ivan firmly, having no desire for him to suddenly vanish in pursuit of a rabbit if he came out with her. Grabbing her lightweight sweater and tugging it and her boots on, she went outside and around to the windows, muttering darkly when she discovered that the farmer's wife had planted a pretty bed of flowers in front of them. There was no light on in Bob's room, which in one way was good since if he'd been feeling ill he would surely have put it on to find his way to the bathroom, if nothing else? His window was also slightly open and she stood with the dew on the grass starting to wet her ankles above the boot tops, listening hard. When she heard him starting to snore softly she realised it must have been a nightmare.

"Well after everything he's seen," she told Ivan, as back in her room she towelled herself dry, "it's hardly surprising if he does get nightmares. But I could have done with an uninterrupted night."

Yet in the morning Bob still seemed very subdued, saying almost nothing over breakfast.

"Are you okay to carry on?" Stella asked worriedly as they drove off. "We could go back to Malvern, you know."

Bob seemed to shake himself mentally. "No, I'm okay. I just didn't want to say anything while the landlady was flitting in and out. I had the weirdest dream last night."

"I know, I heard you scream!"

"Did you? Shit! Sorry about that. I didn't think I'd actually done that, just dreamt it."

"That sounds like a nightmare and a half."

"It was! I was down in a mine, but not with you. It was like I was with the lads who went missing. So there I was in this tunnel, and there were standard army lanterns lighting it up, and I could see some of the lads doing something with some kit down on the floor. I could see a smallish guy up at the front of the line of men, and we were in some sort of cavern – quite a big one – and suddenly the small guy looks over to one side and seems to see something. He goes deathly white and starts shouting for everyone to get out, and there's this big guy in the middle of the group who I guess was a sergeant, and he's on the radio saying we're heading back up. Then someone on the other end is yelling orders at him, but I can't hear what, because suddenly I hear one of the other lads scream and I turn, and he's holding on to his arm that's been nearly hacked off! Blood everywhere!"

He stopped and gulped convulsively, and although she was driving, Stella glanced sideways and could see the pulse in his neck pounding. To rattle Bob that much it must have been bad, but his next words revealed the source of his trouble.

"I've seen as bad elsewhere, but what made me scream was what was behind him. It was tall and slender, and it looked kind of human in a feral sort of way until you got to the eyes. Holy crap, Stella, those eyes were something else! They kind of glittered in the semi-dark, like they were cat's-eye green but with a black, star-filled sky behind them ...like looking through a telescope at the stars close-up but through a perfect emerald lens. And I just knew they hated us ...hated me ...hated humans!

"And then I saw the bloody great sword in its hands – but not metal! It looked like slate, but slate that had been polished and sharpened to a razor edge. And I turned and I saw another man and then another one go down, all attacked by these fucking weird things!"

The sweat was starting to stand out on Bob's brow even just recalling it. "And then someone got some shots off. God knows who, because somehow I just knew that we weren't armed. We weren't expecting to be attacked. And then it suddenly went much colder, like there was a wind coming from somewhere, and this other figure comes towards us ...and ...and," he had to stop and swallow hard again, pausing to have a long swig at one of the bottles of water.

Stella desperately wanted to know more but didn't dare push him. Yet Bob seemed to get a grip on his thoughts and continued,

"I'd say it was female, but again it was like the others, really tall and slender and in the strangest way not quite solid. If there is such a thing as another dimension, then that's where I'd guess they live, but they could certainly come into ours enough to do fatal damage. Those slate swords were very real when it came to hacking men down.

"But the woman! Christ, she was fucking scary! Whereas the male figures were kind of whitish, or at least a sort of cloud grey, she was black. She had like these flowing robes on, but they were see-through in as much as you could see the wall of the cavern through the floaty bits. Not sexy, though! More like, not quite in the real world and yet alluring …as though she was giving off some kind of primal sexy scent your body had to react to, even while your head was screaming at you to get out of there. And her eyes were just black, like inky pools – not solid like coal but something you'd drown in and never be found again. Like those tar pits you hear of on places like Dartmoor, bottomless and deadly. And the men she touched just seemed to fold up and crumple to the floor."

He stopped to get his breathing under control again. "And then we were running, really running for our lives, and I hear somebody shout, 'Toby, get the lads up, I'll cover your backs,' and then it all went kind of swirly …you know, the way dreams do when they shift. And suddenly I'm face to face with this old man, and I know he's not just old in the normal sense, but ancient, like he's from another time or something. And he's saying to me, 'they don't want you here, but you've got to get your friend out. The sane ones can't protect him for much longer. Hurry up!' And then he was gone and I must have just slept normally. But when I got up this morning I was soaked with sweat, and I feel like I went ten rounds with Mohammed Ali in my sleep. You won't have to struggle to keep up with me today, I might be pushing it to keep up with you."

Stella had by now found the small car park where they were intending to leave the car, and pulled in at the entrance, so she turned to him and said,

"That sounds very like what I experienced last night in the pub. It was like someone was trying to warn me off, but your ancient mariner bloke is saying hurry up? That's very bizarre."

"What colour were the faces you saw?"

"*Hmm*, I'd say it was the same face twice, and it was definitely white. Why?"

"Well telling you about this now, it comes to me that the ones who did the hacking down of our men were the ones who were grey, not white."

"What? Like they were heading for the 'dark side', you mean?"

"Well not to go too Star Wars on you, but yes, that's the best description of the woman, because God, did she ever feel evil!" He stopped and scruffed his short hair as if to sort the thoughts out. "I know this probably sounds really barmy, but despite just saying she was as close to evil personified as I've ever encountered, there's something at gut level that's saying to me that she's been driven there ...driven to it, that she wasn't always like that."

If she hadn't had her own experience of a warning, Stella would have thought that coming back out into the wilds had triggered some sort of PTSD in Bob, but however utterly barmy it all might have sounded to someone else, here and now she totally believed him.

And looking at him, Stella was worried, because he already looked knackered. What was going to happen if they got up to this place and they really needed to help someone? It wasn't in their plans to have to leave Bob there with them while she went for help because he'd collapsed, too.

Luckily part of the decision was made for them at the car park. It was another bright morning, and clearly several other walkers had thought to make the best of a nice weekend, because the car park was already full.

"Well that settles it," Stella declared firmly. "We're going to have to take the car as far up the road as we can.

Yet what surprised her was the way that there were clear signs of heavy vehicles also having come up this tiny road.

"Let me have a look at them," Bob demanded, and got out of the car to inspect some deep treads in the mud where one of them had gone right to the very edge of the roadway, presumably to allow something else to come past. "These are army trucks!" he declared. "No doubt about it. I've seen enough of them in my time. This isn't a local farmer's tractor or trailer."

Finding such a positive clue seemed to perk him up more than anything, and when the proper surfaced road ran out, and they tucked the car into a hedge and got their packs out, he was his old energetic self. What was rather disappointing was to find that the woods around the small Llyn Cwm-mynach at the top of the track were owned by the Woodland Trust, and that there were other walkers ahead of them doing the loop around the lake.

"They'd never do something in an area this well tramped over, surely?" Stella said in disbelief, but Bob was examining tyre tracks again.

"Oh they came this way," he said with more assurance than Stella felt. He stabbed a finger northwards. "They carried on on this track and out beyond the woods onto open ground!"

Walking on, they exchanged pleasantries with the various other walkers they encountered, but felt rather relieved when those petered out as the woodland ended. They had come out onto very exposed open land. Gone were the well-tended arable fields and pretty woodlands of yesterday, and instead they were into a landscape of thin, wind-ravaged pasture and stark, knotty crags. This was definitely a place you wouldn't want to lose your way in, and yet Stella could see that it could be all too easy to go astray. The crags off to their right looked much the same no matter how far they walked on, so you could be anywhere within a mile and not have a clue as to your precise position. No doubt GPS would help, but this would still be the kind of terrain where you would be relying on the Mountain Rescue teams if you had an accident.

And that made her think all over again about the men lying in the ward back in Birmingham. If they'd come to grief up here they should have been airlifted off. There was no way you'd get an ambulance up here. So if Toby was right, and the first stage of his journey to Selly Oak had been by ambulance, then how on earth had they got to one?

"I agree," Bob said, bringing her out of her thoughts.

"Eh?"

"You just said, 'you'd never get an ambulance up here,' and I agree. I'm guessing you were thinking about what Toby said?"

"Yes, I was. Hell's teeth, Bob, we might be following army truck tracks, but a modern ambulance is a bit lower to the ground than one of them. They'd be ripping the guts out of the underneath going over some of these boulders that are in the way. They'd no more make it over this ground than my Renault would."

"No question of that. I was wondering whether to tell you that in case it upset you to think of how long the lads might have gone without help, but since you've worked it out for yourself, Christ, that's worrying, isn't it? My gut's all in knots just thinking of my Josh maybe having to carry a mate over this while he was hurt himself, because I can't see any other way that they'd have got out."

"Do you think that maybe some member of the public phoned for the ambulance?" Stella wondered, as they paused for a moment to check the map. "That would make a bit more sense of things, wouldn't it?"

"What, you mean if they managed to stumble down to a more trafficked road?"

"Yes. Well that would explain some of what's been just bits and pieces so far. What if it was just normal paramedics who realised that they had something terribly serious on their hands, and it was them who called for an army helicopter?"

Bob turned to look at her aghast. "Oh shit! Now there's a thought. That would actually explain so much, wouldn't it?"

Stella nodded. "So the paramedics call it in, and they get instructions from some army medic – who in his or her defence, may only have had the bullshit the army got fed as information on where our guys had been. But it's the paramedics who are the ones who administer the drugs, which is why the records all looked kosher enough to deceive the hospital staff. That was something that had been niggling away at me ever since I spoke to that sister, you know. She was no fool, so how had she and the others been so taken in in the first place? Do you see? It makes no sense unless the info they had as the lads got admitted came from a reputable source – i.e. the paramedics."

Bob had been nodding along at every step of her reasoning, and now gave her a hug, or as best he could with her rucksack still on. "Bloody hell, Stella, you've got it!" he declared triumphantly. "And of course, if the paramedics thought the lads had just been on some day exercise in the forest that had gone wrong, they might have genuinely thought that these were injuries only a few hours old. They wouldn't know the difference between wounds – especially not the medics who work out here. The big city paramedics no doubt know all about different kinds of knife wounds and even bullet wounds, but the worst they probably see out here is the odd shotgun accident."

"And they might even have thought that the hallucinations stemmed from the lads having some drug they shouldn't have had on them, and been taking it for a lark. It's hardly as though the army is insulated against drug abuse, is it? I mean, you don't want to think of someone in charge of a serious bit of weaponry being off his head on something, but I bet it's happened at some point. And if that got backed up by some army person on the end of their call for help looking at the list of substances a soldier might have come into contact with, and having to make a selection based just on what they were being told down the phone, you can understand how everything descended into such a mire of misinformation. Neither they nor the paramedics are to blame. They were just doing the best they could with what they'd got."

Bob's frown was back as he announced, "I am so going to enjoy ripping some tosser a new arsehole over this! Because when I find the blame-shifting bastard who's actually responsible for this, they're going to wish they'd never been born!"

Stella managed a thin-lipped smile as she patted his arm and said, "Well I'll be there holding your coat for you, and so, I suspect, will Ade."

Bob huffed, exhaling his anger with his breath. "Thanks! ...But we still have to find proof of where they were. Let's get cracking again. Come on, Ivan! Leave that stick and get your paws working!"

They shortly reached a point where even the rough track petered out, but off to one side they could see the remains of what had probably been old sheep pens, and it was there that they found the evidence of the trucks having turned around to head back down the valley.

"This is encouraging," Bob said. "This looks like it might have been the drop point for any equipment that got brought in, like that welding gear Karl talked about. He said it took a while to get to them – well that's pretty understandable if it had to be brought up to here, and then they had to come out and fetch it."

They crossed a small stream and made their way across the open scrub to the pens. The first ones showed no signs of having been disturbed in any way, but they tramped over to inspect the ones closer to the small crags, and it was as they rounded the first rocky face and saw the next, that they found the right pen. Not only had what stunted grass there was been flattened, as if something heavy had crushed it, but there were pegs left lying in the now yellowing grass, as if a tarpaulin had been pegged into the ground to cover something.

Feeling excitement rising at the prospect of being on the right trail, they began scouting around the area, and it was Bob who turned over an old piece of metal and called across to Stella,

"What was the name of that mine we're looking for?"

"Blaen-y-mynach."

"Think we found it, then!" and he held up what had once been a sign. It was rusty and pitted, but it was still possible to see the white lettering that had said Blaen-y-mynach, and with 'Keep Out' in red beneath it.

"Good grief! I wonder if these weren't so much sheep pens as mine stores and things? Okay, those ones back over closer to the track were pens, but even now these walls are a bit high for pens, aren't they?"

Bob was slowly turning around, scanning the countryside. "This has to have been a mine, because I can't see anything that looks like it was ever once a quarry, however small and returned to nature."

Stella shielded her eyes and squinted southwards into the sun which was managing a few beams through the clouds. "That looks like a path over there, going between the rocks. Maybe that's where it is?"

They followed the narrow track and were rewarded with the sight of some long-abandoned chunks of rusting metal beneath the plant-life, which had taken advantage of the sheltered spot and was burgeoning more than out on the exposed heath. And then suddenly, almost hidden by another natural crevice, they saw the mine opening. Yet this time the mine had been well and truly sealed off. Planks of wood had been nailed across its opening, and by the moss growing on them, this wasn't a new job. Indeed the green of the moss was one of the reasons they'd had such a hard time spotting it.

Even so, Bob went over and gave a few experimental tugs on the timbers. "It could just be some very clever camouflage," he explained, but it was clear that they weren't.

"Damn!" Stella muttered. "I was so sure this would be the place."

"Hey, don't get discouraged. We have to be close. I'm convinced that we found the drop-zone for supplies and stuff back there, so wherever they went to, it won't be far from here. You said there were two mines up here. What's the other one?"

Stella retrieved her piece of paper from her jacket pocket. "Bwlch-y-groes-ddu, but don't bother looking for it on the map. I've been over it with a magnifying glass at home, and I can't spot it."

"No clue in the name?"

She waved a hand around at the landscape. "Do you see anything that looks like it might be called Black Cross Gap? Or to be a bit more literal, Gap of the Black Cross."

Bob involuntarily shivered. "What a bloody creepy name to give a place!"

"Isn't it. ...Makes me wonder whether some old chapel minister came up here and found more than he bargained for?"

Chapter 18

Saturday

Studying the map, they decided to head westwards. That was taking them back in the direction of the main Mawddach valley, and they both agreed that that made sense.

"See, down here, there's an old gold mine," Stella told Bob, pointing at an area within the trees near to the Tyn-y-groes Hotel, "but that's too much of a tourist thing to be what we're after. Same reference to a cross, though, which was why I thought there was a chance that Bwlch-y-groes-ddu might be in the vicinity, if not right on top of it."

"Sound reasoning, let's have a go."

As they walked over the undulating terrain they realized that there were crags up ahead. Even better, with the sun still not yet having come around into the west, the crags were in shadow and looked distinctly black.

"Your instincts have been right," Bob praised Stella. "I doubt the locals were that literal when they gave places names. Just something looking blackish for most of the day would probably do. And that looks definitely black to me."

"Yes, but how close are we to the start of the National Trust land?" Stella fretted. "It has to be getting close."

Unsurprisingly, Bob had GPS on his phone, and so they were able to locate their position quite accurately.

"Actually we're still good for at least another half mile on the flat," he reassured her. "The main boundary doesn't kick in until up on the top of those crags. I can't imagine many tourists come that far, much less scramble down those rocks."

They were that busy looking at the crags that they almost didn't spot the house. There had been one or two more trees dotted around the place now, so they hadn't registered the trio of big old oaks as anything abnormal, and it was Ivan suddenly diving across to them and barking furiously that made them stop and head that way.

"Well I'll be damned!" Stella gasped, as in the shade of the trees they suddenly came across a much newer chain-link fence with large 'Keep Out' notices attached to it. "Clever lad, Ivan! Extra biscuits for you!"

"Talking of biscuits," Bob said, shrugging his pack off, "now might be the right moment to stop and have something to eat. We don't know what we're going to find in there, so let's take the chance and refuel."

They found a spot that was reasonably out of the wind and sat down to eat sandwiches and have a mug of tea each from the flask, but surprisingly Ivan wasn't interested in his dog biscuits, and even turned his nose up when Stella offered him a piece of ham.

"Oh, I don't like this," she said worriedly to Bob. "He never refuses food. God, I hope he hasn't sensed something like at that other mine."

And then the wind shifted, swirled a bit and the smell hit them.

"Shit! Whatever's that?" Stella gasped, gagging.

"Dead bodies," Bob said softly, and when Stella looked at him he'd gone pale. "I'm not sure you should go in there, Stella. I've seen some grim sights in my time, but it might really upset you."

She reached across and firmly took hold of his arm. "Now you listen to me, Bob Ashford! Don't you go getting all heroic on me! I volunteered for this, remember? I'll take heed of your warnings if there's something specific in there that you think is dangerous. But if you think I'm sitting out here with Ivan howling his head off, and gnawing my fingernails down to the quicks while you go in there alone, you've got another thing coming."

He smiled wanly at her. "You've got a lot of guts, lass. But be warned, if those bodies have been in there for the thick end of three weeks, it's not going to be pleasant. I don't want to make you throw up your lunch before we even get in there, because this won't be like what you see of bodies on TV shows.

"By this time they're going to have bloated up and things like the blood will have already begun to decompose. Depending on how warm it is where we find them, things like their nails and teeth will have started to fall out, and don't even ask me about things like eyes and tongues. I've seen old bodies in war zones, so although I'm not exactly keen to see them again, it's not going to give me any more nightmares than I already have. You, on the other hand, truly have no idea of how horrific this might get, so I'm sorry, I am going to play, as you call it, 'the hero.' You can come in with me, but if I say you stay outside a building, you stay out, okay?"

"Alright." Stella still thought that she might be better equipped than Bob realised. Toby had never spared her a single grisly detail when he'd come home, and her neighbour in one of the flats she had rented later on had died, and it had only been the smell leaking through into Stella's that had alerted anyone. She had gone in with the paramedics and police, and though they'd tried to shield her from the view, she'd seen what

Don't Delve Too Deep

old Mr Tomlinson had been like. That had been the point when she had quite firmly decided on cremation when her time came, and understood why her dad hadn't wanted a burial. However, this wasn't the time to argue with Bob over it, not least because she had a shrewd idea that he was capable of tying her up and leaving her outside if he thought it was to protect her.

Nonetheless, she put Ivan on his leash and let Bob lead the way in, after he'd cut his way in through the fence with cutters produced from his rucksack, and which looked like they might be army issue. They'd gone a little way around to the one side from where the obvious view of the house was, not wanting to encourage others to wander in in their wake – after all, they had no idea how dangerous the mine itself might be, and they had no wish to be the cause of someone else's misadventure.

And so they came to what had probably been the mine manager's house from its side. It was a gloomy, forbidding old pile, double-fronted and rising to two floors with attic windows just visible, no doubt where in the past a couple of poor local lasses had frozen during the Welsh winters, while they did the rough work for the lady of the house. It wasn't that grand, just a standard detached house, but it stood in stark contrast to the rows of workers' terraces they had seen elsewhere. If it wasn't wealthy on the wider scale, it had been impressive enough for the locals in its heyday, but its glory had long since faded. As Karl had described, the windows were filthy and covered in the muck of ages, except for a couple of panes which had to be the ones Toby and his men had started to clean.

Bob gestured for Stella to stay back as he went and stood on tiptoes to see in through them. By the way he went pale and then turned to lean against the wall with his eyes closed, it was clear that something deeply unpleasant was inside.

"Bodies?" Stella guessed.

He nodded, then went and rummaged in his pack. He pulled out a cotton neckerchief and a small bottle of tea-tree oil, which he liberally dropped onto the scarf before tying it over his nose and mouth. Before he could say anything Stella had held up her hand,

"I know. I stay here."

"Have you got any of those poop-bags on you? If the bodies have dog tags on them, I'll retrieve them, but we want each one to go in one separately in case there's evidence on them."

"Here, have a bundle. They're the disinfected ones, but that can't be helped. I just hope they don't destroy any evidence."

She and Ivan watched as Bob opened the door and went in. It was telling, she thought, that it wasn't locked, because surely when this was abandoned, the house would have been properly secured? Certainly Ivan had begun a soft whining as Bob disappeared from view, as if he was worried what might happen to him.

"Steady, boy, he's only gone into the house," she consoled him, but knew that Ivan's keen sense of smell must be being almost overwhelmed by the stench of the bodies. No wonder he was distressed.

It didn't take long for Bob to reappear, pale and grim. "Their tags have gone," he said, "and there are five of them in there, so I'm thinking these must be the men who've been confirmed as dead."

Stella felt the tears coming as she realised that one of them must be Little Andy. Damn, she hadn't meant to go all weepy at the first encounter, but it was hard not to when it was someone you'd counted as a friend, albeit years ago.

"At least Wendy and the others will have their proper funeral," she managed to wring out in between snuffling into her tissues. "Where were they? In the bedrooms? Was that their dormitory down there? Karl said the roof leaked."

"No, on the floor in the main room. Looks like they got carried in there and then left."

"Oh for God's sake!"

Bob put his arm around her shoulder. "That might not have been Hardy's doing. It could have been the wounded lads making a grim decision. If they were having to carry one another out, then those already dead would've had to be left."

Stella pulled herself together. "Yes, of course they would. How daft of me not to think of that. And if they were already dead by the time they got brought up to the surface, then that was probably the only option. Sorry, Bob, I didn't mean to be such a girl about it."

"Bloody hell, Stella, I've known big tough blokes take the death of friends harder. You're doing amazingly well!"

"Right, then, let's see what else there is around here," she said with a watery smile at him, and a last blow into her tissues. "If your night-time visitor said that we need to hurry, he surely couldn't have meant the bodies. They can't be pleasant to be around if he's actually near here, but by now there's a limit to how much worse they can get. Time can't be a factor for them, so who is it for?"

They began to search the area around the house, finding that within the confines of the chain-link fence that there were several other buildings with the tin roofs Karl had described, and also the static caravans he'd thought the boffins had been living in. None of the old buildings had ever been anything special, with low roofs and small windows, and it was easy to see why they hadn't been visible from the outside world when they hardly rose higher than some of the scrubby bushes beyond the fence. The new tin for the roofs had also been sprayed a camouflage-green colour, presumably so that they wouldn't be obvious from the air, and Stella thought that somebody had gone to a lot of trouble to keep this place hidden.

This time Bob was quite happy for Stella to come in with him and search, and together they went through the half-dozen vans with Ivan almost glued to their heels. They found nothing of any great help, but it was clear that the boffins had exited in a hurry. Various personal bits and pieces, like paperback novels and cans of food, had been left behind, including a bottle of Highland Park malt whisky, and surely no-one would have left that unless they'd had little choice?

What Bob did discover were the three lockers which looked as though forced entry had been attempted.

"That certainly validates Karl's story," Bob declared. "He couldn't possibly have known about these unless he'd either witnessed them himself, or talked to men who had."

"And just like he said, there's no sign of a phone connection to the outside world," Stella said, as they stood on the step of the last van looking across to the other huts, cramped together within the compound. "Look at it, Bob, there's not a decent aerial anywhere here. They had to have been relying on satellite connections because there's nothing else here." She looked at her mobile. "Not a bloody whisker of a signal up here, we must be miles from the nearest mast. How about you?"

He fished out his phone and checked. "Nothing on the regular signal, only the GPS is working." Then he growled in disgust. "So that's another story that's right. Only Hardy had access to the outside world, and that must have been on a satellite link, not an ordinary network. I'm on Vodaphone, what about you?"

"EE. So that's the two biggest networks in the UK ruled out, and I can't imagine that the others would be faring any better up here in the back of beyond. Jeez, Bob, those poor lads! Even if they found their mobiles, they wouldn't have been any good!"

"Fucking disgusting!" he growled. "The more I'm seeing, the more grateful I am that my boy made it out at all!"

They went and inspected the huts, but found little more than basic equipment had been left behind.

"God rot the bastards," Bob swore savagely, "but it looks like somebody came back up here and took away anything of value. Because I can't believe that there was only this rubbish kit up here. Where's the scientific stuff, eh? Karl's not such an idiot that he wouldn't have known what serious scientists might use. Granted, you wouldn't know which specialist bit of kit did what, but this here is the kind of stuff you could pick up from any half decent computer store.

"I can't believe that the boffins only used this – no way! There had to be more than this. So where's it gone? 'Cause you'll never convince me that the local bad lads came up and scavenged it! They wouldn't know what half of it did. Anyway, they'd have taken everything. But that means that some bastard came here and left our lads to bloody rot!"

Stella was with him all the way, her anger threatening to get the better of her at the thought of Little Andy being left up here, never to be found if it wasn't for them. Who could do such a thing? Who thought more of a bit of computer equipment than a human life? Or if not actually a life, than of the families left behind whose loved ones had died in this stupid, meaningless experiment?

"I tell you something else, Bob," she found herself hissing in fury. "When did those boffins leave, eh? Was it after our lads? Because if so, I shall have a few choice words to exchange with them when we catch up with them. Why aren't there some of them in the hospital alongside Josh and Toby? Did they not help to carry them out? Did they sit quivering in these caravans not daring to come out when whatever it was went wrong?

"It never occurred to me until now, but none of them are in Selly Oak, are they? Or have I missed something? Because if they had come in with the lads, as part of the same military operation, surely they should have been on the same wards?"

"Holy crap, I hadn't got that far, being so wrapped up with Josh and his mates, but you're right, at least one or two of them should have been there if they went to try and help our lads. How did I not see that?"

"Well if this had been just some other mission you'd been on, you probably would have," Stella consoled him. "But this involved your son. That was bound to throw you off your game. ...You wouldn't be much of a dad if it didn't."

He smiled faintly. "Thanks for that, but I'm still going to feel guilty that I didn't ask that question a lot longer ago. ...What's with Ivan, now?"

The big lurcher was staring fixedly in one direction, his tail clamped hard between his legs in a sign of distress, and his ears flat against his head. Something was really upsetting him, and this time both Stella and Bob took notice.

"What's over there, old lad?" Bob asked gently, stroking Ivan's head, in reply to which he got a whiffle of distress. "Stay here, Stella, he could be picking up on something dangerous."

Dumping his bag onto the ground, Bob dug into it, and to Stella's dismay came out with a gun.

"What in God's name is that, Bob?"

He looked up. "It's a SIG Sauer P226. Probably means bugger all to you, but it's the weapon I'm most used to other than a sniper rifle." He grimaced. "I don't know why, but once I'd come out of the forces I felt naked and exposed without one close to hand. That wasn't machismo, or anything. It was more that I knew how many evil little shits I'd pissed off over the years, and I knew that me being out of the army wouldn't stop any one of them coming after me if they had the chance – or if not them personally, then some other lunatic member of their family out for revenge.

"And I'm sorry, but I wasn't about to leave the safety of my family in the hands of some local plod who'd be more likely to end up drilled full of holes on the floor than saving Soph or Deb. So I arranged to get a 'clean' one on the black market. You don't spend as long as I did fighting terrorism without knowing certain ways and means of getting what you need in an emergency – except this time I intended to have it already at hand, if and when that emergency came around."

Stella swallowed hard, but admitted, "I can see why you would feel like that. I'm just not used to guns of any sort." Then a thought came to her. "Was that what you meant by something you wouldn't want going into the local landfill site?"

"Yes."

"Oh. ...Well I can see why you wouldn't."

He pulled out what she supposed was a magazine of bullets and clipped it in. If anything got in his way with that, Stella didn't give much for their chances of survival. Bob wasn't the bragging sort, but she knew in her soul that he would be a good shot and very efficient in his use of the weapon. He wouldn't use it unless he had to, but when he did, something or someone was going to go down and stay there.

"Be careful," she warned him, holding on to Ivan, and together they watched him go across the compound towards where Ivan was staring. He didn't go straight across, but rather skirmished around the perimeter, pausing to check behind every wall and building that there was nobody lurking behind it who might jump out at him. There was no showing off going on, every movement was economical; every glance around a corner, every time he brought the gun up to bear, was done with professional calm, and somehow that made it all the more scary and alarming. It was a stark contrast to the kind of thing Stella had seen on film in that there was almost a lack of drama about the whole thing. And yet there was a chilling deadliness about Bob. He wasn't quite six feet tall, and didn't have single tattoo as far as she knew, but she knew beyond a shadow of a doubt that he would have chewed up some heavily muscled, tattoo-covered thug and spat him out as a pre-breakfast warm-up without even breaking into a sweat.

As Bob reached the other side of the open area she saw him stop in his tracks, then heard him call out,

"Come out with your hands up! Don't think you can take me. I'm armed and I won't hesitate to shoot."

Yet the man who came out of the shadows had Stella gasping. This had to be the old man Karl had talked about, but he wasn't just old, he looked positively ancient, and yet he was also far more sprightly than he had any right to be.

"Ah, you're here!" Stella heard him say in the deep silence that pervaded the place. "Blessed be! You're here in time."

Chapter 19

Saturday

"In time?" Stella heard Bob challenge the old man. "In time for what?"

"You have to help me get him out," the old man said.

"Christ! You mean someone's still alive down there?" Bob exclaimed, even as Stella and Ivan went racing across to join him.

"Yes, I don't know why he didn't fall prey to her charm, but he didn't, and that saved him. She uses it to drive men insane."

"Who does?" Bob demanded sharply.

"The queen."

Stella moved to face him. "What queen? Queen of where, of what?"

The old boy shook his head sadly. "The queen of Trawsfynedd – well they used to call it something else in the days when it was undisturbed by people, but that's the name it goes by now. All of this region was her kingdom. There were others of their kind to the north in the big mountains, and further south, but she ruled from the sacred lake to the bald mountain, the one you call Cadair Idris."

"But who are 'they'?" Stella asked.

"The Fae. Elves you might call them, but not the fairy folk my old mother used to talk about, the wee folk. The ones she'd leave a saucer of milk out for, or what you see in books with wings and things. These are the kingly ones, the ones who, back in the days when they were supremely powerful, rode abroad defending the land itself from anything evil. As a young man I was fascinated with them. Read everything I could about them, never for a moment thinking that I might meet them one day. They're the ones people wrote of as the seelie and unseelie courts, as if they were two totally different things — the white elves and the dark ones. But they're not. They're so attached to the land that they change with the seasons. In the winter they cleared the dead wood away — both in plants and in living creatures. They cleared the sick and the weak so that come the spring the land could flourish and grow strong again."

"All sounds a bit bloody Tolkien for my liking," Bob grunted, but Stella said,

"No, it's the other way around, Bob. Tolkien used the old legends. If you've ever been up to Perthshire, that big mountain that's up there, Schiehallion, has its own legends. The name apparently translates from the Celtic as 'the hill of the fae or fairies of Caledonia.' It's believed to be the mystical heart of that area, so I find nothing odd in Cadair Idris filling much the same role down here. Just because it's not so embedded in the place name doesn't preclude some local legends."

She was hoping that Bob would take her hint over this, because she didn't want to insult or antagonise this old boy if he knew where a survivor was. Luckily he caught her eye and responded.

"Okay," he said with a cynical sigh, "so you've got this elf queen. Why is she so anti-men?"

Now the old man looked incredibly sad. "It was the digging that started it," he began. "The men of my grandfather and great-grandfather's generations. While we stayed up above, they didn't particularly like what we did, how we destroyed the trees and stripped the earth, but they left us alone unless we crossed their paths by accident. Then woe betide you, you'd be in danger! That's where legends of things like the Wild Hunt come from, because those caught by the Fae never returned to tell their side of things, and it was only those who saw their passing and were frightened half to death who lived to recount what they'd seen.

"Once we started digging down into the deeps, though, they became worried. Ancient things dwell down there, they've told me. Things that shouldn't be disturbed. And they feared that in our greed we would go deeper and deeper until we reached the flames."

"Ah, the earth's core," Stella breathed softly to Bob. "Yes, you could understand why they'd fear tapping into that. They wouldn't necessarily understand magma, given that we've had no active volcanoes in these isles in millennia, but they might have a racial memory of it."

"They're old," the ancient gatekeeper was continuing, "as old as the hills themselves in some cases. Beside them I'm a mere child. And because of that age, the changes have come so very fast for them. What have been many generations for us were the merest blink of an eye to them. That's why they can't adapt, it's too much all at once, and that's where the hatred set in."

"So where do you fit in?" Bob demanded. "If you're intending to lead us down into the mine, I'd like to know who my guide is."

The old man sighed, but seemed to recognise that this man, who still held a gun to his face without any sign of relaxing his guard, was going to take more convincing.

"My name is Emrys ap Siôn, and you'll have to go a long way back to find any record of me. My great-grandfather, Rhys ap Gryffydd, was one of the very first men to put a pick into these hills. He worked the slate, see? And twenty years later, my father Siôn ap Rhys, joined him. And for the first few decades all was well. We worked the slate, bringing it up to the surface where the men who could split it did their work. *Duw*, they were craftsmen! One wrong tap of the hammer and the whole piece could shatter in your hands, but those men, ah, they could just give a little tap, and a whole sheet of slate would shear away as smooth as you like."

Old Emrys heaved a sad sigh. "All gone now, though, all gone. ...We'd worked as far as we could towards the Mawddach, but the quality was declining. So Iorweth Beddus, the mine manager, tells us that the owners want us to try other seams." He shook his head. "Folly. Complete and utter folly. We never even saw those men, the ones who condemned us to a terrible fate. No doubt they died in their fancy homes at a great age, never having given the likes of us a single thought. ...They would have if they'd seen what we saw, oh yes, they would then! She came. She came and she cursed every man, but Beddus most of all."

He turned and nodded to the house. "That was Beddus' house, much good it did him. He didn't die down in the mine like my family, but there was a curse on his family ever after. I don't think a single one escaped it. All of his sons died horrible lingering deaths. The same disease as the old queen's grandson, I was told — you know, the one whose father was the Tsar. Or has so long passed by that you don't recall him? I lose track of it down below."

"Are you talking about Tsar Nicholas and the Russian Revolution?" Stella asked. "It was his son who had haemophilia. It got handed down through the family."

Old Emrys stared off into the distance. "I believe that's what they called it, yes, that was it." Then his rheumy eyes suddenly fixed on Stella as he added, "But there was none of that in Myfanwy Morgan's family — that was Beddus' wife — none at all. All of her brothers were fine strapping lads. And none of Beddus' sisters' boys ever had it, only the direct line from him. Not that the local doctor had much of a clue. Not exactly Harley Street was Huw Gregory. He just called it the bleeding sickness, and it was only after they were all long gone, and someone dropped a newspaper up here, that I read about the Tsar and his son."

"How long have you been here?" Stella asked in amazement. "Who was on the throne when you were a boy?"

"Oh, that'd be the old queen — not that she was anything like as old as the queen below, but she would be queen for a long time."

"Victoria?"

"Aye, that was her. And her son was king the last time I came up onto the surface much. There used to be a shepherd who'd come and talk to me, bring me the news. But I watched him growing old and gnarled, and then he stopped coming altogether, while I felt not much older than I'd been when I first met him." He paused and then added, "I was born the year her father came to the throne, you know. My mother wanted to call me William after him, but my father said no, I was to have a proper Welsh name, so Emrys I am."

"How long ago was that," Bob asked Stella in an aside. "My history's crap where kings are concerned."

Stella had been doing some rapid memory searching even as Emrys had been talking, and answered softly, "Something like the early 1830s, I think. I can remember that Victoria came to the throne in 1837, and King William was her uncle, not her father — he'd died before that or he would have inherited instead of her. But given that Emrys probably only went to a local school until he was about eleven, if he was lucky enough to go at all, I'd not quibble over that."

Emrys was staring out at the hillside, as if looking out on a world that no longer existed.

"You must have been terribly lonely," Stella said sympathetically. She wasn't quite ready to believe that this man was the best part of a hundred and eighty-five years old, but whoever he was, he must have suffered terrible psychological trauma if he'd lived here alone for years in the dark.

Emrys nodded. "Terrible. Oh the elves are alright once you get to know them, but they're a bit high and mighty for the likes of me. And they go off into their dreaming, lost to the world for years on end. There are always some of them keeping watch, of course, some better than others for company. They keep me like you keep your lovely dog, there. I'm their watch dog, the human face who can be sent up to warn off strangers. And too much time had passed up here by the time I realised it was moving far slower for me down there. Everyone I'd known was already long gone, so if I'd escaped, who would I have gone to?"

He cuffed a tear from his eye. "I didn't know whether to cry for joy or for fear of what might happen when those new lads appeared. I offered them my services, said my father had worked the mine and that I knew all the secret ways down there, which was all true, just a much longer time ago than they thought. ...It was such a relief to talk to my own kind again, see? To hear those lads talking of their girlfriends and wives, of normal things. The one I didn't like. He seemed to be in charge. Never came down below, not even when things went ...when thi..." He cuffed more tears away. "When she came. When it all went wrong. ...So arrogant he was. I heard his voice on one of those things they talked into in their hands. Told them to keep going, not to stop. What a bloody fool!"

"Yes he was," Bob agreed, relaxing a little.

"I warned them, you know?" Emrys told him. "I told them, 'don't go that way, it's dangerous,' and they didn't, the men didn't, …at least not until he made them. If they'd stayed just in the original mine they might have been alright. But maybe not. Whatever they were doing, she could sense it, you know. It called to her from afar. The elves who were with me didn't call her, she just came."

Bob coughed politely. "Fascinating though this is, you said that there were men down below? How many are alive? And can I go down and get them?"

"Oh yes," Emrys said positively. "She's gone again for now. As long as you don't make a big noise, you'll be fine."

"What about me?" Stella asked and got a black look from Bob even as she queried, "will I be alright down there?"

"Oh I would think so," Emrys said, giving her a smile, but it faded fast. "Anyway, it'll take two of you to get them up to the surface, not a one man job, and I'm too old to be of much help."

With Ivan having settled down now that he'd had chance to sniff at Emrys, Stella tethered him once more to a chunk of old equipment and dumped her pack beside him. "You be a good boy and stay," she told him, giving him a hug and making sure his portable water-bowl was filled.

"Put a waterproof on," Bob told her. "Some of these underground places drip like mad, and it'll be colder down there than up here on the surface."

With flashlights in hand and spare ones tucked into their waterproofs, Stella and Bob followed Emrys into the mouth of the mine. As with the one they'd explored, there was an old railway track leading into the deeps, and for a short while it was easy walking. However, they soon came to what was clearly a worked cavern off which several tunnels ran, but none of them were where Emrys was headed. Instead, he went to where some steps had been roughly hewn into the rock. A new rope handrail had been attached with modern ringbolts, speaking of this being the way the army men had come, making Bob turn and give Stella a surprised look over his shoulder. Apparently he hadn't expected Emrys to lead them so directly.

"Watch your step," Emrys warned. "These steps get a bit slippery with the wet."

Their descent was quite short, and they came to another chamber, but clearly the seam of slate had descended further, because it was possible to see even by just their lights that attempts had been made to go deeper. This time, though, the miners must have given up on the hard work of cutting steps, and there was a solid modern ladder waiting at the top to be lowered down.

"How did you get up to us, then?" Bob asked suspiciously, as he and Stella extended it to its full length and manhandled it into place to lower it down.

"I know the back ways," Emrys said.

"So couldn't you have brought the lads up that way?" Bob's internal ambush warnings were sounding loudly in his head.

Yet Emrys shook his head mournfully, "No, *ffrind*, I couldn't. For one, that would have meant me taking them deeper into Her territory, and She would have sensed them passing their warnings – don't ask me how they work, but work they do. I just see crystals in the rock. And anyway I'm smaller than your friends." That was true, Stella realised, he was shorter even than her and wiry, not stout. "There are gaps I can just about get through, but they wouldn't have. I wish it could have been that simple."

He paused and then seemed to make up his mind to show them something. "I've been with them so long I've started to become like them. I can touch you," and he reached out and put his hand on Stella's and Bob's. It was cold to the touch, too cold. "But if I try too hard..." and he tried to grip the ladder.

To their shock his hand seemed to sink into the metal.

"I've been able to handle the odd loaf of bread, or some of the cans of food, as long as they're light," he confessed, "but when the others came and pulled this ladder up, I couldn't move it back."

"Woah! Hold on a moment!" Bob exclaimed, straightening up and glaring down at Emrys. "What others? You didn't mention them! Who? Who came?"

"More men. They came about a day after it all happened. I tried to call to them, but they had guns and they shot at me. I kept calling to them that there were men down below, but all they did was come and take the machines away. They never came back."

"The fucking bastards!" Bob fumed. "So we were right! Somebody did come for the technical stuff!"

"And they left men to die." Stella choked on the words. "Didn't they even come here to check, Emrys?"

"They came to this ladder. I think one went down it. I can't get to the intermediate level beneath this one, you see. But the one called Dafydd said the ladder had gone from the bottom level when I found him, and when I went to look I couldn't see it either."

"Dafydd?" Stella squeaked. "Dav survived? Is he the one you're talking about being down there?"

Emrys had barely got the word 'yes' out than Stella had swung her leg onto the ladder and began a rapid descent.

"Oh fucking marvellous!" Bob groaned. "I'll bloody have your guts, mate, if she comes to any harm!"

He was swinging himself onto the ladder as Emrys's reply of, "No she won't!" came to him, and he realised that the little man was scurrying off down a tunnel as fast as his bent old legs would carry him.

"Oi! Where are you off to?" he called after him, but by then Emrys had vanished.

"What a cluster-fuck!" Bob muttered darkly, going down the ladder as fast as he could, already hearing Stella calling,

"Dav! Dav!" and the sound of her feet almost running, which meant she had already reached the bottom of the ladder.

With the Sig braced on the wrist of his hand holding the flashlight, Bob moved with speed after Stella, the beam of light seeking out every hollow and crack in the walls where someone might be waiting in ambush.

"Stella, wait!" he yelled a couple of times, hoping and praying that she was going in the right direction, given that they'd come down onto a tunnel which ran in two ways from the ladder's base.

At first he got no answer, and his pulse was starting to jitter. It was one thing going into enemy territory with his highly trained team-mates, another heading into the unknown with a feisty school teacher who hadn't a clue about how fast things could go base up. Then he saw the light. Stella seemed to have propped the flashlight against something so that it was shining onto the roof of the tunnel and cast an eerie glow around her. She was struggling to move something, and as Bob got closer he saw it was another ladder.

"Don't even do that to me again!" he remonstrated with her as he caught her up. "Bloody hell, woman, you nearly gave me a heart attack running off like that!"

Stella turned wide eyes in a face that didn't just look pale because of the bluish light of the torch. "But I heard him, Bob! I'm sure I heard him – Dav!"

"Sodding hell," Bob growled under his breath, realising that there'd be no point in telling her that what she'd probably heard was an echo of her own voice. The only way to get Stella back up to the surface was to go with her, and find whatever was down there. But in his heart of hearts, Bob was sure that they'd find only corpses, and please God they'd be less decayed than the ones up above, because if they were like those, Stella would be having nightmares for months.

Together they heaved the ladder down, Bob being surprised that at its full extent it was more than long enough to reach the bottom this time. If the first ladder had only just safely reached, this time the top was poking up high enough to nearly reach the top of the tunnel.

"Right! I'm going down first this time!" he told Stella firmly, and precluded any argument by swinging out onto it before she could beat him to it.

He'd hoped in vain that she would wait until he was fully down before following him, but at least he'd had the chance to scan the tunnel before she reached the bottom rungs. Yet now they could have done with Emrys to guide them. Once again there were modern ropes bolted to the cave walls, but they ran off in two directions, and with no way of telling which was the one they wanted.

As Stella drew in a deep breath to shout, Bob softly hissed, "No! Don't shout! ...Look, Stella, I don't buy into all that bollocks about elves, okay? But there's something dangerous down here that we don't know about, so we proceed with caution, right? And that means no shouting! It could be some wild animal sent a bit loopy by the dark, and if the poor thing's been living off bats and rats it could be bloody hungry by now. We don't want it thinking a new all-you-can-eat buffet just landed on its doorstep."

"Animal? Like what? Come on, Bob, what could do that much damage?"

"Have you never seen a big old boar badger? The ones you see as road-kill in the gutters are usually that year's cubs, you know, the ones that haven't learned about traffic in time. The old males are three times that size if not more, and they're bloody powerful. They can break a fence with ease.

"I watched one do it once when we were holed up watching some bad lads. We were under camouflage netting and had been there for days, so it wasn't bothered by us, but I watched it break into a pretty stout garden shed to get at the fruit that was stored in there. Those big digging claws made short work of pine planks, I can tell you, and there's a damned good reason why badger baiting is outlawed – it's not just for the badgers, but because they can rip the face off a big dog like Ivan with one swipe of those claws. So will you please listen to me and stick behind me with no more shouting?"

Stella realised that she had been pushing Bob's restraint rather too hard. "Sorry, Bob. I just can't bear the thought of someone being down here alone for all that time and maybe hurt."

He reached over and looped an arm around her shoulders to give her a brief hug. "No lass, me neither. But there's a right way and a wrong way to go about searching, and while you're with me we're going to do it the right way, okay?"

"Okay."

He sighed and looked around. "It'd be bloody useful if that Emrys would show up again."

"Did he not follow you? ...Oh, no of course he wouldn't! Silly me! He couldn't have grasped the ladder, could he?"

"No, he couldn't, but the last I saw of him, he was running off down one of the tunnels. I just hope he hasn't led us astray."

"I don't think he has," Stella reassured Bob. "We've found obvious signs of the lads, haven't we? And if Emrys couldn't use the ladder, then you can't think that he somehow undid the bolts the platoon put in and moved the ropes. That wouldn't be possible for him. I bet he doesn't even know how to use most of the kit they had with them."

"That's true," Bob conceded, feeling the threat level dropping by just a whisker.

She was right, that old man all by himself couldn't have shifted things around that much, and if he'd tried, then there'd be holes in the walls where the previous ringbolts had been. He played the light over the walls and was reassured to see that there were no signs of disturbance. Yet there was a wholly new kind of worry niggling away at his senses, because if Emrys was telling the truth – however, that bizarre it might be – then what was he? What had he become? Bob had seen with his own eyes the way the little man's hands had sunk into that metal, the same rungs that not moments later he'd gripped himself and knew they were solid.

So what was Emrys? Some digital projection? And if so, why had someone gone to all the trouble of putting such cutting edge technology down here in a mine where nobody was ever likely to go? Anyway, although Emrys' hand had been too cold for a normal person's, nonetheless, he'd been far too tangible for just some hologram. Bob had seen enough proper holograms – as opposed to Arnold Rimmer on *Red Dwarf* on TV – to know that the one thing you couldn't do was touch them. But the deep, unsettling confusion he was feeling about Emrys was doing nothing to quash his professional anxiety that they were walking into some form of elaborate trap, despite not knowing why it would even be there in the first place. Everything was off kilter down here, and Bob didn't like it one bit.

Chapter 20

Saturday

They began to walk the one way, just hoping that it would be the right one, not that it was easy to tell. Once again, there were rail tracks down here from the days when small wagons filled with slate must have been pushed along here, running both ways all day. The gap through which they'd come on the ladder was certainly wide enough for some sort of bucket system to have operated, but thinking back to the museum they'd been around and that mine, Stella thought that this one must always have been a small operation. There would probably only ever have been a handful of families earning their living from this place, and so any more complicated lifting system probably hadn't been worth the cost.

That worried her now, though, because how were they going to get Dav out if he was too wounded or weak to climb? If there'd been so much as a pulley system with buckets, then she and Bob together might just have managed to haul him out, but she was getting the nasty suspicion that those miners of old might have brought the slate out in sacks over their backs, just the way she remembered the coal man hefting sacks nearly as big as him around when he'd come to deliver to her dad's, back when they'd had a coal-fired Aga range. But Dav wasn't a sack of coal or slate, he was six feet two tall, and even if he'd lost a lot of weight down here –

which was surely inevitable – then he was still a very big man for them to get out with just the two of them.

Yet what on earth could they say to any Mountain Rescue team they called upon? And unlike Bob, Stella found herself believing what Emrys had said to her, simply because nothing else came even close to fitting what they knew. So if there really was some evil – or perhaps more correctly, totally insane – elf-queen protecting her territory with all the venom of a queen wasp, then was it fair to bring unsuspecting rescuers down here? It all worried Stella terribly.

They passed one chamber and Bob went in alone, coming out holding a fragment of something in his hand.

"One of the devices they triggered, or what's left of it," he said, pulling a face. "Looks like a worthless piece of junk to me. I think you were right, Stella. Some greedy sod has been trying to sell the army useless tat, and has been massaging test results to make it seem like it's the real deal."

They pressed on, finding five more worked out caverns where there were the same pieces of metal scattered about the place.

"I know I don't know your friend, Dav," Bob said, turning one of the pieces around in his hand, "but I can tell you, my lad would have smelled a rat where this thing's concerned, and so would Ade's Tom if he's even half as good with explosives as his dad says."

Stella agreed. "Toby was an idiot where I was concerned, but as a soldier he was nobody's fool. He'd have known something was off here, and as for Dav, he's as sharp as a razor. If this is as shoddy a piece of work as you say it is, then I can't imagine he'd have been fooled for long at all. And don't you think that this all backs up the stuff that Karl was telling me? You know, about Toby challenging Hardy nose to nose? It makes even more sense when we've got evidence like this, doesn't it?"

"Yes it does, and for the life of me I can't understand why Hardy wasn't complaining harder to those above him. He must have had little short of a full scale mutiny on his hands here by the end, and unless he was a complete fool, he would surely have known that if this went to a court-martial that the men would have been completely exonerated? So in many ways he would have been better standing by the men."

"Unless he had a very dark secret that somebody was holding over him?" Stella suggested with a shrug. "God knows what that might have been, but if it was bad enough, then maybe he was trapped?"

"Maybe, but hell's teeth, Stella, it would have to be something pretty bloody awful in that case, wouldn't it? You're talking about something that would carry a worse sentence than the one he'd have got for leading his men deliberately into harm's way when he knew there was no need to, and, God help us, maybe even against army regulations. What could he have done that would top that?"

"I have no idea," Stella sighed. "He hardly seemed the sort to have buried his wife under the patio, did he?"

"No, but I've just had the thought that maybe previously he led a platoon into a bad situation and then lied about it afterwards? If there were serious casualties, then if that came to light in an enquiry where he was already being accused of poor leadership, it might have meant that he wouldn't have seen the outside world in a very long time. Military prison is no picnic, and for an officer …well you can imagine, especially since most in there would have had trouble with officers in the first place."

"Good grief, now there's a thought. Every time I start thinking that Hardy was just another victim, another question about him has me thinking that maybe he did get his just desserts, awful though that is. …Ooh! I wonder if that had anything to do with that new evidence the two detectives found? We really must get in touch with Ade as soon as we can."

"We've got to get out of here first," Bob reminded her, "and to be on the safe side, I want to follow this rope all the way to its end. That way I think we'll know that we've covered the extent of where the men got to."

"I don't understand why they put the rope in even across some of the openings, though. Yes, the ground is a bit uneven, but not so much that you need to hold onto something."

"But if the lights went out for any reason you would," Bob told her grimly. "You wouldn't want to be groping around here in the dark, going into some of the chambers by mistake, and then coming out and going back the way you came because you'd got disorientated."

"Oh my God, now you're giving me the creeps! …Oh that's an awful thought, being down here in the pitch black and never finding your way out," and Stella shivered and moved a bit closer to Bob.

He felt a bit bad for having scared her like that, but if it made her more cautious then perhaps it wasn't such a bad thing. Who knew what cave-ins might have happened in the long years since the miners were down here? One missed footing had the potential to be fatal, so if he'd made her hang on to his heels instead of running off, then that was all to the good.

They walked on but then Stella suddenly tugged at Bob's sleeve. "I hate to say this, but can you smell that?"

Bob inhaled and immediately got it – there was at least one dead body not far from here and maybe more.

Moving cautiously forward, they played the lights around in all directions and then Stella suddenly let out a squeak of dismay, and Bob turned to see her with her free hand clasped over her mouth, and the shaking beam of her torch picking up a huddled shape on the far side of one of the small chambers.

"Stay here!" he commanded, and skirmished into the cavern, checking both sides as he slunk in, just in case something was lurking where he couldn't see. Satisfied that he was alone, Bob then moved to the slumped figure, which closer to turned out to be wearing what had once been a white lab coat, the buttons from which having been what Stella's torch had picked up on.

Bob bent down, having pulled the tea-tree soaked neckerchief up over his nose once more as a partial barrier against the smell. To his horror he saw a definite bullet hole in the scientist's temple, and one of the scientists he surely had to be, going by his hands, which had never seen rough work even in their now less than perfect state. The cold down here had delayed their decay compared to those on the surface, acting like a huge stone refrigerator, but that didn't make them any more pleasant to look at. There were no calluses on the scientist's hands, and they were small and almost feminine in size, not the kind of hands that would heft weaponry around with ease. No, this wasn't one of the soldiers simply dressed up to look like one of the scientists, and in one way that was a relief, because it meant that the boffins hadn't just walked away and left the soldiers to their fate. They must have been dead, or been killed at the same time as when everything went wrong.

He stood up and retrieved his phone from an inside pocket. Taking some careful images, he made sure that he got a close-up of the bullet wound, then tucked the phone away safely. If he had to, he would find a way to seal the mine off, but the boffins were somebody's husband, son or father, and they also deserved to know what had happened to them.

Returning to Stella he told her what he'd found and was impressed when she said in a slightly shaky voice, "Then we have to carry on along here, don't we? I don't want some enquiry blackening their names when all the time they're down here in this damned oversized grave. Karl said that there were four left by the end, so, heaven help us, there must be more bodies down here."

Bob reached out and squeezed her hand. "Brave lass! Keep focused on that. We're clearing their names."

This time as they carried on he could feel that Stella had hold of the hem of his jacket at the back, and he couldn't blame her, this was starting to creep him out too.

It took until they had found three more old chambers before they found the other bodies. All three were huddled together and looked as though they had had their hands up in defensive gestures when they had died, going by the way the bodies had slumped. Stella hung on to Bob as they crossed the floor, and in the twin beams of light even she could see the neat round holes in each forehead.

"Oh my God, Bob," she sobbed, "those poor men!"

He pulled her to him and let her cry, knowing what she meant. These weren't soldiers. The poor bastards probably hadn't had a clue as to what was coming until they'd turned around down here and seen someone's gun pointing at them. But something more was really starting to bug Bob now. Both Karl at the hospital, and the strange man Emrys, had been quite adamant that Hardy had never set foot in the mine. So who had done this? Who had turned traitor on these men? Because every indicator was that it had to be one of the soldiers, and Bob really didn't like the sound of that. And worse, what if it was this Dav who was far from the stand-up bloke Stella portrayed him as? How on earth was he going to handle that if Dav was still alive?

When the first bout of sobbing had passed, Bob gently released himself from Stella's grasp and repeated the photo taking.

"It's evidence of a sort," he told her, "and at least the images will have the date and time embedded in them." Then as he was bent down, and having swung his light away so that it wasn't in the phone's camera lens, he noticed light glinting on something. "Hello, what have we got here?" He went over and realised that one of the bullets must have gone through the scientist and bounced off the cavern wall. Ricocheted was probably too strong a word for it. It probably hadn't had that much momentum left in it, but when he picked it up with one of the plastic bags Stella had given him, he was appalled to realise that it was a hollow-point bullet, or what was left of it.

"Crap," he muttered softly, knowing that its calibre meant it had probably been fired by a Glock pistol – in other words, standard army issue. And a hollow-point? That was something you used to make sure that someone went down and stayed down, and made a real mess in the process, because the alternative full metal jacket ammo would go straight through, leaving just the neat hole of its passage. It had probably made one hell of a mess of the back of the scientist's head, and he was glad he hadn't tried to move one of them – the net result would probably have had Stella throwing up, and she was coping incredibly well so far without more grisly images to haunt her. But it only confirmed his worst fears that someone within the platoon had not been what he seemed.

"Bob," Stella was suddenly whispering in his ear. "Something's coming! I can feel it!" And as he turned her way he saw her switch her torch off and point urgently back the way they had come.

Grabbing her arm he hustled her to the cavern wall backing onto the tunnel before switching his own torch off; that way they would be least exposed to the sight of whoever was on their way. Yet straining his hearing though he did, Bob could hear nothing. No footsteps, no voices, not even the rustling of fabric. He had just turned to Stella to whisper had she been sure, when he felt it himself.

Like a cold draft but without the actual touch of one, he felt it approaching, and was suddenly glad that he too had switched his light off. He reached backwards to touch Stella and felt her shivering as his hand connected with her middle. She was terrified.

He inched forward, silent footstep by silent footstep, until he could just feel the start of the opening with the tips of his fingers, then brought the Sig up to bear. If something went past, he would still be hidden from its view – and he didn't know why he was thinking of an 'it' instead of a 'someone' – but its back would be in his firing line if only he could see it.

The eeriest of sensations drifted by him, and then in the total blackness he saw them. Two figures, both very tall, both in something flowing. The one was an almost painfully brilliant white, as if lit by the moon from within, and was graceful in a feral, feline sort of way. The other was a darker grey, and rather than a steady glowing light, tiny sparks spasmodically went off, but black, not white. Even its movements were different. It seemed to shudder and shiver along rather than gliding.

They passed out of view, and Bob realised that he'd been holding his breath. Turning and putting his mouth right to Stella's ear, he whispered very softly what he'd seen, adding, "I think they'll come back. Stay still!"

He felt her slide down the wall and realised that she'd slumped down into a crouch. Better that, though, than her legs giving way at the wrong moment, and he rested his free hand on her head in reassurance as he stood guard.

Sure enough he felt the chill again before they came into view, yet they must have changed places, for the white one had been on his side on their way out, and it was still there as they came back. He brought the Sig up to bear, though what it would do against beings that transparent he didn't know. Thoughts rather than words drifted into his mind, and he knew that the white one was saying to the other.

"You're mistaken. There's nobody down here. It must just be the bodies breaking down."

Just for a second Bob glimpsed the grey one's face and it was a gut wrenching sight. Teeth were bared in pain in what had once been a beautiful face, but was now covered with what on a human he would have thought of as something like powder burns, such as ones he'd got from firing weapons. Yet these creatures could surely no more hold a gun than Emrys could?

It was the white one, though, that really took his breath away. Impossibly beautiful, it wore an expression of profound sadness as it watched its companion, and just as it passed, it twirled as if to look back, but instead, looked straight at Bob and raised an ethereal finger to its lips in the universal signal for silence.

"There," he felt it think at its companion, *"nothing more than gases escaping from a corpse. Come, let's leave this place, the smell sickens me."*

And then they were gone.

Bob gave it until a count of ten before putting his flashlight back on, at which point he realised that Stella was on all fours at his feet, forehead resting on the cold ground.

"Christ, Stella, are you alright?" he asked anxiously, bending down to her.

Her white face came up to meet his, eyes huge with fright. "I had to see them, Bob, I had to know."

He helped her to her feet and she put her torch back on.

"Here, have some of this," he said, handing her a chocolate bar from out of his pocket. "Get some sugar into you, it'll help with the shock. We can't move for a while anyway."

Having gratefully munched her way through the kind of sticky sweet bar she would normally never had gone near, Stella asked,

"Do you think we're nearly at the end of this tunnel, then? Only those," and she choked a bit on the next word, "*elves* didn't go much further on, did they? It was only a couple of minutes, though to me it felt like an eternity."

"No, I think you're right," Bob agreed, "and that makes me think that this is the original tunnel that the platoon came into. We've not come across the big natural caves Karl talked about, for a start, but the other thing is these bodies. Whoever did this to them would surely not have done this where the others were going to stumble across them? They had to be sure that this was down in a part of the system that the other lads would think they'd finished with."

"I think you're right," Stella agreed, "the only question being, are these the first lot of scientists that went missing or the last? Let's face it, I'm bloody frozen down here. It must be as cold as any morgue, so they wouldn't be decomp…" She gagged on the word. "You know what I mean …so fast as the ones on the surface."

"So they might have been down here longer," Bob finished for her. "Yes, that's another possibility, isn't it? Knowing now that at least one group of the scientists were murdered, we have to question whether these are the first lot, or whether they somehow went home or elsewhere, and these poor buggers were the ones left behind, just like our lads?"

Stella blew her nose again, then wished she hadn't as she inhaled the smell again. "Damn, I'm running out of tissues! I never thought I'd be crying this much when we set out. I'm not normally the weepy sort."

"I think the weepy sort would have folded up at the knees and I'd be carrying them out slung over my shoulder," Bob said with a wink. He wasn't feeling cheerful inside, but knew that he needed to reassure Stella that she was doing well. He couldn't imagine any other woman he'd known coping as well with this and he'd meant the compliment.

It worked, and Stella managed a watery smile. "I know what you're doing Bob Ashford …but thank you!" She wafted her hand in front of her nose. "Can we get out of here please or I'm going to barf."

"Absolutely. We'd better just check up to the end, don't you think?" He didn't want to say, 'do you want to wait here while I go look for more bodies?' That was a bit too brutal.

"Yes, we'd better."

Yet at the end of the workings they found no more remains, and as they began the return walk, Stella said thoughtfully,

"I don't think those other scientists can have got out alive, you know. Wherever they are, all my instincts are screaming at me that they're dead, and it's because they of all people would have the knowhow to prove that these tests were fake. But more than that, they would have been part of the company running this, whatever it is.

"Those mercenary bastards in charge could only do so much with regard to our lads, couldn't they? I mean, you lose too many soldiers and somebody higher up is bound to ask questions. You can't just obliterate half a dozen off the rotas and pay sheets without someone asking why. But those scientists would have been on their own records, so it would be far simpler to just erase all trace of them being there. That would be so much better, from these rogues' point of view, than having living scientists around who might get called upon to give testimonies at any court hearing."

"They might even have thought it cheaper to compensate any relatives for the death of their husband, or whoever, under the guise of an accident pay-out, than what they would have to fork out in fines, quite aside from the possibilities of prison sentences."

They had been talking very softly, now acutely aware that they weren't alone down here anymore, and so they picked up the faint rustling of movement coming their way. Bob tapped Stella's arm and gestured into another small cavern. It was far smaller than the one with the bodies in, and would hide them less well, but it was the only one close enough for them to get into in time.

This time Bob wrapped an arm around Stella and didn't bother with the Sig. Bullets would probably pass right through those ethereal beings, so there was little point in aiming at them. But as he watched, Bob suddenly thought of something else that Stella had relayed from Karl. He'd said that he'd heard someone getting rounds off when the elves attacked them, and that he'd thought none of them were armed. Well whoever that was stood a good chance of being the murderer, and suddenly Bob hoped that Ade was keeping a close eye on Karl too. Far too many witnesses in this unholy tangle were ending up dead.

But here and now there were the patter of feet heading their way. Then the feet stopped as if someone was looking and listening.

"Are you there?" Emrys' Welsh lilt came softly through the darkness. "It's alright, I'm alone."

Letting held breath go, both of them switched their torches back on and stepped out into the tunnel.

"Christ, you took your time!" Bob remonstrated.

"I know, I'm sorry, the old legs don't work as fast as they used to, and I had to go the long way around. One or two of them are getting jumpy, see? I couldn't seem to be rushing down here or they'd have got suspicious."

"We've already had a near miss with one pair of elves," Stella said, and told him of the white and grey elves, ending with, "but why did one of them seem to want to hide us?"

"That would be Dailarian, he's one of the truly sane ones left, and he knows that if too many die here, then it will only end in more people coming, more invading what space they have left. He wants you gone as soon as possible, like the others, but in one piece."

"We found the bodies of the scientists," Bob said, wanting to see what Emrys had to say about that. Of anyone, he was the one who might have witnessed something. What he wasn't expecting was for the old man's face to crumple in misery.

"Oh yes …those. After what happened to the first four who came down here you'd have thought they'd have learned their lesson."

"And what happened to the first four?" Bob demanded.

"She took them."

"The queen?" Stella guessed.

"Yes."

"Took them where, though?" Bob wanted to know.

"No, not that kind of taken. Not *to* somewhere." Emrys shook his head sadly. "When the full moon is up, she's at her most powerful. At times like that she has the strength to do what the elves of old could do, to take a life force. It's how they used to cull the weak and the lame from amongst the animals thousands of years ago, their way of maintaining the natural balance, see? But not people. It doesn't do them any good taking our life forces – too close to them, see? It's almost a kind of cannibalism."

"Bleedin' hell!" Bob growled. "So where are they now, then? You said life force, so I guess you mean like their spirit, their soul? But their bodies must remain. Where are they?"

"Dry husks down in the deeps," Emrys sighed. "You'll never get them back. She gets her darkest warriors to carry them down, after she's stunned them, and then she feeds on them slowly in her chambers." A tear trickled down his wrinkled cheek. "It distresses the good ones terribly when she does that. It's a perversion, you see? Something they were never meant to do, and this was the first time they've ever known her do it. It shook the sane ones something awful. The elves in their uncorrupted state were all about life and light, you see, and to see Arian-y-mynyddoedd sink so low, to be so twisted and full of darkness, it breaks their hearts. Some have even said that it would be better if she passed into the Summerlands beyond the veil than live like this, because this is a new corruption beyond any they've witnessed before."

"You mean for her to die?" Stella asked gently.

"Aye. They don't know death like we do, but they're still not wholly immortal either. It is possible for them to leave this world, and that happened to the ones to the south of here. But they chose to go. All that digging and corrupting of the land, they couldn't bear to see it. It was like watching their beloved child being killed over and over again. So they chose to go so deep into the dreaming that they passed beyond.

"But that means that the only others we could call upon are those to the north of us, and they have troubles of their own. Yet forcing one so mighty as Arian-y-mynyddoedd down such a path, when she does not wish to take it, is no small undertaking. It would take all of those still able to think clearly to do it, and for them not to be distracted by those who have also become infected by the poisons as she has."

"You talk of poisons," Stella wondered, "but you don't have the pollution problem here like in other places. Are they so very sensitive that just these old mines disturb them so badly?"

"It's not the mines. It's what's up at the sacred lake. That's what's turned things so bad these last few years. They call it the dark star. Brenaur, another of the light ones, told me about it when his brother came back from there all twisted and going dark. 'They've taken fragments of dark stars and buried them in the ground,' he told me. 'Such things are not natural. They shouldn't have been allowed to exist. It should never have come to earth. Yet these fools of men encase them in metal and worship them. We can no longer save them from themselves.' And whatever that 'dark star' is, it is most terribly poisonous to them."

Stella was frantically wracking her brains trying to think what he could be referring to. There'd been no environmental disasters, not oils spills, no nuclear... "Oh no!" she gasped. "That's it! It's Trawsfynydd Nuclear Power Station he's talking about! The cooling water comes from Lake Trawsfynydd! That's what the dark star fragments are, they're the nuclear rods in the reactor!"

Chapter 21

Saturday

"What's a nuclear power station?" Emrys asked as Bob groaned in dismay.

"It's a means of generating electricity," Stella began, then saw Emrys' incomprehension. "Oh dear, of course you can never have seen electric lighting. You'd have been lucky if gas lights had come along before you left the real world."

"Oh, I remember those," he said with childlike wonder. "One of the last times I went far afield was to Cardiff, and there was a place there that had those lights. Amazing!"

"Well out in our world now, every house is lit by lamps you put on with just the flick of a switch," Stella explained, "and they're powered by electricity. That's the stuff lightning is made of. We've learned how to make it and harness it. But one of those ways is what your elf friends call the dark star, and we call nuclear power. There are a lot of people who think that's a step too far, and that the dangers from places like Trawsfynydd outweigh the benefits, yet we need the electricity it produces in our modern world. It's a huge argument that's been going on for years, and I'm not even going to try and explain all the sides of it to you, but suffice it to say, I understand what the dark star is and why the elves are bothered by it."

"*Duw*, there's a thing!" Emrys said in awe. "Well I never! So do you understand what's happened to Arian-y-mynyddoedd?"

"Understand fully? No. But I can make a good guess that because she and hers live beneath the ground nowadays, that she would feel its presence, and even more so through the waters of Llyn Trawsfynydd. I think the power station stopped generating a few years ago, but that probably makes no difference to her if the rods are still there. Anything that tuned in to nature would be bound to feel them, I would have thought.

"We'd only notice if there was something very wrong with what keeps radiation contained, but we aren't that sensitive. And nowadays we know of something called radiation poisoning. It could well be that she and her dark warriors are all suffering from their own form of that, and it makes them much sicker with far less exposure than humans would have to suffer."

"Fascinating though your explanation is," Bob interrupted, "we really need to crack on! I don't want to be lingering here when ...what did you call him?"

"Dailarian."

"When Dailarian and his mate come back. So come on Emrys, lead us to where the men are."

The old man took them back to the ladder and then on down the other spur of the tunnel, and for the first time they saw what Karl had meant about the sudden change from mined chambers to natural caverns. The huge cavern he had spoken of was like a great hole in the earth, and though there was now a secure set of ropes on the sheer-drop side of the old iron walkway, and new steel grills laid on it to make a more stable foothold, nonetheless Stella felt faintly giddy if she looked out into the void by her feet.

"It's a long way down," she gulped, and Emrys in front of her stopped and looked over the edge, with no sign of the stomach churning Stella experienced even just watching him doing it.

"Oh yes, a long way down to the black pool," he said, as if it was the most normal thing in the world.

Bob also looked over the ropes' edge. "A pool you say? It wasn't someone chucking rocks in that which woke the elves up, was it?" The sceptic in him was still thinking of someone watching too many re-runs of *The Lord of the Rings* films.

"*Naww*," Emrys said with little laugh, "they didn't need waking by the time your men got here. The soldiers had set those things off already, see? And somehow they could hear those through the rocks from a long way away.

"Up until then there'd just been a few of us here. Dailarian, Brenaur, Breuddwydiwr and Seren-nos and me. The rest had gone back to Cadair Idris in the hope that those who had been infected by the dark star might recover there. They love to get out in the moonlight, you see, and up on the mountain top they're undisturbed at night. And there's a deep pool up at the top of old man Cadair where they can bathe in the clear waters – not that they'd let the sick ones do that, just in case they turned the water bad.

"So they were far away when I first led the men down here. I had no idea that they were going to do something so stupid, but as soon as I saw Breuddwydiwr fall over screaming with his hands over his ears, I knew that someone else would be bound to hear it."

Bob looked to Stella. "Didn't Karl say something about sonic devices?"

"Yes he did. God, that must have resonated through these natural caves for miles."

"It did," Emrys confirmed. "Two nights later she came with a handful of her dark warriors, and she's been worse than ever since then."

"I can't help but feel sorry for her," Stella said to Bob's surprise. "Well think of it, she's been here for thousands of years by the sound of it, and then suddenly in her old age, first of all men start blasting tunnels through the rocks of her world – 'cause even back then they can't have chipped it all out by hand. Then just when that seems to go quiet, or at least 'just' as it would have seemed by her sense of time, someone goes and puts in Trawsfynydd, and that really poisons her. And then to cap it all, when she's sick and half out of her mind already, along comes the army and sets off a series of sonic 'bombs', or whatever you want to call them. It must have been like us feeling rough as hell with a hangover, and someone coming and beating on a saucepan by the bed. *You'd* want to rip someone's head off if that happened to you, wouldn't you?"

Bob harrumphed. "Except that when I've got a hangover I don't go around sucking the life out of people and sending them round the bend." They had reached the next run of tunnel, and were close to the second cavern by now. "So is this where the confrontation took place Emrys? ...Holy crap on a cracker!"

"Bob?" Stella was concerned by the way he took one look into the cavern and went pale, thinking that he'd seen more bodies, but his croaking reply came,

"This is the place! The place I saw in my dream! How the hell did I see this?"

Emrys gave a small polite cough. "I believe that Seren-nos reached out to you. She said that she was going to try. It was Brenaur who saw you at the other mine, you see, and he was so angry that more men were coming. But Seren-nos, she said that maybe you were coming to look for the lost ones? So she said she would try questing for you. It's not something they do much these days. They find people's minds so full of machines and ugly thoughts that it's disturbing for them. They're trying to show you the wonders of starlight on water and moonbeams through trees, and all people want to see is some machine that has no soul."

"That I can sympathise with," Bob said wryly. "Having tried to have a conversation with two daughters who are permanently glued to their mobile phones, I know just where they're coming from!"

He stepped into the cavern then stopped and tried to grab Stella's arm, "No don't...!"

It was too late. Stella could already see the men in fatigues lying on the floor. Three of them had a strange, desiccated look about them, and having been looking at other dead bodies so very recently, even Stella could tell that they hadn't died the same way. There was no natural slump into the stickier, nastier parts of death; they were more like the husks spiders left behind, stiff and lifeless.

But laid out much more carefully were four bodies, as though someone was taking care of them, even though they hardly seemed to be breathing. Then a fifth detached itself from the shadows and staggered towards them.

"Stella?"

The voice was a mere wisp of the vigorous one she remembered, but Stella would have known that voice anywhere.

"Dav? Oh, thank God! You're alive!"

"Only just," he said, almost falling over as Stella shot over and threw her arms around him. Then he spotted Bob. "Who's your friend? 'Cause I know Emrys by now."

"Bob Ashworth," Bob said, coming and holding out his hand to Dav. "Ex forces. My son is…"

Dav's face was already creasing into a grin, "…Josh. Yes, I know! He's talked a lot about his old man. Pleased to meet you, Bob." Then a flash of concern came over him. "He did get out okay, didn't he?"

"Out, yes. …'Okay', well that might take a bit longer to decide."

Dav's shoulders slumped and he looked miserable. "There were casualties, weren't there? I just knew something was wrong when Toby didn't come back to look for me. He'd have come even if it was only to drag my corpse out." He shot Stella a sad look. "I know what he was like with you, but when the chips were down, Toby never left a man behind."

Stella went and hugged him again. "Well Teflon Boy managed to get out of it again, you'll be pleased to know, but this time with amnesia which is taking its time to wear off. Something about what happened to you down here had all the lads who made it out hallucinating like crazy for weeks."

"That would be Arian-y-mynyddoedd," a voice as clear as a mountain stream came from behind them, and Bob and Stella nearly leapt out of their skins.

"This is Breuddwydiwr," Dav said remarkably calmly, as they spun around and saw one of the white elves standing behind them. "He and his friends saved my life. One of them has always been watching over me since the attack."

"And now that we can get you out, you should go," the elegant elf said firmly. "You have been lucky so far in that She has been satiated by those She claimed during the attack, but it will only take one of my kin telling Her that you still live down here, and She will come for you. We would do our best, but against Her with the strength She has now we would not prevail."

"Yes, come on, Dav, time to go home," Stella urged him, but Dav resisted her pull on his arm.

"No, Stella, you don't understand, these four are only in a coma, they're not dead! Seren-nos helped Dailarian put them into a deep sleep so that they wouldn't suffer from their contact with Her."

In his time down here, Dav had picked up the elves' inflections where every mention of their queen seemed to come with a capital letter.

"Buggering hell," Bob swore, and cast a baleful glance Stella's way. He knew who would be doing the lugging of those dead weights up the ladders. "Right, Dav, I want you to go and climb up to the next level now the ladder's back in place. Emrys, can you go and find my pack please? It's somewhere with Ivan. Inside it there should be some lightweight nylon rope. With luck you should be able to lift it. If you can find it, I want you to throw it down to Dav at the middle level. In the meantime, Stella, you and I will start carrying these lads to the bottom of the ladder. We'll get them up stage by stage. Am I right in thinking, Emrys, that if you couldn't access that landing area in between the two ladders, that the elves won't be able to either? ...Emrys? ...Oh bollocks, he's gone already!"

"You are both right and wrong," Breuddwydiwr said. "Right in that we have no way of getting to the middle stage. Anyone who is there will be safe from Her. But you are wrong if you think we cannot get to the surface. The reason we could not carry your men up is partly because we have the same trouble lifting heavy things that are fully in your world, just as Emrys now does. Had we been able to do so, we would gladly have brought them up to where they would be found.

"But the other reason is that to get to the ways to the surface, we have to go close to where those who are most affected by Her madness are. Even had we been able to lift your men, we would have had to fight our way past our own kin to get them out, and we sane ones are getting fewer in number with each passing solstice. It does not help that She insists on going to try and expel the dark star every time She has recovered Her strength, and too many have gone with Her in the past before we realised the harm it was doing to them in the process."

Bob was nodding thoughtfully as he listened. "Okay, then this is what I would like you to do – if you don't mind, that is? Once you've seen us get the last man to the ladder base, would you go up to the surface and help Emrys? I need that rope, because I'll need one end around me, and the other around the man I'm lifting just in case I lose my footing or my grip. But also, if your folk can get up to the surface, I'd be very grateful if you'd keep watch for us. I can't carry a man up and be on guard at the same time in case the ones who started all of this come back."

"Of course, anything we can do to help."

Bob refrained from saying that that wasn't much in his books, but pasted what he hoped was a smile of thanks on his face. After all, these few had done their very best to keep the lads safe – it wasn't their fault if they didn't have access to modern medicine or the means to call in for help.

"Come on then, Stella," he said with a sigh. "Let's get to it."

It proved less exhausting than he thought getting the limp forms of the four men to the base of the ladder, partly because Stella insisted on taking their shoulders and she was far fitter than he was used to seeing in a woman. "You'll have the heavy weight on the ladders, and I'm not strong enough to carry any of them then," she said firmly, "so it makes sense if I take the heavy end down here."

She also volunteered to scramble up the ladder to find the rope, since Emrys hadn't appeared by the time they needed it.

"I've tied it to a great big metal cog up on the first stage," she told Bob as she shinned back down. "It must be a long way around given the time it's taking Emrys, but then he was a long time when he came down to meet us."

"It is," Breuddwydiwr confirmed, "and there is a stretch where he cannot seem to be in a hurry or one of our sick brothers may notice."

"Fair enough," Bob said. "Right, Stella, can you help me get this lad up over my shoulders?"

"I brought the ropes I use to secure my tent if they're any use?" Stella offered. "I thought we might be able to tie them to you?"

"Consider yourself kissed," Bob said with relief, yet again glad beyond words for Stella's sound common sense. "Yes, that's just what we need. Hand it over," and he made a couple of carefully knotted loops. "Okay, let's get him up, then you can drop that rope over him and me and pull it tight."

With Bob bending over, having helped Stella to lift the first man into a vaguely upright position, they managed to drape him over Bob's shoulders in a fireman's lift. Stella then helped Bob to stand upright, and then carefully dropped the looped rope over both Bob and the inert soldier so that he was strapped with two crosswise loops to Bob around the chest, Bob having wriggled an arm through each of the loops. It was far from ideal but it was better than nothing.

"Here goes, then," Bob declared and grabbed the ladder. Immediately it was clear that with the weight of the man pulling him backwards, that Stella was going to have to go up to the top and hang onto the top of the ladder, otherwise it was going to swing outwards with such an unstable load on and throw them off. Yet they managed to get the first man up with less trouble than they'd expected, although Bob was still glad to get him onto the floor.

They then also used another of Stella's spare ropes to tie the ladder to one of the great metal cogs which littered the first landing area.

"Do you think that once upon a time they actually did have some sort of winch down here?" Stella wondered. "This thing doesn't look like it came off the railway."

"Given what I've just done, Christ, I hope so for the sake of the poor bastards lugging rock up!" was Bob's heartfelt response.

Yet he wouldn't stop for a proper rest until all four men were up at the interim stage, and were moved across to the base of the ladder up to the surface.

"Come on up and have another mug of tea," Stella insisted. "They're as safe as they can be now, and if they've lived this long they're unlikely to deteriorate if you have an hour's rest."

Up on the surface they found Dav sitting with Ivan, who seemed delighted to have his friend back. In her trip to the surface, Stella had put a pack of sandwiches out for him, and the second of the three flasks.

"You can't imagine how much I've dreamed of tea," he said, taking another grateful slurp. "Just let that go down and I'll do my best to help you. ...But tell me, what happened to the others? Why was there such a delay in coming to find us, and why was it you two? Not that I'm not grateful," he added hurriedly. "I'm delighted beyond words to see you! But you aren't exactly the official rescue party, are you?"

And so as the setting sun began to turn the western sky red, Stella and Bob told Dav of what had happened, and how they had come to have their suspicions that all was not as Hardy had told it.

"I always thought there was something fishy about him," Dav said as they finished. "You'll understand this, Bob, but when you've been in the army for as long as I have, you get a sixth sense for an officer who's a bad'un. I wouldn't have wished him murdered, but he was clearly serving more than one master by the time things started to come unravelled here.

"We were sure that these tests were bogus, and yet we couldn't get the sod to admit it, and the way he nearly had kittens every time I or Tom Bailey went to him to demand that we be allowed to speak to base was telling, too. And I tell you something else odd, Toby was acting as sergeant for his squad, because his newish sergeant had got sent off with the others to Afghanistan. Who sends men out without even a sergeant, eh? Right from the word go, Toby, Tom, Andy and me were suspicious, but without knowing where we were, there was a limit to what we could do.

"And the other thing was that we had no idea of how long we were supposed to be here for. So at first we decided to just hang on, since we assumed we'd be going home within a couple of weeks. We thought we'd have plenty of time to report to someone more senior when we got back. How wrong were we with that!"

"I can sympathise," Bob admitted. "You don't want to rock the boat unnecessarily – all that could do was get you into hot water, and with nothing sorted. ...So when did you start to worry this wasn't going to be what you thought — you know, getting home soon?"

"About the middle of the third week. That was when the first group of scientists went missing. Suddenly they were down to half their number, and they were scuttling about looking scared to death. And that was also when we first thought we saw the ones I now know are Breuddwydiwr, Brenaur and Dailarian. We'd had this sensation of being watched for a week or so, and we were pretty sure it wasn't Hardy sneaking down below.

"But then we saw them at the entrance to the mine at night. Fair put the shits up us, I tell you! It was Ed who said they might be elves, and we all pissed ourselves laughing at him at first, but then after a bit we started to think he might be onto something. We had a couple of really clear nights, when although we were past the full moon it was still really bright, and we saw them come out into the open and stand looking up at it."

"Emrys, you said that the full moon was when the queen attacked the scientists?" Stella asked, the old man having come to sit with them, as had Breuddwydiwr.

"It was," he answered solemnly.

She turned to the elf. "So was that the point when you realised that the men were in trouble?"

He nodded, his long white hair floating on the slight breeze as he did so.

"She was in an uncontrollable rage. We saw those men die, saw Her drain the life from them, and we knew they were not warriors. She should not have done that, but we got there too late to even begin trying to stop Her."

"Will she come out here?" Bob asked.

"I do not believe so," Breuddwydiwr replied. "She has no reason to, especially now that Dafydd in particular is beyond Her immediate senses. The others are so deeply asleep that She will not be interested in them."

"Then let's get those lads up here and then camp for the night," Bob declared. "There's no way I'm going to try and get back down the valley in the dark unless there is a real danger in staying here. Daf, I know you want to help, mate, but you're as weak as a kitten, and I don't want you going head first back down the ladder, so will you pitch the tents for us? We'll put the sick lads in them, and we three will just have to sleep in the open for the night."

"Yes, and when we're done, I want to hear your version of events," Stella told Dav. "I want to know how come eight lads made it to hospital, and yet you got left down there!"

Chapter 22

Saturday

It took some heaving and sweating on Bob's part, but they got the four men up out of the mine. Stella had tied off this ladder too, and so she insisted on going ahead of Bob up the ladder, hauling on a rope around the inert body he was carrying, and even then they needed Dav's help on the rope to get the last man up as Bob's strength faded.

"Stop being so pigheaded," Stella told Bob sternly when he baulked at Dav trying to pull on the rope. "You're exhausted! Let us help."

And so between them they got the men out and into the tents, at which point Bob dug into his pack and came out with some packs of army issue ready-to-eat meals.

"Got them just in case," he said with an apologetic grin. "They've got a long life on them, and I don't know why, but I grabbed them with my stuff when I left home."

"A month ago," Dav said through mouthfuls, "I never wanted to see one of these ever again. Now it tastes like the best meal ever!"

"We did come and get him what food we could," Emrys explained, "but we could only take it down a bit at a time, and the ones who came later took most of what was there."

"Short rations," Dav muttered through one of Stella's biscuits, which he'd now started on. "Thought I was going to starve to death!"

Emrys gave an apologetic smile. "I'd forgotten that I had longer to adapt to what's around down below. It didn't occur to me until way too late that you were suffering."

Having ascertained that it would be okay to build a small fire, Bob had got one going and now they were brewing up tea in one of the kettles that Dav had found in the house's kitchen. Bob had warned him not to go into the main room, and though Dav couldn't avoid the smell, at least the kitchen was at the back and accessed by its own door. There was only an ancient coal range in there, which was why the men had had a mess elsewhere, but they'd brewed up tea on a primus on its top and the kettles hadn't been taken. So once the humans and Ivan were fed and able to unwind a little, Stella turned to Dav.

"I meant it," she said firmly. "Before you get swept off by the army again, I want to know what the hell happened to you down there."

"Can you take us through that last foray down into the mine?" Bob asked. "We've got some suspicions about things, but we'd really like to hear a firsthand account."

Dav cleared his throat and took another swig of tea. With a puff of his cheeks he said, "Where to start?" Then seemed to get a grip on his thoughts and began,

"By the time we went down there the last time, there was a really bad atmosphere about this place. Like I told you earlier, we were pretty sure by then that four of the scientists had met a bad end. At first we thought they'd just been swept off by Hardy while we were down in the mine one day, and didn't see the transport coming to take them away. After all, a bunch of squaddies like us could have rushed a bus and forced the driver to take us away, and there was one day around that time when he absolutely insisted that we all go down below, even when we weren't all needed.

"As it was, we'd already planned a break-out for the night following our last expedition. We'd had enough by then, 'cause it was clear that this was all a scam of some sort." He sighed. "We'd talked about whether we could take the boffins with us, you know? We could see that the poor buggers were scared to death by then. But initially we'd decided that the best thing to do was to get out ourselves and then go back for them."

He turned and grinned weakly at Bob. "Your Josh said we should aim for Hereford. He set a lot of faith in your lot. Said he knew some of your old mates who were still in, and that they'd listen to him if he asked for help."

"That's my boy," Bob declared with a glow of pride.

Stella smiled too, but said, "I'm guessing that you never got chance to put any of that into action, though?"

Dav shook his head. "No. On that morning we got up and realised that we hadn't seen any of the boffins since dinner time the previous day. Toby, Tom and me challenged Hardy over that, and he told us that they were setting up the next experiment down below, and that we'd be going straight down to help them. Well that didn't ring true. They'd *never* gone down before us before, but we talked it over in the short time we had, and we decided we should still go down, because there was always the possibility that the boffins were being held against their will down there in the dark, and that Hardy might threaten to shoot them if we didn't cooperate. Our plan suddenly changed, you see, to free them and then for all of us to get out.

"So down we trooped, and this time we were directed to go to the far side of the second cavern and into the tunnel. We were supposed to set off one of those useless bits of tat in there, but we'd had one apart the last time we'd gone and couldn't see anything explosive at all. A lot of components wired up that made no sense to us, but nothing to cause an explosion. Emrys says the elves heard the sonic bang, so I have to assume that that, at least, worked some of the time."

His expression became grim. "Well we got down there and just dumped the stuff, intending to go searching for the boffins. And that was when the three guys we didn't really know showed their true colours. We'd had seven lads transferred out to other platoons, you see, and then these three came in, and at first we just thought they were regular guys from another platoon. They never really gelled with us, though, always staying together. Not badly so, but in that time stuck in the damned house, we never truly got to know them – and God knows we had enough time on our hands.

"They covered it well, though, making out that they were all backgammon fiends, and going off into a huddle to play it at every chance. They gave us some bull about having learnt it on a previous mission where they'd been sat around watching some place for ages; and maybe we should have smelt a rat sooner over that, but to be frank, us older ones were just hoping that this would be it – the last mission – and we'd be allowed out of the army afterwards. So there wasn't much incentive to be making new buddies at that stage for us, and lads like your Josh knew they'd be moved on too."

Bob nodded, "That's all reasonable. And though it must have felt like a long few weeks, it was weeks, not months."

"Exactly," Dav agreed. "You don't become bosom pals with anyone in two weeks unless you're thrown into something really extreme, and that hadn't happened to us yet. Yes, it was grim, and boring, and distinctly dodgy, but not the kind of situation where someone saves your life."

"I'm going to start writing this down," Stella declared, "because I think we need to keep track of what happened when, and who was where, so that it's clear before you start getting cross-examined. So Dav, did all of you go down below that last time? Surely to God they didn't need all of you for that?"

He shook his head. "No. And we were angry and a bit off-kilter because Hardy split us up – and the bastard had done this several times already, which we weren't happy about at all. So Tom Bailey got ordered to go down, but not with his whole squad. Your lad, Bob, along with Tom Fernleigh and Ed Martin, were told to stay up top. That meant that Tom B. was going down with just those three odd ones, not any of his old squad at all – and that didn't feel right."

"What were those three's names?" Stella asked, pen poised over her pocket-sized notebook that went everywhere with her. "The new ones, I mean?"

Dav gave a sniff of disgust. "Jim Burney, Adam Smith and Dave Wilson – traitorous bastards! Burney was the worst, and I'm glad he died down there, as did Wilson. Smith is one of those in the tents. I really hope he wakes up and starts singing like a canary, because I'm convinced those three were company men."

"Did you know the company name?" asked Bob hopefully.

"Mercantor & Girelle, we thought – could have been French, but equally might not. We found that name and a logo on some of the boxes of equipment that came in, but the name itself meant nothing to any of us, and the one thing we found with any sort of address on it said it was registered in the Caymen Islands."

"A tax haven," Bob snorted. "How convenient!"

Stella wrote it down but then wondered, "Do you think that they might have been trying to break into the arms market, then? Because presumably if none of you had ever seen the name before, then it wasn't someone who regularly supplied to the armed forces?"

"Could be," Dav conceded. "To be frank, though, we cared less about them than who Hardy was immediately answering to, because that wasn't some managing director. He called him 'colonel', just like you heard, Stella, and we really wanted to know who he was because he was the bastard giving the orders. We never did find out, though."

"We'll track him down," Bob said with deadly certainty. "So this Tom Bailey – he was a good bloke?"

"Tom was one of the best," Dav said sadly, "and he got the shitty end of the stick with those spies in our midst, because his was the squad that was still two men short despite their addition. He'd lost five of his trusted lads, you see. I was short one, and so was Toby after he'd moved up to acting sergeant when 'Homer' Simpson got moved on. ...His proper name was Hugh, but you know what the lads are like, Bob, stupid nicknames stick.

"The only one of Toby's squad that you'd remember, Stella, was Stuey Bogdanovic. God, I'm gutted that he didn't make it!" and he cuffed a tear away. "But I'm getting ahead of myself, and you won't understand what the fuck happened with me rambling on like this." He coughed and rubbed his tired eyes before continuing,

"So Tom B. got sent down with me. I had Andy with me, and I thought I was taking the rest of my squad, but then Hardy stops us and orders Flynn and Biggie to go back to the house." He saw Stella pause with her pen and look up at him. "Oh, err, yes ...that's Errol James and Craig Biggins, to you guys." He saw Stella doing a quick name count and added, "The others in my squad were Karl Wright, Tim 'Tiger' Woods – he's another of the comatose ones in the tent – Tommy Wilkes and Jamie Clarke," he choked over the last two names, "who are two of the dry husks down in the deeps."

"Oh, Dav, I'm so sorry," Stella gasped. "Your whole squad except for Karl and Craig gone – that's awful!" Even as she said it she felt Bob's elbow dig her in the ribs and knew she'd been tactless. Of course Dav hadn't known that Errol 'Flynn' James was dead until just now, and in his state, probably hadn't understood his losses in quite such a stark a light. "Oh shit! God, I'm sorry, Dav," she gulped as his face crumpled and a sob escaped.

They had to give him a few minutes before he could continue and then it was Bob who said very matter-of-factly,

"So what about Toby's squad, then? Did they go down into the mine with you that last time?" and his tactic to get Dav thinking again worked.

Dav threw his hands up in frustration. "Again, only some of them. You see what I mean about splitting us up? Toby got ordered to stay up top with half of his lads, but Stuey, Brian Jones and Cory Bates were with me." He gave another distressed glance to the tents.

"Brian and Cory are the other two lads in a coma over there."

Stella wrote the names down, then frowned. "I'm really sorry if this distresses you, Dav, but was there another Jones with you? Only there's a lad in the hospital with Karl, and I'm sure his surname is Jones, but I don't remember it being Brian when I got a brief glance at his name."

Yet this time Dav actually smiled. "Bloody hell! Tufty made it? God, that little sod would walk out if they dropped the fucking bomb on him! He's a total pain in the arse in camp, but throw him out into the wilds and he's got the survival instincts of a ninja fox. Comes from some awful estate on the edge of Nottingham, and his folks are travellers who'd lift anything that wasn't nailed down, so compared to that, life in the army has been a doddle for him."

Stella smiled back. "That would be why Karl said he could get past any lock, then!"

"Oh hell, yes! He was the one who got into the boffins' lockers for us."

"Karl told us that too," Bob said, glad that this was good news. "He's not out of trouble fully yet, but after we'd pieced together that the ones brought in to Selly Oak hadn't had immediate treatment, they changed the meds, and the last we heard from Ade, all of them were doing much better."

Dav's smile had faded, but he still looked a bit brighter and said hopefully, "So remind me again, who made it to hospital?"

Bob ticked them off on his fingers as he listed the names. "My Josh, Ade's Tom, and Toby – which is why we three teamed up in the first place, of course. But Flynn and Craig were on the same ward as our three, although you now know Flynn didn't make it. Not wishing to freak you out or anything, mate, but those two had – have – something weird in their blood that the hospital couldn't get to grips with at all."

"That was Her," Dav said without having to think about it. "When she attacked …oh bugger, I'm going to have to go back a bit again, aren't I? …Okay …so I've told you who came down with me, right? Well there we were in that bloody awful tunnel, all of us with the hairs on the back of our necks standing up, 'cause the whole level of creepy had gone through the roof. And one minute we're on our own, and the next what I now know are the dark elves come at us with their swords.

"God it was bloody terrifying! They just seemed to melt out of the stones, but I now know that there are narrow cracks that they can kind of slide through because they're in an existence …parallel universe …whatever, where those are wider. There were only four of them, but you can imagine the shock factor, can't you? Nobody ever remotely expects to come face to face with elves in real life!

"So Andy's farthest from the way out, but he's the one who turns round and sees them and calls the warning. But before we can do much they're on us. That's when I knew that fucking Burney was dodgy because he just produced this Glock – when the rest of us hadn't so much as seen a gun in weeks – and started blasting away at them. And then fucking Wilson's doing the same …and …and I'm screaming at them to bloody stop, because we've got bullets ricocheting off the walls like sodding rain, and all they're doing is passing straight through the elves! But whenever the bullets went through them *they* were screaming too, and then going even wilder – and Christ, but they knew how to use those swords!"

He was panting just at the memory, and Stella reached out to put a calming hand on his, yet he shrugged it off and nodded at her that he was okay.

"So we're fighting tooth and nail, but I see Stuey go down with half his arm hanging off, and God bless him, Karl dives on him, hoists him over his shoulder and runs with him. That lad deserves a medal, you know, because he was the one who made it to the surface and warned the others. Not that they were far away, because Hardy must have been fair screaming into the radio by that point, and I'm sure Toby was on full alert.

"I saw Andy go down, and I managed to dodge the one trying to fillet me enough to yank Andy closer to me, and I'm just hoisting him onto my shoulders when She came." He shuddered. "She's insane, totally insane. ...So She floats in and it's like she drew Wilson, Smith and Burney to her like fucking wasps to jam. Talk about like calling to like! And even as I'm running for the bottom of the ladder with Andy, and ordering the lads to get out, I see Her reach out and touch Burney, and it's like someone sucking the juice out of a bottle – he just went rigid and keeled over like an empty husk. Then She grabbed Wilson, but he got a couple of rounds off into her, so although She sort of crumples for a second, he still dies like his twisted bloody mate."

Dav paused and drew in several sharp breaths. "By then I was heading out of the cavern, and I'm dumping Andy on the ground by the bottom of the ladder when I hear Toby calling my name, and I know help's coming. So I head back in, and it's chaos. I see Tom Bailey crawling along the floor cut to pieces, and then one of the elves just ran him through. Jeez, those swords were something else! Brian and Cory were doing their best to defend Stuey – who's on the ground by now – and they've had the sense to resort to their knives, which make a bit more of an impression on the elves. Somehow they don't like the metal."

Emrys' soft voice startled them as he said, "It's elves and iron, see? I've never known why, but the Fae really don't like iron – it's poison to them. That's why their own knives and swords are made from this slate. They have some way of sensing which shards of slate are the strongest, and of sort of melding them so that they don't shatter on impact, but I couldn't begin to tell you how, beyond that they seem to sing *at* the piece they're working on – like they put something of themselves into it."

Dav nodded. "It was certainly more effective making cuts with the steel knives than trying to shoot at them. But what was freaking us all out a bit was the effect we could see. They didn't go down with any of the cuts we made, but where the knives had passed through them that fucking weird dark sparking got worse – like black lights going off inside of them. Oh crap, I know that sounds weird. How can light be dark, eh? But that's the only way I can describe it. It was black, but not a matt, dead sort of black; more of a glowing blackness as if someone was shining a light through thick, black oil so that you couldn't see the light itself, just the effect it was having."

He shivered and Stella went and brought her sleeping bag to wrap around his shoulders. It wasn't that cold a night, but Dav was clearly reliving the shock he'd felt. He didn't want to stop, though.

"No, let me tell it, Stella. I might as well get used to talking about it – God knows there'll be enough questions when we get back to civilisation."

"You'd got as far as Brian and Cory trying to defend Stuey," she prompted him gently.

"Yes. And Tiger, Tommy and Jamie were doing their best to cover their backs, but the elves were driving them towards Her. Then Karl comes back in and yells that help's on the way, and he grabs Stuey, who's a big lad when you're Karl's size, and he somehow lifts him and starts making for the tunnel with Brian and Cory still behind him. But it's all happening too slowly! She turns and seems to kind of scream into Smith's face and he just folds up onto the ground – no great loss there, but it was fucking scary the way it happened. I'm trying to cover them all and then Tiger's screaming at me to duck, and I do, but then Her scream sorts of flows over above me and hits Tiger full on, and he keels over too.

"Then I hear running feet, and Toby and the other lads are down with us, and I hear who I think are Tommy and Jamie yelling at them to use their knives, and they wade into the fight. Mark gets trapped up against the cavern wall by two new dark elves who come in at their backs, and suddenly Toby's lot are in as much trouble as us. Mark goes down cut to ribbons, and Simon manages to get to him when the two new elves turn on Ed.

"So there's Simon dragging Mark away, and Josh and Tom then take Mark off him and run with him to the ladder. Meanwhile, Flynn and Craig are trying to haul Tom Bailey's body out - 'cause I think by this time we're all so freaked out by all of it, that we're thinking there's no way we're leaving anyone behind if there's even a minute chance that they might be alive."

He gulped some more tea. "Toby's yelling at Tufty and Simon, who're both big lads, to get up to the next level and chuck ropes down, then start hoisting the wounded up. It's not good, and we know we might be doing them a heap of harm, but it's better that than them getting cut to ribbons. I get why he did that. His lads were that bit fresher and had a bit more in reserve.

"That's when Tommy bought it, 'cause suddenly it's like some silent command's been given and the warriors are parting to let Her through, and that's the first time I really see Her doing this thing where She just pulled him in and *kissed* him! But you could almost see the life running out of him and into Her. God, it was obscene! But poor Tommy went down in a dried husk too, and yet what was crazy was that just for that last moment or two, his face lit up like he'd just experienced something wonderful, and I'll swear he wasn't fighting Her in those last seconds.

"And there I am, tugging Jamie along, trying to get the daft bastard to move back into the big cavern – 'cause we'd fought our way that far back by then – and it's like he was sleep-walking! I couldn't get him to fucking move! We're at the back by this time, and suddenly I realise that the others are on the metal walkway and the elf warriors have pissed off – and I realise it's 'cause it's iron, and they somehow can't follow us onto it.

"But I've still got to get Jamie out, and She comes right up to us, and I'm thinking, 'Oh fuck! This is it! This is where I get my ticket stamped!' and she reaches out and Jamie bloody dives into her arms. ...Couldn't believe it!" and he threw his hands in the air in an emphasis of his frustration and disbelief.

"Then she turns to me, and I say something like, 'Come on then bitch, if you think you're hard enough!' but she seems shocked that I'm not falling at her feet. I couldn't understand back then why I wasn't turned into another giant Rice Crispy lying on the ground, 'cause she's kind of panting damned near in my face, like it's a real effort for Her too. Didn't need any telling when it didn't work, though! I turned and legged it along that walkway like the hound of the Baskervilles was snapping at my arse!"

He stopped and took another long drink of tea, holding his mug out for a top-up.

"I thought we'd made it once I got nearly to the end of the walkway," he said with a sad shake of his head, "but then suddenly I hear the sound of fighting up ahead of me, and Brian and Cory come scuttling back to join me on the walkway yelling that the bloody elf warriors have come around the back of us from some hidden way, and are attacking Toby and the other lads. So I yell at Toby to get clear and go and get help. To be honest, I didn't give much for our chances – us three left in the cavern, that is – so there was no point in the others getting killed to just rescue three more corpses.

"So we're hanging on there, scared to bloody death, and we hear someone – I suspect Toby – shouting that he's the last man up, and I know that they're at least in with a chance of making it. But then She appears around the other end of the walkway, and we're backing into the middle of it."

He paused and looked sadly at Breuddwydiwr. "That was the first time we saw you and the white ones like you." He turned back to Bob and Stella. "They were doing their best to stop her, you know, but she was just scattering them out of her way like bloody fallen leaves. They tell me that the lives she sucked up gave her energy, and when you think that two of them were as corrupt as Wilson and Burney, that had to feed her dark side. ...Well then She got to the very edge of the walkway, and we saw her pulling in what looked like a really deep breath, and Brian turns to me and says, 'It's been good knowing you, Dav.' We knew this was it, and Cory's just taken my hand to shake it when she screams, and it, like, echoes in that cavern, and that's the last thing I know for a couple of days."

Chapter 23

Saturday – Sunday

"Oh!" Stella gasped. "So if you were unconscious for that long, you have no idea what happened when the other men came, or what they found?"

Dav shook his head. "No, I don't." He turned and smiled weakly at Emrys and Breuddwydiwr. "I learned some of it from Emrys and the friendly elves like Breuddwydiwr, here. They told me that when they got up to the surface – believing that I had succumbed to Her breath as the others had, and was dead or at least very close to it – that my mates were already patching up the wounded and talking about getting out of here."

Emrys added, "I saw the one you call Toby knocking the man called Hardy so hard it took him off his feet and across the yard. *Duw*, it reminded me of a boxing match I went to when I was a boy! I haven't seen anyone go down as hard or so fast since!"

The little man smiled tentatively. "I believe I heard him saying that Hardy could 'fuck right off' if he thought they would listen to even one more order. *Dewi Sant*, but he was upset over losing the big man, y'ere!" and he gestured to Dav. "'You've cost me my best friend,' he screamed at Hardy. 'Don't you dare come the high and mighty with me anymore!' And you know, I think that Hardy finally realised that he was actually in danger from these men, because when he came too, he scuttled off into one of the sheds."

To Bob and Stella's amazement it was Breuddwydiwr who then continued, "Dailarian said he would lead them through the forest. It is by far the faster way to where your people are than back along your track across the highlands. We knew it would be mostly downhill, too, once they had got past those crags on the sun-rising side." He seemed genuinely sad when he added. "We wished we could have helped with carrying those who needed to be helped, but please, I hope you understand now, that just was not possible?"

Stella immediately reassured him, "Oh yes, I think we can see now that you couldn't hope to have lifted the weight of a grown man without him quite literally sliding through your fingers."

"Thank you," Breuddwydiwr said with a gracious incline of his head.

"So how many left here with Toby?" Bob wondered, and Dav immediately began listing,

"From what Emrys told me, of Tom B.'s squad, only Josh and Tom Fernleigh. ...Out of my lads, just Flynn, Craig and Karl. ...And then Toby with his lads Tufty, Simon and Ash."

Stella let out a worried gasp. "Hold on a tick – Ash? Are you saying this Ash made it out of the tunnels alive?"

Dav nodded, and Bob said, "There are only the five bodies we knew about in the house – the ones Hardy reported to the army and we knew about. And from everything you've said, Dav, those are the ones who got hacked about by the dark elves' swords. They must have been close to bleeding out by the time they got to the surface."

He turned and clapped a sympathetic hand on Dav's shoulder. "I've been in situations like that, mate. One's where you look at someone and think, 'if we move him he's dead anyway, but how much blood has he lost already?' They must have assessed the situation once they got up here and realised that with no way of calling in an air ambulance, that the chances of those five living to get out were beyond slim.

"Unless Hardy called for one," Stella said bitterly. "Don't forget he had contact with the outside world."

Yet Emrys shook his head. "No, I don't think he did at the end. That Toby fellow tried to take something out of his hand, and when he did I definitely heard him screaming, 'what have you done with the card?' I don't know what that means, but the men were all shocked over its loss, and someone said that meant that they couldn't even call for help. That's when that Hardy got smug about it and Toby hit him across the yard."

Bob and Dav were swearing softly and fluently at that, Bob looking to Stella and adding, "The bastard took the sim card out! What the fuck was he so worried about?"

Stella could feel the tears rising again. "I don't know, but for once I think I misjudged Toby. He must have been frantic by then." She sniffed and then said, "But to get back to my point – where is Ash? He's not in the hospital, unless they have someone there without a name. He's not here. God in heaven, where is the poor soul?"

Bob and Dav both looked at her in horror, and even Emrys and Breuddwydiwr seemed worried.

"Oh no!" Breuddwydiwr said. "I shall go and find Dailarian! He may know since he led them down to the road – or at least, near to it," and he hurried off, still somehow managing to look as though he was half floating over the ground despite his haste, as evidenced by the way his white robes flowed out behind him.

Emrys was about to move off too when Bob caught his arm, or as best he could. "No, hang on a moment Emrys, I need to ask you something now that none of the elves are here." The little man looked perplexed but sat back down.

"What is it, Bob?"

"Okay, listen carefully. I can't explain all the ins and outs of this, but please take my word for this: I used to belong to an elite part of the army, alright? Their main camp is at Hereford, and with the miracles of modern transport, they can be here in no time at all. So I'm going to catch a few winks of sleep, and then as soon as there's enough of the dawn that I'm not going to break my neck doing it, I'm going to climb up to the top of that crag over to the west and see if I can get a signal on my phone," he held up the smart phone and waved it at Emrys. "I know you don't understand these things, but it allows me to talk to my old friends over a long distance, okay?"

Emrys nodded but seemed more than a little bemused. However Bob went on,

"You'll know they're coming because you'll hear a *whump-whump* sound in the air, and you'll see something big and grey coming towards you up in the sky. When that happens, you get underground and stay out of sight, right?"

"Alright, if you say so."

"I do, Emrys! I don't want you to get hurt! ...But now I need to know something: if we could blow up the tunnels, could we seal the queen elf in there? And if we did so, would even the white elves attack us for doing it? Or would they see it as a kindness to end her suffering? You see, my old mates will come heavily armed and with weapons that fire a lot of metal. So I don't want the good elves to get hurt – which they will if they try to attack these men. Rather than that I would just blow up the entrance to the mine, so that nobody else could get hurt by her."

"You could do that?" Emrys asked.

"When my old mates get here, yes I could," Bob said, making sure that he was looking Emrys straight in the eye so that the old man would know he wasn't lying. "But what I'm asking you is, should I speak to the white elves and offer to bury their queen in a very deep grave? Or will they see that as a betrayal after having looked after Dav so well for so long? Because I'm not unappreciative of the fact that they've had to go against their own folk in order to do that."

"That's very kind of you," a silvery voice came from behind them, and they turned to see four white elves had come up silently behind them without them even knowing. "I am Seren-nos, and Arian-y-mynyddoedd is my mother's sister."

"Oh no! That's awful!" Stella gasped. "How terrible to see one of your family suffering like that!"

Seren-nos gave her a sad smile. "Thank you for your compassion, and yes, it is. Her name means 'moon of the mountains', and for most of her long and illustrious life she has been just that — our guiding light. For her to have fallen into such darkness pains us immeasurably."

She turned and looked at Bob, her face a picture of misery. "I heard what you just said, and while it is a decision I never dreamed in all my long years that I would ever have to make, I would say this to you: if you can bring the caves down upon her so that she passes beyond the veil without suffering, then do it! As she is now, she is dragging all of our kin down into darkness with her, and that is not right."

"Would they be likely to recover if she's not there?" Stella wondered.

The female elf shrugged. "I do not know. We have never in all our years had a situation like this. All I can say is that without Arian-y-mynyddoedd, there will be none of our kind who could command others to follow in the same way. So those who have only recently become infected by the dark star might, in time, recover. And there are several who, if we can keep them in the quiet places, will at least be able to do no harm to your kind. Others are badly affected and one or two are almost as sick as she is – they are her two brothers and three of her lovers. If they do not die with her, they may still choose to go to fight against the dark star; but at least they do not have the long-standing loyalty to call upon others, nor the right to command, as Arian-y-mynyddoedd has."

"Then listen very carefully to me," Bob said standing up and moving to right in front of them. "My friends will bring something called C4, if I tell them there's a mine which needs sealing. What I need from you is two things. Firstly, you need to tell me *exactly* where to place this stuff so that we trap Herself inside a ring of it, because we can bring the roof of the mine tunnels down on her. Do you understand?"

They all nodded.

"But then I need you to make sure that everyone you *don't* want trapped below has moved out by the time my friends get here. You won't have long! It will take me an hour or so to get to that ridge once I leave, so if you say that they might be here by the time dawn fully breaks, that's all the time you'll have, okay? You must be out of the way! I'll just need someone to be that bit ahead of us to point me and a couple of others to where the explosions will take place."

"I'll do that," Emrys immediately volunteered.

"But Emrys, dear friend, you cannot move fast enough to get out if what this man says will occur!" Seren-nos protested.

But the old man shook his head and carefully took her hand. "Dear lady, you've been kindness itself to me. But my kind were never meant to live for so long. And I've become so lonely for their company. I was only ever a poor pit boy. I don't understand your poetry and your songs, your love of just watching the stars for nights on end. I was born to a simpler life, and I've reached the end of what I can endure. Please let your old servant leave with a little dignity, and knowing that I've done some real good at the last. I'm ready to pass on – I have been for many years – I just didn't know how it could be done. Well now Bob has given me a way, so please let me take it."

Bob and Stella would later say that they both realised at that point how fond the elves were of Emrys, because all four seemed deeply distressed at the thought of him leaving them. Yet they also respected his wishes.

"Very well, we will begin rounding up those of our folk here whom we could hope to save," the one Bob and Stella thought was probably Brenaur said. Yet as they turned away he was putting a comforting arm around Seren-nos who was clearly crying at the thought of Emrys' impending death – possibly more than that of her aunt's.

Bob turned in immediately after that to get some much needed sleep, and though Stella lay down, and soon heard the soft snoring of both men, she couldn't seem to really fall asleep. Toby in the role of hero was a new and troubling concept for her, not least because she wondered how many other times in the past he'd done something like this and then played the cocky idiot when he'd come home, so that she'd never really got to appreciate he had that side to him. Could she – dare she – offer him a place to convalesce, in that case? Even if this was a first for him, he'd certainly come up trumps for his men this time, and that did an awful lot to redeem him in her eyes. But was it enough?

As a result she was still half awake when she heard Bob starting to move around again.

"Is it time?" she asked him wearily.

"Yes. ...Dav?"

"It's okay, I'm awake."

"Good. You stay here with the lads who are in a coma, alright? I hope I can tab back from wherever I need to go to find a signal in time to be on the ground to meet my lot, but if I don't, they need to be met by someone they'll recognise as regular army. I'll give them your name. What's your surname again?"

"I'm Sergeant Dafydd Jirel," Dav supplied, Bob responding,

"Jirel – got it! ...Stella, you stay put too!"

"No."

"What do you mean, no?"

Stella shook her head. "I'm sorry, Bob, but no! Didn't you hear what the elves said? Dailarian led the other men down to the road, so he's going to have to lead *someone* else down there if we're going to find what the hell happened to this lost squaddie, Ash. Well that can't be one of your mates, can it? How would they react to an elf? And you have to go for help, because nobody else can make that call. Dav can't go and shouldn't go. He needs to get medical help himself as soon as possible.

"So the only other one is me. You've got my mobile number, and surely the closer I get to habitation, the more likely I am to get a signal? I might have to get a bit further down into the Mawddach Valley than wherever Ash is, but at least I'll be able to call you and tell you where I am – that's more than poor Ash has been able to do."

Bob looked as if he was chewing wasps at the prospect, but grudgingly had to agree.

"Go and find Dailarian," he said to Emrys, "and tell him that if he loses Stella, there's not a fucking hobbit hole on this earth that'll be deep enough for him to hide from me in!"

The reference was totally lost on Emrys, but he certainly got the inference, and so he hurried off.

"Where's your pack?" Bob demanded of Stella, and when she produced it, proceeded to repack it with first aid supplies, refilled water bottles, and some of the sugary chocolate bars. "Now you take care!" he said urgently to her. "If that poor bugger is down some gully, or wedged stuck in some rocks, don't you dare go down to try and help him! We won't be far behind you, and there'll be some professionals who can help him much better than you." He didn't need to say that he didn't want her to get hurt – it was written all over his face.

When Dailarian appeared, Bob and Stella got out through the wire fence the way they'd come in, and then Bob turned westwards for the high crag, while Dailarian pointed an ethereal finger eastwards and said to Stella,

"This way."

He led Stella and Ivan briskly eastwards, and with total assurance up a narrow path which climbed up the crags without ever becoming a difficult scramble for her. At the top she needed to pause to catch her breath, and turning to look westwards out over the slightly lower area where the mine was, she could see a small figure which had to be Bob moving remarkably fast towards the crags that faced them. He wasn't hanging about, and

Stella realised that he'd been saying nothing but the truth about help not being far behind her.

"This was the hardest part for the men," Dailarian said, as her took her past a tiny lake and then on past some more craggy outcrops. Yet after that Stella could see why he'd brought the men this way as the land began to slope sharply downwards. They also now came to more Forestry plantations, and it was easy to see where the men had gone. The serried ranks of close-planted pines allowed little in the way of undergrowth, but the pines' lower twigs were brittle, and had been snapped off as the men had stumble past them.

"They look like they were in serious trouble," Stella said worriedly, as they came to a muddy patch, and she could see the remains of footprints which seemed to be staggering.

"They were," Dailarian said sadly. "We had not appreciated that even these men had caught some of Her breath upon them, which dazes and confuses. But two of them were worse than the others. They seemed to be seeing things, and I feared that they would wander off and get lost. I am afraid that I had to menace them somewhat to get them to go in the direction they needed to, and the longer they walked, the more of them I needed to do that to."

"I think I can pinpoint which ones they were," Stella said in gasps, as she fought to keep going at Dailarian's pace, despite being tugged along by Ivan. How to explain a hospital to him, though?

"The people who look after our sick," she panted, "they can look at people's blood and see what's made them sick. ...Not with everything, you understand, but they did it with these men. ...And they said that there were some things like tiny crystals in there. ...Does that make sense to you?" She was desperately hoping that he would be able to tell her something she could then relay back to the hospital. Unfortunately, though, his elegant face simply creased into a frown of incomprehension.

"I see you think that this is important," he said, "but I cannot tell you how what we do works – not because I do not wish to, but because I truly do not know. We have accepted this as being the way things are for as long as I can recall. Some of our kind who studied such things might once upon a time have been able to tell you what you need to know, but we have become isolated from them for such a long time I would not know where to send you to find them."

Had she had the breath left, Stella would have sighed over that, yet suddenly they came out onto a logging trail, and Dailarian was leading her to a clearly marked footpath.

"This goes straight down to the place you call a road," he said. "It is not far. Your friend Toby said something about a quarter of a mile, if that means anything to you?" Suddenly he seemed very uncomfortable.

"Dailarian? What's wrong?"

"I fear I made a terrible mistake that night."

"What sort of mistake?"

"One I have apologised for many times since to Dafydd. You see, on that night I was thinking very much of my own people, and how we did not want any of your kind to ever come back. We did not know then that Dafydd lived, nor that you might have the means to rouse the four from their slumbers – we have only seen others in the past sleep until they fade away, and that was a very long time ago by the way you reckon time.

"So I believed all that were at the mine were dead, and with these men I was leading now being so close to where they would get help, I …I'm afraid I too breathed starlight upon them. ...I only meant to confuse them, Stella. For them to forget just where they had been. I had no idea that any would take permanent harm from it."

He was genuinely distressed by what he'd done, Stella could see, and although on the one hand it angered her, on the other she could understand why he'd done it. He and the others were already fighting what must have felt like a losing battle against their leader dragging everyone into sickness and insanity. The last thing they needed was another bunch of curious men tramping all over the place and provoking their queen even more. And if your only experience of men in a few centuries was Captain bloody Hardy, then she could hardly blame him for not finding it a particularly positive one.

Then another thought occurred to her. "Actually, you might not be wholly to blame. If as you say,Ariany-mynyddoedd had already breathed her toxic breath over them, what you did was possibly nothing more than just enhance it. And the terrible nightmares the men have been suffering from were probably induced by the memories of seeing her, combined with the hallucinogenic properties of her breath."

"She is terrible to behold these days," Dailarian said sadly. "She disturbs all of us. I can only imagine how she must have seemed to those men. ...But thank you, Stella, it makes me feel a little better about what I did, but I should still have seen them safely to the road. I shall not make that mistake with you!"

Stella smiled at him. "Thank you, but if I tell you to disappear, please do it. I don't want you to suffer on my account, and to be frank, you appearing in the middle of the A470 might cause chaos! We don't want freaked out motorists crashing their cars," then realised that he probably hadn't got a clue what a car was. "Err, that's those metal boxes that move really fast up and down the road."

"Yours is a strange world, Stella."

"You'd better believe it!"

And so they scrambled down the steep path towards the main road. The path was clear, but Stella could imagine the difficulty Toby and the men would have had, especially carrying the wounded.

As if to prove the point, she began finding snagged pieces of cloth on trees. This was obviously the point when Toby had got those splinters of twigs and other bits of wood impaled in him. No wonder it had confused the doctors. On the one hand he had the cuts and gashes from the fight with the dark elves and their strange weapons, and yet also must have looked like he'd been dragged through a hedge backwards when he arrived at hospital, with the two sets of wounds not matching up.

Yet they got to the bottom of the trail and found no sign of Ash's body – and surely, Stella had told herself in warning, if he'd been lying there wounded for nearly three weeks without help, food or water, a body was what she was looking for.

"Where the hell is he?" she wondered aloud, turning around on the path and looking for any likely places. Yes, she was close to the River Eden here, but although that drained into the Mawddach not far away, it wasn't deep enough at this time of year to wash a body away. So why hadn't Ash been picked up with the others?

Dailarian was waiting for her back inside the tree-line, and she climbed back up to him.

"Let's back track a bit and just see if there's any sign of him having wandered off earlier," she suggested.

It took until they were almost halfway back up to where Dailarian had left them before they found it, a crushed patch of undergrowth that looked as though somebody had lain there for a while. Now Dailarian could follow him, seeing minute changes in the natural surroundings that defeated Stella's powers of observation, and they clambered off the track and began following his progress off to one side.

"He must have been doing this in the dark," Stella guessed. "Nothing else makes any sense. Was it dark when you left them? I've kind of lost track of the times of day when things happened, but I got the impression the Toby and Dav went into the mine in the morning."

"They did," Dailarian confirmed, "and though it was getting towards dusk when I led the men through here, it was not so dark that they could not see their way – I would not have left them to stumble blindly in the black of night!"

Stella paused to wipe the bits of earth and foliage off her hands on her jeans. "Then I think Ash may have passed out back there and not come to until it was truly night. Heaven help him, he may even have lain there for the whole of the next day."

"I would agree with you. That is the one telling of events which makes any sense."

And so they tracked Ash onwards, until suddenly Stella gasped, "Oh my word, that's the Visitors' Centre roof I can see through the trees, I'm sure of it! Dailarian, you have to leave me now! This is a very busy area, and you could get spotted at any moment. Please, go! I'll be fine now, you've no need to worry, and if you get a chance to speak to Bob before I can get a message to him, if you tell him I'm at the Visitors' Centre, he'll know exactly where I am."

Reluctantly, Dailarian faded away into the foliage, and Stella slithered her way down to the centre's car park. She brushed herself off and tried to make herself look a bit more respectable before going in, also pulling several bits of twig off Ivan and smoothing his ruffled fur, then pushed the door open and went to where a man and a woman were manning the main desk.

"I know this is probably one of the more bizarre things you've been asked," she began with an apologetic smile, "but a friend of mine was out with some others about three weeks ago, and we're getting very worried that he hasn't been seen since. I don't suppose you know if you've heard of anyone being picked up around here? A hitchhiker maybe?"

The middle-aged woman rolled her eyes. "It's been a month for weirdos," she said cynically. "First there was that bunch of druggies picked up on the main road just south of here. What a palaver that was! First this trucker comes in screaming in Polish and waving back down the road, just as we're trying to close up. Then when Morgan got some sense out of him and rang the police, we were here until late with the police and ambulances. If they want to get off their faces, why don't they go and do it in some town somewhere instead of coming out here and spoiling the countryside for the rest of folk? It really upset a family with two kiddies who were here. And then we get that pervert wandering in in just his underwear…"

Stella's patience snapped. She was worn out and emotionally exhausted, and the woman's self-righteous attitude hit a raw nerve.

"Those 'druggies' were soldiers!" she snapped viciously. "One of them was my husband! And they'd come across some chemicals up in an old mine in the hills." The tell-tale *whump-whump* of a huge doublerotored Chinook helicopter passing low overhead appeared as if on cue, with a second close behind it. "That's more of the army going to deal with the place, by the way. Men died up there! And I promised Toby that I would come asking, because he thinks that one of his lads made it out but not to the hospital. The army think he's buried with the others in the rock-fall in the mine, but we need to know for sure."

The woman's face was a picture. She went very red in the face and stamped off into the back room, leaving Stella seething with just the male attendant.

"I've told her about making assumptions before," he apologised. "This is the first season she's come to help us, and at this rate it'll be the last."

Stella looked at his name badge. "Well can you tell me, Rhodri, what was that about a man in his underwear? When did that happen?"

"Oh, only about two or three days after all those other men got found. But we didn't think he was anything to do with them. He stank of alcohol for one thing."

Stella recalled that there had been some sort of alcohol in the first aid kit up at the mine, probably for washing wounds out with. If Toby had given some of that to Ash to carry down with them in case they needed it, and he'd then broken whatever it was in, then yes, he would have stank of the stuff. Would someone like Rhodri know the difference between vodka and sterilising spirit? Probably not. And if that was a glass bottle, in his dazed state Ash would probably have just stripped the uniform off rather than trying to get the shards out of his pocket.

"Where did he go?" she demanded.

"Don't know. Local police came and got him, see? Probably got taken to Dolgellau police station. They'll tell you where he is. Possibly locked up for a drunk."

Chapter 24

Sunday – Monday

Back at the mine, Bob was nearly there when he saw the Chinooks' familiar outlines coming towards him against a dawn sky shot with delicate pinks and golds. A huge sense of relief had come over him when he'd been able to speak to someone he knew and tell them what he needed. He'd had to edit things, of course. He could hardly say, 'there are this bunch of elves up in the Welsh hills and we're going to assassinate their queen.' His old mates would have been clutching their sides laughing at him if he'd said that.

Instead he'd played up the corrupt company side, emphasising that some miserable bastard had been playing with a bunch of ordinary squaddies lives, and they'd been in serious trouble up at an old mine.

"We need to blow the bloody thing up so that no other poor sod stumbles in there and comes to grief," he'd told his old colonel. "This Mercantor & Girelle, whoever they are, just sent in a clean-up squad to grab the equipment. Jesus, boss! They left bodies in the house just lying there!" and he heard his former colonel swearing at that. "We'll need plenty of body bags, and lots of C4. I'm not walking away and leaving that place as it is. The squaddies should never have been left like that, and there are also the bodies of some poor boffins down in the deeps too. They ought to be brought up and given a civilised burial, too. They can never have dreamt they were signing up for something as dangerous as this."

And so now Bob stood just outside of the chain fence and waited for the Chinook to land. It had barely got to earth when men began jumping out and running towards him, the one in the lead being someone he knew.

"Chuck? Bloody hell, they made you a sergeant? What were they thinking?" Bob laughed as they greeted on another. 'Chuck' Harrison had been the young kid of the team in Bob's time, albeit a very promising one – and Chuck wasn't for Charles, but for the battered chuck key he carried as his good luck charm ever since it deflected a bullet and saved his life.

"Fuck me, Serge!" Chuck declared in turn, unable to call his old senior NCO anything else. "Can't you stay out of bleedin' trouble even on civvy street?"

Bob gave a wry smile, "Oh if only you knew, lad, if only you knew!"

He led them inside the compound, explaining that he hadn't wanted to cut the fence any more than he had already for the sake of anyone else who passed the place by. At the house he gestured to where the main room was,

"Sorry, lads, you've got a grim job in there. The five squaddies in there have been festering for about three weeks," and the men with the body bags grimaced, but didn't baulk from going inside.

"You didn't just call us in to act as undertakers, though, did you?" Chuck said with a questioning glance.

Bob shook his head. "No. I want to blow up that mine down there. We've got the bodies of the scientists to bring out, but then the whole thing needs sealing. I also need men with impeccable credentials to witness the absolute crap that these lads were meant to be using.

The few who survived are in a terrible state in hospital, because there's something nasty down there, and they're too befuddled to ever be able to go into the witness box and testify that they were being forced to use something that was never going to work properly.

"Can you believe that these tossers were getting them to set off some kind of sonic device in a mine? Defies belief, doesn't it? But that's also why I asked for you to bring breathing apparatus with you, because in the process they either released something or disturbed something. It's in the air, whatever it is, and I don't seem to have been affected yet – but then I only went in and out to get these comatose lads out."

"Yes, the medics are landing behind us. Sounds bloody nasty."

"It is! So when we go down, we go in fast, grab the evidence, plant the C4, then get out and blow it. Whoever this damned company are – and it wouldn't surprise me if they turn out to be just some shell corporation with no physical existence beyond a few pieces of paper – I don't want them thinking that in a few months time they can come sneaking back in here and try this again. ... I don't think they will, mind. Stella came up with the idea that it's some bunch of accountants trying to rip the army off, and so now that it hasn't worked, they'll be busy trying to cover the paper trail."

"Stella?"

"Ah ...quite a lass is Stella. Her ex-husband is the one who led the last of the lads out. So when she went to see him in hospital, he told her that their old friend was missing, and as my lad Josh was one of the others, we sort of joined forces. This is her friend. Sergeant Chuck Harrison, meet Sergeant Dafydd Jirel of the Mercians."

Chuck blinked. "Jeez, mate, you look rough!"

"Three weeks scavenging off bits of rations left behind," Bob explained. "Dav got knocked out down below, and in the dark his mates didn't realise he'd been left behind. Came to a day or so later and had to crawl his way out, then hasn't been fit enough to try and walk out yet."

"I'm getting giddy turns," Dav said as additional explanation, and Chuck seemed to accept that.

As Chuck and the remaining men went back to the Chinooks for the explosives and breathing gear, Bob softly asked Dav, "Have the elves gone?"

Dav made sure that he was facing away from the returning soldiers as he answered, just in case anyone was good at lip-reading, "Emrys popped back up to say that they have an underground route that will take them part of the way to Cadair Idris. They've called all the ones they dare and are setting off. They should be clear of the explosions by the time you set them. He gave me a message from Seren-nos. She said to blow this part first," and he showed Bob a page of Stella's notepad on which he'd sketched a plan of the mine. "If that goes, the queen will feel it and come from this direction here, so you need to have charges already set at that point there, but don't set them off until you can practically feel her."

"Thanks Dav."

"Any word from Stella?"

"No, but I haven't got any signal again, and I don't want her mixed up in this if I can help it. Not this bit, anyway – you know, the messy bit getting the bodies out."

With everyone kitted up, Bob led the way down into the mine, glad this time that he wasn't the one having to lug the ladders about. At the bottom he sent one team off to get the boffins' bodies, then led the other four-man team through the caverns. As they passed through the huge first one he heard the murmurs of surprise from the men.

"Blimey, you don't think of places like this being down here!" he heard someone say, and for a moment felt queasy. He couldn't say to them to keep silent, because then he'd have to give a reason why. But the voice echoed around the cavern and he feared that the queen might just hear them. With that in mind he led them to the point where Emrys and Dav thought it would be best to bring down the roof.

"You see the problem," he explained to Chuck as they set the charges. "Some daft pot-holer could come into here from a totally different direction and stumble across this stuff." He was glad that the breathing gear partial masked his face, though, while telling such a blatant lie.

They moved back, meeting with the other two men who had gone to set the charges they would blow first, finally backing up and setting another lot just at the exit end of the huge cavern.

"It's a shame to seal off a wonderful piece of nature like this," Bob admitted when one of the men questioned whether they needed to do quite so much, "but I don't imagine anyone's going to spend money analysing whatever's in the air down here when it has no commercial value. So it'll never get made safe, and that means we have to do the necessary and ensure nobody else falls sick."

With the boffin's bodies back on the surface, and the med-evac' team having scooped up the comatose men and already left, Chuck pulled everyone out of the mine except him and Bob.

"I want to do the honours," Bob said, and was relieved to hear Chuck laugh behind the mask and say,

"You just miss blowing the crap out of things, don't you! Come on admit it, you miss it!"

"You got me," Bob laughed, playing along with him, and then pressing the detonation switch which blew the first of the C4.

A deep, rumbling thump came from back in the cavern, and even up on the middle stage, Bob and Chuck felt the vibration. They saw a billowing of dust go past beneath them where the ladder had been.

"That's one down," Bob said with relief. "Okay, Chuck, up you go. I'll blow the next one and then come up to the surface." He saw Chuck hesitate and chivvied him, "Go on, bugger off! For old times' sake, eh? Let me do this."

"Don't you dare get yourself stuck, serge. The paperwork would be a bastard, and I'd never live it down."

"Don't be daft. How many times have I done this?" And then Bob heard her. An unearthly scream of rage echoed through the caverns and Chuck froze, one hand on the ladder and a foot in mid air.

"What the fuck was that?"

Bob waved him to carry on climbing. "We think there's some crazy old badger down there. Poor thing's half starved, but Dav said you can't get near it to help it."

"Christ! Sounded bloody human!"

"I know, put the shits up me the first time I heard it. Go on, up you go!" He heard Emrys's soft call of 'now!' And offering up a silent prayer for the old man's soul, Bob blew the next section of tunnel, then went up the ladder after Chuck at speed. At the top he blew the last of the C4 sealing the cavern, then when they were sure everyone was well clear, he did the honours with the final explosives and they saw a great cloud of dust come billowing out of the mine's entrance.

With a wheeze and a groan, the aging wooden props at the mine's entrance gave up and collapsed in a further puff of dust, after which the roof sank to the ground and then silence fell.

"Thank God for that!" Dav's voice said with relief, and Bob turned to see him being supported by two of the soldiers. "I couldn't leave without knowing that it was done," he explained, and Bob could understand why.

"Right, let's get you lot back to base," Chuck said firmly, and gestured for them to go to the Chinook.

It was a full two days later when they all met up again. Dav had been flown to hospital and reunited with a very relieved Toby. However, Stella had had to call for a taxi for her and Ivan, and get it to take her to where her car had been left. She had left messages on Bob's answer phone and he'd rung her back, contrite in the extreme over her having to pick up the remaining pieces while he rode home in style in the Chinook. However, he had begged a lift from another old friend, who'd brought him out to the B&B so that he could drive home with her.

They were then able to report back to the Mercian HQ that Ash had indeed been picked up by the Welsh police, but had been thought to be mentally unbalanced and been sent to a psychiatric hospital. It relieved the local constabulary considerably to know that they weren't dealing with a suddenly new escalation in hallucinogenic drugs, and it was at that stage that more came to light.

With Ade joining them at Toby and Dav's bedsides, he gleefully told them. "The army was already doing its collective nut over this, it turns out. They've been trying all ways to get in touch with this Mercantor & Girelle, and getting more and more furious when they can't track them down.

"The CO won't say anything outright to a civilian like me, of course, but I got the distinct impression that a few heads have rolled in the tendering department. One or two seem to have been marched off by the military police, and are realising that those nice backhanders they took have come at too high a price. The army aren't mucking about over this – especially as the body count has doubled, and with four more likely to die."

"No chance of them coming out of the comas, then?" Stella asked.

Ade shook his head. "No. It would be different if they'd been kept properly hydrated and stuff, but one of the nurses told me on the quiet that they're just giving them pain relief and letting them go, because there's nothing anyone can do for them. Even modern medicine and machines can only do so much. Terribly sad, especially after your efforts to keep them going, Dav, but the docs say that if they ever came to – which is beyond remote – they'd just be vegetables, and that's no life at all."

Dav looked glum. "That wasn't what Brian, Cory and Tiger deserved. But I wish that bastard Smith had come through for a totally different reason. He was the only one left who might have been able to finger someone."

"Speaking of that," Stella said, anxious to move the conversation on to prevent Dav dwelling on the deaths, "but have you heard anymore of what happened to Hardy?"

"Oh, that's the best bit!" Ade said with relish. "He turns out to have been a thoroughly bad piece of work, or at least, someone you can't have a lot of sympathy for."

"Yes," Toby said with a smile. "The CO turned up asking for my version of events now that I'm thinking a bit more clearly. It seems that our Simon's the one who got discharged from the cardiac unit. Being as near *compos mentis* as any of us at that point, he was pretty pissed off and realising that too few of us had made it out. And he hadn't forgotten who the bastard was who was there with us, either.

"So he lurked around the hospital until he saw Hardy come out. That night you followed him, Stella, you weren't the only one! Simon borrowed his mum's car and tailed Hardy back to his house. Then when everyone had gone to bed, he broke in and put a knife to Hardy's throat – got him to write a confession!"

Ade was quick to continue, "Turns out that Hardy, was already in trouble of a sort. He'd been disciplined for bullying, but he also had a gambling problem – that's how that shell corporation got to him. They threatened to expose his dirty secrets to the army unless he played along with them. Hardy knew that with an already blemished record, by the time all the other stuff came out he'd be looking at a dishonourable discharge at best, and he couldn't afford that – literally!

"He was into some bad boys for pretty large sums of money it seems. So the back-hander he got for this job was doing nothing more than sorting most of his debts out. That's why he wasn't living the high life, Stella! He was getting enough money that he could have done it, but all it was doing was keeping the thugs' collectors off his back."

"So what's happening to Simon?" Stella asked worriedly. "Please tell me they're not throwing the book at him? Surely there are extenuating circumstances, here?"

"It's not official by any means," Ade admitted, "but I think they're going for the balance of his mind being disturbed. Given that they've already decided that he needs further psychiatric treatment, and has no desire to carry on in the army, I got the impression that he'll be sent to some nice safe place and given the help he needs. He certainly won't end up in a civilian prison, anyway."

Better news from Stella's point of view was that Dav could be discharged from hospital if he had somewhere to go. With Bob already having decamped to a guest house in Malvern – though his kit was still in the back room – Stella immediately offered Dav the bed.

"I always thought you might need it," she said with a grin, but then when she disappeared off to the ladies, Dav said softly to Bob,

"Are you sure about this? You and Stella, you seemed to have really clicked. Surely you haven't rowed?"

Bob's smile was instantly reassuring, but he was glad that Toby was turned the other way and happily chatting to Ade, while he was on the far side of Dav to them. It gave him chance to say quietly to Dav,

"Not at all. We're fine! But I realised up at the mine that I'm serious about this lady, and so I'm not going to muck it up by diving in too fast. She's had one bad experience with a soldier, I'm not going to give her another."

"So you're not just leaving?"

"God, no! But I do think I need to do this properly. You know, take her out for dinner and things, not just sit at her table and act like I expect to be waited on. So I found the guest house just as a stop-gap while I find a flat. I only need one of everything, and there are enough on the market to rent. And I want my divorce to go through – or at least be well in motion – before doing anything permanent, so that she doesn't get dragged into that. I'm not having Jane portraying Stella as some man-hunting husband-stealer.

"But I also want things sorted so that the lawyers see Jane living in that great posh house in Harborne which she'll inherit half of, and me in something very much further down the scale, so that at least I get to keep my army pension. That's not being nasty, Dav. If Jane was struggling, or the kids were still small, it'd be different. But even the girls are out at work and over eighteen."

"Well I'd make it a two bed place," Dav warned him. "Josh has only gone home with his mum under sufferance yesterday. He told me to ask you to ring him as soon as you can, because he's feeling suffocated already. I think you'll find him on your sofa rather than staying in his grandmother's house."

Bob felt both sad and cheered by that news. Sad that Jane was well on the way to alienating her son, and yet glad that he would at least have contact with one of his children, because he knew the girls would view him as the bad guy and their mum as the innocent victim. And having Josh staying with him while he recovered was another good excuse to take things steady with Stella, especially with Dav in her spare room.

"How's Toby taking it, though?" he asked Dav with a worried glance across to the next bed, where Toby was still regaling Ade with some tale. "Is he pissed off that he's not the one going home with Stella?"

Dav gave a small shake of his head. "No, and I admit I expected him to at least posture a bit over that. But something's changed there. I think he finally recognises the damage he did to her. That all his pratting about wasn't funny for her, and that at times he really hurt her. He's never acknowledged that before, you know, Bob.

"He says he's going to divorce C.D., and if they'll have him, he's going to re-sign-up for another stint, even if it's in an office job while he gets some psychological help. I never thought this would happen, but I think Toby's finally grown up. He says he needs to sort himself out, and I think he just might."

At that point, Stella came back, and the conversation shifted again, but before they left, Toby had one last question.

"What I don't understand," he said with a pained expression, "is how come, when that awful queen whatever-she-was was throwing all her charms around, and blokes like Jamie were doing their kamikaze bit, throwing themselves into her arms, why did you not fall for her Dav?"

Stella perplexed the others by immediately going into a fit of the giggles, but Toby's face when Dav replied had the others joining her.

"You daft sod," Dav said with a roll of his eyes. "In all the years we've known one another, have you never realised that I bat for the other team?"

Toby looked blank. "Eh?"

"I'm gay, you soft bastard. She could have ripped her kit off and done a fan-dance in front of me and it wouldn't have worked. The only thing that had an effect was the same stuff the others could do. That made me more than a bit hazy, I'll admit, but all those pheromones, or whatever they were, they were never going to work on me. Now Dailarian …he's a different thing all together!"

Three months later

"Are you absolutely sure about this, Dav?" Stella asked, knowing that she'd asked this many times already, but still needing to hear him reply.

His discharge papers had come through, and as far as the army was concerned, Dav was a free man. It had been something of a shock, though, when he'd told Stella of his intentions to go to Cadair Idris and see if he could find Dailarian and the others.

"Yes, I am," he told her as he loaded his bags into her car. "I'm not Emrys. I've read widely, I'm far more educated, and I miss their company. They value the kinds of things I do. …I can't do it, Stella. I can't walk back into civilian life, I've changed too much. I don't fit in in this world anymore – not to live fully in it, anyway. You've got a glorious little house up here, but even so, even if I could find another just down the road from you here, I'm feeling a desperate call to go back to Wales. …I have to try. If we get up there, and after hanging around for a few nights I don't find anything, then we'll come back and I'll try again on the next full moon."

"And if we don't find them? How long will you keep trying, Dav?"

"Well at least until the Christmas solstice. After that …I don't know. What I do know is that you and that man of yours need to be able to come back here without me sitting on the sofa playing chaperone, especially as Josh is around a lot while he's waiting for his regiment to come home. One or other of you needs a place you can come to, and it shouldn't be Bob turfing his son out."

"You're a wonderful man, Dafydd Jirel," Stella said, hugging him. Part of her hoped he wouldn't find the elves, but the other part of her knew that he'd found something he desperately wanted with them, some of which went by the name of Dailarian.

A battered Land-Rover clattered to a halt behind Stella's car, and Bob and Josh got out.

"You didn't think you were going to get away without us coming along, did you?" Bob asked with a mocking wag of his finger.

Dav came and took his hand. "Good! I didn't want Stella crying her way home," he said softly and got Bob's squeeze of his hand in understanding.

"Right," Bob said more cheerily, "let's get going! Come on Josh, get in Stella's car, this'll be something you can tell your grandkids one day – we're going on an elf hunt!"

Author's Notes

There are disused slate mines all over the northern half of Wales as described in the book. And I've kept the general areas as they have been historically described, so there really were groups called Bethesda, Dyffryn Conwy, Blaenau Ffestiniog, Mawddach, and Corris, to name just a few. Aberllefenni, Cymerau and Ratgoed are genuine old mine workings in the Afon Dulas valley, but Pant-y-Celyn isn't a real place, and Chwarel Coch (the red quarry) which I've placed in the same area is wholly fictitious, as is Mynydd Cwm-goch (the red mountain valley) mine. Blaen-y-mynach (front of the mountain) mine is also purely my creation, along with Bwlch-y-groes-ddu (black cross gap) mine, and I'm not aware of any real slate mines up on that western shoulder of the Mawddach valley. As far as I'm aware the Ministry of Defense has no interests in that particular area at all.

However, Trawsfynedd – pronounced Traus–vineth – is a very real place, as is the nuclear power station on the lake, which although it is no longer operational, has plans to reactivate it; and while I appreciate that they operated to a very high safety standard, nonetheless it was a rather creepy experience driving along the main road at night and seeing it all lit up so that it seemed to glow. It was easy to imagine that a people deeply attached to the land would find it frightening.

In contrast, the Mawddach valley and the Coed-y-Brenin Forest are stunningly beautiful places, with several waterfalls and some lovely walks you can take. There are many places you can stay, and it's an area worth visiting. Likewise, Cadair Idris really is quite accessible on its lower flanks, although the crags at the peak probably aren't for inexperienced walkers. This whole area of mid Wales is very different to the stark mountains of Snowdonia to the north, and the mine-scarred area around Blaenau Ffestiniog – if ever elves had wanted a home, this green landscape with its multiple rivers, streams and lakes, and woodlands, would surely be it.

Living in Worcester as I do, I've known and worked with various ex-soldiers over the years who were either in the Worcester Regiment (the Woofers) or latterly in the Mercians. Our local pub is one of the reunion spots for ex-members, so again, we run into a few, and I hope I've portrayed them in a way that they would not be ashamed of or insulted by. Having also had a father in the 'Hereford Hooligans', I have the greatest respect for the men and women of our armed forces.

What might surprise many of you is that the story of the old gypsy lady is actually true, although not regarding the Mercians in Afghanistan. It dates rather from my father being shipped out to fight in the Korean War in the early 1950s in the days when he was still with the Royal Corps of Signals (prior to being seconded to the SAS), and the old gypsy lady really did pick out those lads who never made it home. As my dad said, there was no possible way that she could have known this by normal means, and given that she never actually said to those lads that their lives would be cut short, it rather precluded any psychosomatic inclinations to take risks or otherwise force the prediction, although I can't imagine why any of them would have wanted to anyway! I've known a small number of true Roma myself, as opposed to just travellers, and they really are quite a distinct people. Their values might not be the same as ours, but they do abide by quite a strict moral code in stark contrast to many of the people who get mistaken for them.

And remarkably, the story of the eminent professor and the vacuum cleaner is also true, but this time it was my mother whose office the bag exploded over when the handyman came to try and 'repair' it. The prof' in question really was one of life's geniuses, but the practicalities of life were beyond him, as proven by him then repeating the same lack of awareness with an electric shaver – this time the handyman was prepared for what he would find! All concerned are sadly now dead, so I'm not slandering anyone, and it was an affectionate memory that I wanted to share and it fitted this story.

Thank you for taking the time to read this book.

I hope you would like to read other books like this, and the fastest way to do that is to sign up to my mailing list. I promise I won't bombard you with endless emails, but I would like to be able to let you know when any new books come out, or of any special offers I have on the existing ones.

Go to ljhutton.com to find the link or find me on Facebook

If you sign up, I will send you free ebooks (paperbacks aren't viable, unfortunately), but also other free goodies, some of which you won't get anywhere else!

Also, if you've enjoyed this book you personally (yes, *you*) can make a big difference to what happens next.

Reviews are one of the best ways to get other people to discover my books. I'm an independent author, so I don't have a publisher paying big bucks to spread the word or arrange huge promos in bookstore chains, there's just me and my computer.

But I have something that's actually better than all that corporate money – it's you, enthusiastic readers. Honest reviews help bring them to the attention of other readers (although if you think something needs fixing I would really like you to tell me first!). So if you've enjoyed this book, it would mean a great deal to me if you would spend a couple of minutes posting a review on the site where you purchased it.

About the Author

L. J. Hutton lives in Worcestershire and writes history, mystery and fantasy novels. If you would like to know more about any of these books you are very welcome to come and visit my online home at www.ljhutton.com

Also by L. J. Hutton:

Time's Bloodied Gold – the first Bill Scathlock novel

Standing stones built into an ancient church, a lost undercover detective and a dangerous gang trading treasures from the past. Can Bill Scathlock save his friend's life before his cover gets blown?

DI Bill Scathlock thought he'd seen the last of his troubled DS, Danny Sawaski, but he wasn't expecting him to disappear altogether! The Polish gang Danny was infiltrating are trafficking people to bring ancient artefacts to them, but those people aren't the usual victims, and neither is where they're coming from. With archaeologist friend Nick Robbins helping, Bill investigates, but why do people only appear at the old church, and who is the mad priest seen with the gang? With Danny's predicament getting ever more dangerous, the clock is ticking if Bill is to save him before he gets killed by the gang …or arrested by his old colleagues!

The Room Within the Wall

A Roman shrine with a curse, a man accused of a murder he did not commit, and an archaeologist who holds the key to saving his life.

When archaeologist Pip comes across Cold Hunger Farm and the ancient Roman shrine to Attis embedded in its wall, it rakes up demons from her own past. Yet as she digs deeper into its records, shocking revelations come to light of heroic Georgian-era captain, Harry Green, accused of a vile and brutal murder – but who is the sinister woman manipulating his fiancée into making those claims? She sounds frighteningly like someone Pip knew, so how did she get into the past, and can Pip follow her to put things right again and save Harry's life before he's hanged?

Printed in Great Britain
by Amazon